Trencher's Breakout

Trencher's Bunker Book II

Shane Noble

Cover Design by Elijah Hollis
Instagram: elijah_hollis

First paperback edition October 2022

ISBN: 978-1-7360486-2-7 (paperback)
ISBN: 978-1-7360486-3-4 (ebook)

10 9 8 7 6 5 4 3 2 1

In memory of James Robert "Robby" Reeves

(December 11, 1985 – October 7, 2020)

You inspired the character that makes me laugh the most.

Trencher's Bunker

Side View

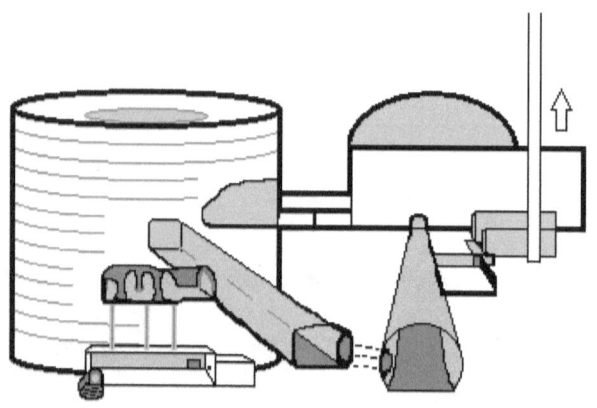

Top-Down

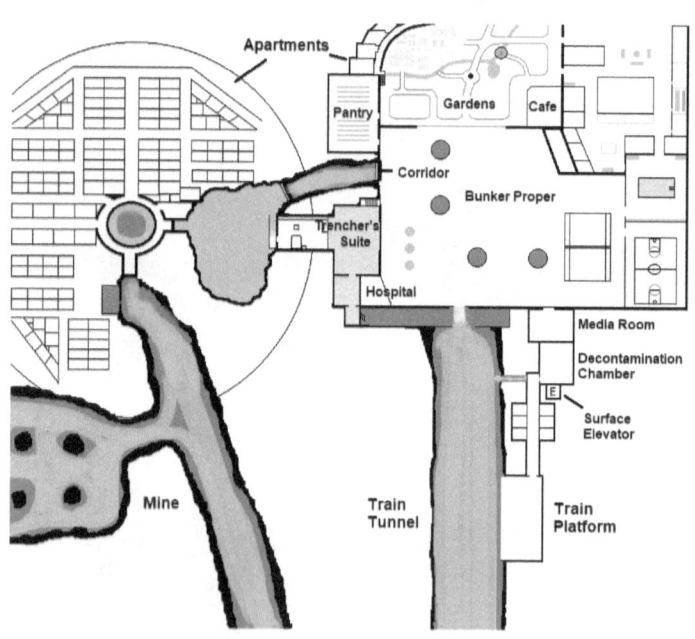

Prologue

Part I

Marcus Trencher closed the study door behind Senator Greg Granger, dampening the pulsating party music. Before the ball dropped, he gathered the senator had a mistress and illegitimate child to stash.

"They plan on killing you," the senator said. "You know that, right?"

"Who? The woman and baby?" Marcus said, bracing for a tasteless joke.

"Not them – the engineers at your site."

Marcus laughed.

"My engineers? I haven't mistreated them at all. They have nothing to complain about. They have bunker bids."

"They're not disgruntled. They're also not tasked with doing the actual deed, I should clarify."

The senator helped himself to the beverage cart.

"Not following. Are – are you serious?"

"Your bunker is not *your* bunker. Never was, and never was going to be."

"That is already clear. They cut me down to only fifteen bids. At the start, they promised the entire capacity for who I handpicked. And now they want to kill me and take the rest?"

"I'll cut to the chase. It'll make sense a whole lot quicker. Marcus – there is no asteroid on a collision course with earth."

He waited for the senator to admit he was joking.

The senator didn't because he wasn't.

"I was at the Pentagon with every living president, industry titan, world elite..." Marcus said. "They snuck Putin into D.C. for that meeting! You're telling me they lied to all of us? Or, what – they deflected the asteroid?"

"Putin sure sold it, didn't he? No, no deflection. There was never an asteroid to deflect. That's what I'm saying."

"Then...what is this all for?"

"A reset. They plan to geoengineer the cooling of the planet, build back the ice caps. We're talking years of freezing temperatures. That's why the bunkers are necessary. On top of that, they're running a depopulation program. To sum it up, an ice age and a global holocaust, for lack of better terms."

"Who are *they* exactly?"

"Wish I knew. High-ranking officials across the globe are complicit, but someone else is pulling the strings. They say we've blown past environmental tipping points and drastic measures must be taken. If you ask me, I bet it's the civil unrest. Rich folks like yourself aren't sitting around waiting to be eaten."

He finished his whiskey and tossed the glass over his shoulder.

"That's what always killed me about these Ayn Rand idiots," he said. "The rich aren't going *shrug* anything. They won't hide in some cloaked valley or on a manmade island – they are going to take the damn atlas."

"By freezing everyone to death?"

"Worse, but let's not focus on that. Gotta keep you alive first. I'm sending you five soldiers. Three are bona fide war criminals and one has a brain injury, but they'll take care of your engineering problem."

"You're positive the engineers are in on this?"

He nodded. "They plan to work as staff, keeping the place running for their privileged cohabitants."

"I was on pace to be the world's richest man. I designed and oversaw the bunker's construction. How can they push me out?"

"Someone more well-connected likes what you built, and they want it for themselves. But we won't let them. The soldiers will handle the engineers, and I'll report a catastrophic collapse to cover it all up. The privileged will move on."

"If my government overseers believe the bunker capacity is greatly reduced..."

"You can fill it with your people from Sherman after all. It'll be tricky, especially when that train tunnel breaks through, but no reason to leave that half of the bunker empty. I only humbly ask you take Nora and the baby."

The senator stood and wobbled. It was 2am.

"Why are you helping me?"

3

"I like you, Marcus. You're one of the good guys." The senator lingered at the door. "And not now, but somewhere down the line, I think you might be able to stop them."

Prologue Part II

One week before the public announcement,
3 months prior to "impact."

The core crew of forty engineers congratulated each other deep in the bowels of their mammoth, and finally complete, eight-year project.

The job required relocation to restricted land in rural Indiana, but the offer was lucrative, and once details were disclosed, impossible to pass up.

They nicknamed the on-site housing development "Los Alamos, Indiana." It had its own doctor's office, café, and community pool. Children rode their bikes in the street. Drones fetched groceries and their online impulse buys.

The dormitories had emptied out shortly after major construction was finalized. At the height of the project, the population swelled to 400. None were permitted to travel into the nearby town. Few ever learned its name.

The eight years were worth it. The reward was more than money. Much more.

The last task was a simple niche in a corner of one of the bunker's more expansive chambers. It was carved out by noon. Nothing more than a storage cubby. It was not in the original blueprints, which was a first.

The hand-drawn plans they received at the start were flawless. They merely had to follow instructions. The late tack-on elicited groans, but after eight years of 12-hour shifts six days a week, they tackled it with slap happy enthusiasm.

An echo of an opening door bounced down the chamber, making them straighten up. The reclusive man leading the project was making a rare appearance. After the initial meeting to layout the plans and purpose of it all, they only ever saw him briefly. Sightings were spoken of as if he were Bigfoot.

He relayed concerns through curt communiques on a bulletin board, rather than face-to-face. He walked the site daily between shifts and recorded his critiques in minute detail.

He was easy to hate.

They didn't mind he had to die.

The man (or *Bigfoot*, or *the Wizard*) looked them over. No one doubted who the smartest person in the room was.

He set a boxed cake and two 2-liters of soda on a card table, there per his instruction. He waited for them to quiet.

"You made great sacrifices to take on this ambitious project," he said. "Eight years you endured challenges, intellectual and logistical, psychological. I'm sure there were days you wanted to cuss me out and drive off into the sunset. A few of you probably wanted to kill me!"

They laughed politely, nervously.

"But here we are at the end of our journey and look at all you've accomplished. I need not explain the importance of it all. This *will* save lives."

He looked down at his notes.

"Julie, we watched your son Jacob grow up, from walking and talking to playing pranks. Mack and Teresa's daughter, Emma, returned to us an MIT grad. Emma, I hope you enjoyed college more than all those years we contemplated fencing you in."

Again, they laughed. His assistant assured him the line would get the desired effect when she wrote it for him. He thought it was nonsense. Emma *was* fenced in. The whole site was.

"Your ultimate reward is clear, but I thought a little cake would start things off nicely."

He cut forty perfect squares of cake and beckoned the engineers forward.

"Also," he said over the chatter, "prohibition in the village has been lifted!"

They cheered. Being released back to the village would have been fine enough. They hadn't resurfaced in a week, and for whatever reason, they were stuck on the "depressing side" of the bunker.

He hung around long enough to shake every hand, and spoke to a few, realizing one was Mack in the nick of time to keep things from getting awkward. Still, anything like this was awkward to him.

He moved to make his escape. The celebration was theirs, he told them. Before he could free himself, a young girl with auburn hair appeared before him, blushing.

"Hi, Mr. Trencher. I'm Emma," she said. "I wanted to thank you for helping me get into MIT."

Marcus Trencher shook her hand with both of his, looking into her eyes with his famous gaze.

"You made it all on your own."

He contemplated taking her with him. At least outside the chamber.

Instead, he continued his departure alone down the drab gray, pillar-lined chamber. If there were yellow stripes on the floor, it would look like a parking garage. Eventually, it would fill with coal.

Outside, he met five soldiers wielding assault rifles.

"Kill them all. Put the bodies in the niche and wall it up. There's concrete is in the corner. Don't forget to mop."

Book I

Chapter One

Henry Plyman, Robby Reed, and the others waited before the corridor like frightened gladiators facing lions and better-equipped fighters – the corridor that linked two bunkers that were really two halves of one all along.

Four days had passed since the doors opened between them, and the angry masses poured over.

They had lived their underground lives in relative comfort. Now, they found themselves facing trial for crimes of which they were unaware, but left with, courtesy of Marcus Trencher.

Henry had barely begun to heal since bearing the brunt of the mob when they crossed over. He was punctured by a pickaxe and stomped by steel-toed boots. Simple breathing hurt, but he insisted on being present for the trial.

He also insisted it could be worse. Jenna Dothmayer was in the bunker hospital with bullet fragments in her liver. Nobody was more a victim of Marcus than she was.

A guard checked his diamond-encrusted watch, no doubt looted from Marcus's collection. "It's time," he said. "Let's move."

Mariya squeezed Henry's hand.

"It'll be okay," Henry said. "Cooler heads will prevail."

They were greeted with boos as they emerged on the other side. A raucous crowd filled the chamber and spilled out into the atrium. They were escorted to a set of aluminum bleachers.

Ashley Cameron's former suite served as the judge's chambers. When the door opened, the crowd hushed in anticipation.

Jurors strutted out like celebrities on the red carpet before filing into their own bleachers across from the Defendants. A woman screamed, *"I love you, Danny!"*

The prosecution consisted of two young men. Jacob was a couple years into a low-level law career in Indianapolis before the end of the world called him home. The other, Charles, had a few semesters in a poli-sci program at DePauw under his belt.

Both held great conviction that they were representing those who had been wronged.

But few could claim to have been more wronged than Timothy Spencer. He slaved away in the coal mine and was injured in an explosion. He lost his wife, dealt with famine, and his eldest daughter had fallen ill. He even evaded an assassination attempt by soldiers that, curiously, disappeared during the chaos of the crossover.

Yet, Timothy volunteered to represent the defense.

Judge Robert Culler stepped out wielding a makeshift gavel – a mining shovel. He was once an actual judge in Sherman, Indiana, before being pulled out of post-apocalyptic retirement. His age was disregarded when filling the bunker, as he was more physically and mentally fit than most down there. He banged the shovel on the railing before him.

Just when it got quiet, a yokel yelled, *"Give'em the electric chair!"*

The crowd erupted in laughter. Judge Culler banged the shovel gavel harder.

"Who said that? Was that Darryl's boy? *Get his ass out of here!*"

Deputies dragged the heckler out to more cheers.

"Sherman's finest," Robby said through pursed lips. "Y'all thought this was going to be civilized?"

Melonie elbowed him to keep quiet.

"I will not tolerate any such nonsense in my courtroom!" the red-faced judge said. "Now before we begin, Doug Sheppard and others took a trip to the surface. Come on up, Doug. Tell us what you saw."

Doug walked to the center of the chamber. A woman handed him a karaoke microphone.

"We didn't make it far. It's darn cold up there. Me and the fellas planned on getting a truck and some guns to go deer hunting, but like I said, it was too cold to go any further than we did. That's about all I got."

Robby leaned to Brad Farris in front of him.

"Priority number one, get guns to shoot deer. Welcome to southern Indiana."

Robby's lack of subtlety caught Doug's attention.

"You got something to say, Robby Reed?"

"I was just explaining how important deer hunting is to our culture."

"Damn right it is! I'm trying to feed my family. We was starving over here!"

"Alright, enough," the judge said.

Timothy glared at Robby, who finally acknowledged he should keep his mouth shut. Judge Culler motioned for the parties to stand.

"We are gathered here today to start proceedings in the trial of *This Side* v. *That Side*. The Defendants lived as lavishly as any could on their side, while the Plaintiffs labored and suffered on this side. The disparity was allegedly unbeknownst to those on the more fortunate half, thanks to a set of very heavy doors between us."

The judge motioned to the corridor.

"No one dares argue it wasn't unfair. The question is whether the Defendants were aware and therefore complicit in the arrangement. Our esteemed jurors shall discern if there was culpability, and if so, what is just punishment."

He leaned his shovel gavel against the wall behind him.

"We won't be so strict on the rigmarole, but we'll do our best to uphold decorum. We will hear opening arguments today and begin presentation of evidence and calling of witnesses."

He motioned to the prosecution. Jacob, the eldest and one with a law degree, stepped forward. Charles wheeled the karaoke machine over.

Both worked in the mines with Timothy, but never the same shift. Despite their oppositional roles, the clean-cut professionals made a good impression on him during pre-trial meetings.

That impression did not last long.

* * *

"Let me take you back," Jacob the prosecutor said. "We were on the surface living our precious last days with no hope any of us would receive bunker bids. Who could expect smalltown Hoosiers to be saved on the precipice of the apocalypse? Lo and behold, a miracle occurred. Sherman's golden son, Marcus Trencher, wielded his great influence and did just that.

"We were rounded up by the National Guard, driven out to the airport, sedated, and then... woke up, in this very chamber. It was an elaborate trick to have us not know where we were. Why go through all that? I'll tell you why, not that you don't already know. It was because we were brought here to be their slaves!"

He pointed to the Defendants.

"They lived *right* over there. While we lost loved ones in a mine explosion, they swam and played tennis! While we starved – they ate like royalty. They enjoyed endless libraries of music, movies, and video games. Can anyone explain why nobody bothered to run a wire across to share? They never cared about our well-being. They only wanted us to mine coal and keep their lights on.

"And here is what they expect us to believe: *they didn't know! It was all Marcus Trencher!*

"The honorable judge tells us that we must decide if there was wrongdoing on their part. Let me tell you..." he began to choke up. "My grandmother made it to the airport but not down here, and my father died in that mine. You are damn right there was wrongdoing, and someone must pay. *They* must pay!"

Jacob dropped the microphone and the crowd erupted in cheers. The judge threw his hands and looked left and right for his shovel gavel.

"Order! Order!"

Timothy was blindsided by Jacob's sudden ruthlessness. He looked at his Defendants' frightened faces. If it was not clear before, it was now – their lives were at risk. The agreed upon punishment ranged from hard labor to banishment, but now none felt they could rule out violence.

Banishment, Timothy thought. *Hell, I want to get out of here.*

Guilty verdict or not, it was best they all move along after the trial. From what little he could gather, there was in fact a breakthrough in the train tunnel that Marcus fled down. They were now connected to the neighboring bunker beneath Bloomington, Indiana.

"We will now hear from the defense. Any disruption and you will be removed from the chamber."

Timothy stood on Jell-O legs and made his way to the karaoke machine.

"For those of you who don't know me, my name is Timothy Spencer. I was not over there living it up. I was here, with all of you. I, too, have suffered. I was knocked fifteen yards in the mine explosion. I count my blessing that I am alive. Men I worked right next to were not as fortunate. Many of you know I... I lost my wife to the misery of this place.

"So, yeah. I am angry, too. My anger drove me to investigate. You want to know who opened those doors? I did. When I crossed over to their side, they were as shocked to see me as I was to see them. I had no idea they were over there. None of us did. Is it not reasonable to think they were the same as you and me in that regard? I would not take up their defense if I thought there was even a slight chance they knew.

"I get it. It is unfair that their prison was so much more luxurious than ours, but that has been addressed. They have conceded their living quarters. Food has been redistributed. We cannot lash out on innocent people. Henry Plyman is one of your own. He was nearly killed during the crossover. Robby Reed, another Shermanite, created public works of art across your county."

The ball of ice in his stomach melted away and the lump in his throat was gone. All eyes followed as he paced closer to the Defendants.

"She is a veterinarian. This one is a doctor, that one a nurse. She keeps the water clean and running. You all know and love Kent the computer guy who has been hooking up all your new devices. These are highly skilled individuals.

"The last thing we need is to go *Lord of the Flies* right before we establish contact with the other bunkers. As soon as tracks are laid in the tunnel, we will have visitors. People will move.

"One man bears responsibility, and that is Marcus Trencher. The second person who knew anything is Ashley Cameron. And still, I implore that we practice forgiveness and move on. We have work to do, and we need to come together."

The chamber was silent. He set the microphone by the karaoke apparatus and returned to his seat next to the bleachers.

"That concludes opening statements," the judge said. "We'll take a short recess before evidence and cross examination. Adjourned."

They were escorted back to the café in the Gardens. As they emerged on the other side of the tunnel, Dr. Nora Weinstein waited to greet them.

Their faces were not encouraging, but she had good news to share.

"Jenna woke up. Her fever is breaking."

Chapter Two

Marcus Trencher had sat despondent at the end of a dark, dead-end tunnel for three days, contemplating the unspeakable. He lost his mind, his friends. There was no going back. He peered into the void, and just when he was ready to step in, the ground shook.

By dumb luck – his least favorite kind – a tunnel boring machine broke through at the last possible moment. He regained a grip on the reality he was ashamed to have lost. It was a grip that would again slip without certain action.

He knew he had a limited window of lucidity to work with before opaqueness, madness, and paranoia resumed.

He hitched a ride to the bunker beneath Bloomington, Indiana, in a truck that tailed the tunnel boring machine. A quiet kid named Chris drove. He answered questions but didn't ask any. Five stars.

The rest of the crew remained to fortify the connection. The digging was done, but they still had to lay tracks and cables. When they returned, news of his embarrassing loss of control would catch up to him.

His stay in Bloomington – "The Quarry" – had to be brief.

* * *

Marcus stared at a white ceiling in a white room from a sterile bed with white sheets. Quarantine. He and the driver were swabbed, given food and water, and left to wait.

A bulky duffel bag sat on his chest. His arms were outstretched above, hands wringing. He cracked each knuckle, flipped one hand over the other, pinched between his thumb and index finger, clicked his wrists forward and back. He watched as if someone else were doing it, unable to stop the compulsive pattern.

Finally, a knock startled him out of the loop.

"Good news, Mr. Trencher. May I come in?"

A doctor wearing a white coat stepped in.

"Dr. Howell," he said. "I am happy to inform you that your tests were all clear."

Marcus smiled and feigned the same level of enthusiasm the doctor showed. Mirroring emotions was a key component of social interaction.

"I am good to go?"

"You are now free to roam about the Quarry! That's what we call it." He laughed but quickly stopped when Marcus didn't. "We'll have someone here momentarily to give you a guided tour."

"That won't be necessary. But I did want to let you know that there was a flu outbreak at my bunker.

You might want to keep that in mind before calling the rest of the crew back."

The doctor bowed and departed.

It was a lie, but he needed to buy time.

He grabbed the pistol from his duffel bag and shoved it under the mattress. He did not trust himself with it, more than anything.

The quarantine area was on the opposite side of the tracks from the rest of the bunker. A skywalk led over the mouth of the westward tunnel that led back to his bunker. He climbed the steps and stopped halfway to look around.

The train station resembled Assembly Hall, where his dad dragged him once a year to watch his beloved Hoosiers play a bottom-of-the-barrel non-conference team. Over the eastward tunnel, five crimson national championship banners hung. They were the real thing.

A man approached and gave a friendly wave.

"We had a sixth banner in our sights, by God! Finally had the coach and players to do it, but the darn world ended! Ah, well. What can you do?"

Marcus descended to the bunker-side platform.

"Jim Cox, big fan of your work."

They shook hands. Cox was a polite middle-aged Midwesterner, and inexplicably, very tanned.

"Ready for the tour?"

"I appreciate the offer, but a tour won't be necessary."

"I imagine you'd find your way around just fine," Jim said. "You know, we met a decade ago. Your critiques on the blueprints were brilliant! But we did throw in our own touches here and there."

He motioned to the Assembly Hall-inspired train station.

"Sorry, I remember the blueprints but not the people. Typical me."

"I was lead architect, plucked right off campus here in Bloomington. My team implemented all 53 of your suggestions. C'mon, I'll show you the cool stuff."

If there was any company he could tolerate, it would be that of another bunker builder. Especially one who listened to his advice.

"Alright, Jim. You talked me into it."

"We are located just beneath the limestone shelf famous in the area. As you may recall, the train station is at the deepest point in the Quarry. Everything else is north and higher than the station, and quarantine area."

"When do the trains come and go?"

"It's a single train, and it stops here every two weeks. Darn near requires the Geneva Conventions to exchange visitors. We're better about medical transfers, but otherwise it's been a mess."

"Don't expect anyone from my bunker anytime soon. Flu outbreak."

"Flu, aye? They'll take it seriously. Some fool from Louisville showed up with bedbugs and caused a diplomatic crisis. Turns out he was exiled for sexual assault on top of that, and those scoundrels didn't tell us. Let's just say we aren't talking much to Louisville right now."

He led the way up a wide set of stairs reminiscent of a subway station.

"Another thing with the tunnels," he said ten steps up and short of breath, "we are connected to the other bunkers virtually, with a sort of internet between us. Once we link up to yours, we'll get to pull in everything from your data center. Rumor has it you stored entertainment. Movies, music, and games?"

"Yes, and worthless NFTs," Marcus said.

"We have a few games on our servers. All the tech wizards down here keep building on to the *Metaverse*. People enjoy the escapism, I guess."

At the top of the stairs, they looked out into a spectacular space.

A rotunda dotted a long rectangular concourse. The height was approximately 120 feet, and more to the west accounting for the descending ground-level tiers. Artificial sunlight poured through the dome windows, hitting the limestone walls in bright parallelograms.

They faced 12 stories of balconies. The outer escalator stack gave it a shopping mall vibe.

Black netting draped down the western half. Marcus thought it could be a safety measure on the balconies, but it did not make as much sense on the barren limestone walls – until he heard a metallic clink. A man at ground level, pitching wedge in hand, stood frozen in his backswing. Another man stood at the edge of a tee box, leaning on his own club.

Jim, having caught his breath, sighed loudly.

"These yahoos decided to turn this into a Par 3. They went to great lengths to pull the net down from a local Top Golf while the world was ending. Nearly killed a guy putting it up. Tee times are booked months in advance."

The golfers interrupted with an outburst. Marcus spotted the green in time to see the ball roll inches from the cup.

"There have been fifty hole-in-ones, if that gives you an idea how obsessed they are."

They crossed the rotunda and walked into level one, stopping at the edge of a track.

"Can't stand here long. The cyclists are as serious as the golfers. If you want to walk or run the track, keep to the inside."

On cue, a team of cyclists zoomed by.

Movie posters lined the outer wall and led up to theatre doors. A matinee and evening film played daily. They crossed to the inside of the track and turned parallel with the golf range.

Yoga, dancing, and racquetball were on display in plexiglass boxes. A sprawling cardio and weight training area wrapped around them. They descended to the ground level where enough overhead clearance allowed for basketball and tennis courts. An artificial turf area took up the far corner. A soccer game was in play.

They crossed the recreational space and entered a dim hall with doors every ten feet. Windows glowed red, blue, and purple.

"Welcome to the farm," Jim said. "Blue light helps the roots, and the red light promotes flowering and fruit production, I think."

"How many real meals per day do you get?"

"Two. These farms grow food so fast, it's astonishing. We keep chickens, and the other meats are mostly lab-grown from Louisville."

Marcus feigned interest in the passing labs. Cabbage, bell peppers, kale.

"I really wanted to show you this."

They approached windows facing an orchard of four rows, forty yards deep. Apple trees, as far as he could tell. Each had a lamp apparatus above.

As interesting as the trees growing hundreds of feet underground were, the people sunbathing between them was what drew the eye.

It solved the mystery as to why Jim was so tan.

"We realized we could tweak the lighting and create some resemblance to the outdoors. C'mon, let's step inside. We won't be able to speak because of the fans, so just follow me. And put this on."

He donned a St. Louis Cardinals ball cap and followed Jim into the orchard. Giant industrial fans created a hypnotic wall of sound. Searing, hot light added to the bombardment of his senses. It made him sleepy.

Jim weaved through the rows to another set of doors. Marcus delicately touched the tree leaves as he passed, sparking a surreal flashback to a summer day on the surface. They exited and the heat and noise dissipated in an instant.

"In the back, grown-ups are allowed to go all nude, FYI," Jim said as he tossed his hat on a shelf. "Soothing, isn't it? We assign teenagers to patrol like lifeguards, so folks don't fall asleep and fry. The fans simulate wind, so the trees grow upright, not to cool the sunbathers, but it works out."

They turned a corner and caught a glimpse of an Olympic-sized swimming pool before stepping into a stairwell.

"Promised the old lady I'd get my steps in," Jim said, again out of breath. "Farms and sanitation are stacked through the first three levels. There's another orchard on three that grows oranges and lemons, but it's not doing so hot."

They emerged into a mixed-use space on level four. There were salons, places resembling shops, and a salad bar restaurant. Jim led him into a grocery store.

"We have a sophisticated ration card system. A fellow from the humanities department leads the program with great fervor. He'll explain the merits of bunker communism if you have a few hours to spare."

Jim scanned his thumb, grabbed two green apples, and gave one to Marcus.

"In real time, we know what food we have and what is being bought. It gives the illusion of choice and normalcy. The restaurants are the only places we serve meat. There were far too many kitchen fires in the apartments. You'd be amazed by the number of people who can't boil water responsibly."

They left the grocery store and passed by a gaming lounge full of children wearing headsets. It may have been a computer-based school. He couldn't tell which.

"For a population of 18,000, we're not doing bad. Food production is strong, and the almost limitless electricity helps. I'm sure you want to see your power station. We can head that way."

"Maybe another time. I was curious about something else." Marcus scanned the storefronts. "This was to be a pharmaceutical haven, correct? I have a prescription I need filled. Nothing serious, but it was something that slipped my mind while stocking my bunker."

"We have labs and production facilities, but also a regular pharmacy, like the old days. It's one floor up, right above the grocery or thereabouts. I can show you the way."

"Thanks, but I'll find it on my own time. It's no emergency."

He had sobered up and rehydrated in quarantine, got a healthy meal in, and the new scenery was distracting his brain in a beneficial way, but compulsions and paranoia would resume. It was more urgent than he let on.

"I was also hoping to track a few people down."

Jim motioned to a kiosk behind him.

"It's a directory. Search a name and you can leave a message. You have a panel in your room that does the same. A few people have been removed from it due to security issues. Celebrities, and for domestic dispute-type stuff."

"Really?"

"Sure," Jim said. "Would you like..."

"Yes, please. I'm a private person."

"Not a problem." He handed him a keycard. "This is to your place. You can set up biometrics and throw the card in a drawer. The council will see you tomorrow. Details will be sent to your room panel. I'm sure you're tired, so I'll let you go."

Jim smiled, saluted, and was off.

Marcus ostensibly tapped the kiosk screen.

When Jim turned a corner, Marcus went to the stairwell.

He really needed to get to the pharmacy.

Chapter Three

Judge Culler banged his shovel gavel as the crowd settled back in.

"Court is back in session. Evidence will be presented, and witnesses will be called."

He motioned to the prosecution. Jacob took the microphone while Charles set up an easel and flip pad.

"As with any crime, it is crucial to understand the order of events," Jacob said. "We will walk the court through Exhibit A, where we have pieced together a timeline."

Charles flipped to the first page.

"To start, the bunker had to be built. According to folks living near the site in eastern Sherman County, the first signs of construction were back in 2021. Now fast forward to the last year on the surface."

Charles flipped two dramatically blank pages, save for the horizontal timeline.

"Almost a full decade is a long time for Mr. Trencher to *not* to tell his best friends that the world was ending, or that he was building a massive doomsday bunker. Yet the defense claims they knew nothing."

Charles flipped another page.

"Here is where the rest of us learned. The global announcement, January 23rd, 2030. For the weeks following, we waited for bids we never really expected to come. Some of us started digging shallow bunkers in our backyards. Most of us accepted fate. Then, the entire town got a blanket bid, July 14th."

Jacob scribbled the date above a dot in the line.

"Through that July night and all the next day, we were loaded into buses and sent out to the airport. With loudspeakers barking directions, and all the windows papered over, we didn't even notice that not a single plane took off."

Jacob put the cap back on his marker and turned to the audience.

"We drank our sedatives and awoke in this chamber with none of our belongings and no clue where we were.

"Then, *boom*! Impact, July 23rd. The whole place shook. We felt it and heard it. The Defendants claim it was special effects, that there was no asteroid. All I know is we've been up to the surface and the sun doesn't shine and the temperature has dropped twenty degrees in the last three days. Alas, that is a debate for another day."

Charles flipped to the last page.

"Last week, Timothy Spencer crosses over. For nearly two days he hangs out over there with his new friends. What took him so long?

"It is absurd to believe none of these people knew a thing – over the years the bunker was being constructed, and over the months we've been underground. I welcome the defense's explanation."

He sat and the audience got in hushed murmurs with their neighbors.

"We will now hear from the defense regarding the timeline," the judge said.

Timothy flipped to the page with the date of the public announcement. He scribbled a dot a few inches in front of it.

"Here is when I learned that Marcus Trencher was constructing a doomsday bunker. This is when the Defendants learned."

He inked another dot between his and the announcement.

"Marcus and I had a falling out over how few people he wanted to take. I objected to the low number. He still wanted me alive, I guess. That is how I ended up with all of you."

He received sympathetic laughter.

"Before I drank my sedative, he told me we were being flown to a bunker in Minnesota. It made sense at the time. He worked closely with a senator there."

He flipped to the last week.

"I crossed over here, and yes, I spent a night debating with them on how to go about opening the doors. Look what happened to Henry Plyman. Caution was warranted.

"People – this is all Marcus Trencher. He may have saved us, but he is not our savior. If you want to accuse anyone of being a slave master, it is him, not them."

He returned to the defense bleachers.

Judge Culler checked his watch. "I think we can get a witness in before a recess. Go on, Jacob."

"The prosecution calls Timothy Spencer to the stand."

He had just sat down. The audience got in a laugh. He made his way to the chair right of the judge.

"Mr. Spencer, how did you know Marcus Trencher?"

"We met in college when he was a boy genius at Rose-Hulman. I got forced into a group project with him. Nobody wanted to work with a little kid. He showed me plans for his invention and I saw how revolutionary it could be. We started working on that instead of the assignment. I was further along in computer programming, so I built out that side of it. After a few years, we received major funding. We hired execs who knew business and I kept to the tech side. Marcus was adamant in being CEO. And, well, *Trencher Industries* took off."

"Walk us through when he shared plans with you for this bunker."

"He drew the plans by hand in architectural drafting books and locked them away. I never saw them up close. I did have access to his mini nuclear reactor designs since they were kept on his computer, not that I could comprehend any of it."

"What did you do with those designs?"

"I leaked them to the Pentagon. He was only going to take a handful of people when he had the capacity to save so many more. The idea was that the government would force him to take in more, and as far as I can tell, it worked. He reached out, told me he was sorry and that I should accept a bid for my family to this bunker."

"You spoke of a falling out with Mr. Trencher. Did you remain employed at the company?"

"I wasn't technically fired, but I moved back to Iowa. There was no desire to draw unwanted attention."

"So we agree that you were essentially fired?"

"I took a stand because Marcus didn't want to save all of you, and sure, I was fired for it."

"No further questions, Your Honor."

"That wraps up today's proceedings. We've all got duties to attend to. We shall resume tomorrow."

Judge Culler banged his gavel shovel.

Timothy returned to the defense's bleachers, tentatively satisfied with himself.

Ashley Cameron sat at the front left end. Tension was obvious, considering he was doing anything but defending her. She stared him down as he approached.

"You don't have the slightest clue what you are doing," she said.

Chapter Four

Marcus entered the Quarry Pharmacy beneath a neon-lit sign.

Like pharmacies of old, there were shelves of over-the-counter drugs, all of which were in plastic bottles with generic labels. A window in the back dealt with prescriptions.

Marcus jotted down his medications before stepping behind the last person in line. The prescriptions were pre-filled and there was no payment process. The line moved quickly.

"Hi, I was hoping to have these filled."

Marcus slid the paper under the window. The pharmacist looked confused. Others before him scanned their fingerprints.

"Is this your first visit?"

"I took these before, you know, the end of the world."

"I'm sorry, sir, but you need a prescription."

"I had one. I just told you."

"You need a psychiatrist to sign off. Their offices are on seven. Make an appointment, get evaluated, and they'll write you a script."

"Seriously? How many people come in here asking for these?"

"Just following the rules."

Marcus nearly pulled his *"Do you know who I am?"* card, but instead put his head down and left.

He didn't know what a visit to the psychiatrist would entail, but he thought it best to first stop by his room and drop off his bag. It was bulky and heavy with an item far too valuable to lug around.

* * *

"The Stacks" were the sprawling living quarters of the Quarry. Its halls were narrow and the ceiling a claustrophobic seven feet high.

His room had a bed, chair, and a flat screen. Shallow shelves were carved in the walls, limestone dust still piled on the floor beneath. A VR headset hung from a hook. A countertop served as a place to eat next to the kitchenette.

The bathroom was the size of a closet, with the toilet and shower nearly overlapping in the space. Marcus tested the hot water, and as he suspected, it was very hot. One of the perks of living with a nuclear reactor on the premises.

Square footage came in somewhere between a dorm room and a prison cell. It was easy to see why Quarry residents flocked to the public spaces or wore VR headsets all day.

A wall panel displayed a message inviting him to meet the council. He confirmed attendance and shuddered at how much it reminded him of his old Outlook calendar.

He tucked his bag under the bed, took three deep meditative breaths, and was back out the door.

* * *

On seven, he found the psychiatrists' offices tucked in the Department of Mental Health Services. He peeked into a waiting room with a receptionist.

"I need a sign-off on some prescriptions."

The perky receptionist smiled. "Can I get a name?"

"I don't need an appointment. Is there someone I can see today?"

"Let me check with the doctor."

The receptionist ducked her head in an office. He could only make out, "...*It's Marcus Trencher.*"

"Right this way, sir."

A tall woman with glasses and a power haircut greeted him in the well-furnished office.

"Doctor Sara Cline. Please, have a seat."

"I won't be long. I only need prescriptions filled." He handed her the crumpled list of drugs. "They were prescribed to me before everything."

She looked over the list. "Right...Why don't we take a seat. I take it you've been off these for some time?"

Marcus restrained frustration and sat. "Since we went underground."

"These are serious medications to quit cold turkey. I don't mean to chastise; the end of the world is as good excuse as any." She re-read the list. "Half the Quarry is on the stimulant. A lab upstairs makes batches. The atypical antipsychotics require a bit more information."

Marcus ticked his head to a side. "I don't want to be rude, but I know what works."

She fanned her hands out over her desk in a calming motion.

"To get this medication right, I need certain information. I cannot simply put you back to the dosages you were at. You do understand that?"

Marcus conceded with a nod.

"Now, walk me through the symptoms you've been dealing with."

There was a long pause. He did not want to – there was that – but he also struggled to unlock the language to describe inner struggles.

"...Hand wringing. I get into this, I don't know, trance, where I crack my knuckles and wrists and press my hands together a particular way, over and over. It usually happens while I space out and start thinking about...recent events, and thirty seconds go by, or two minutes, or ten."

"Do you want to talk about these events?"

"No."

"Compulsive handwringing. Medication can help with repetitive post-traumatic loops like this. Talking about it can help, too. Sometimes more."

"If I feel like talking about it, I'll come straight to you. Otherwise, I'm content with medication. Am I good to go back to the pharmacy now?"

She removed her glasses.

"Mr. Trencher, if handwringing, which I do take seriously, is all you are experiencing, then I'm keeping you off a couple of these."

Marcus tried staring her down. His eyes bugged out and his gaze averted, inadvertently. Since he could not control his eyes, he closed them.

"That...that is another thing."

"What is that, exactly?"

"I used to be able to, I don't know, look at people, or almost *through* people. Eye contact has become like trying to put repelling magnets together."

"You could be disassociating. Think about the internal symptoms you are experiencing and tell me about those."

He contemplated giving up on the pursuit, but could he really continue with his unmedicated coping mechanisms? The ones that had him firing a gun at people? The ones, only days before, had him contemplating suicide? He was in a late-stage glimmer of clarity, reaching out for the help he needed. It was life or death.

"I've had bouts of acute paranoia. Um, intense delusions. I don't *think* I've seen hallucinations, but I can't be sure. I've struggled to control my temper. I started drinking heavily, which is bizarre because I've never done that in the past. I've sobered up, drank a lot of water, and ate good meals since I've arrived. I feel okay this minute, but... I will swing back, and when I do, I don't think I'll come back. I need this medicine."

Doctor Cline finished her notes.

"We'll start you back on the same medications, but at lower doses. Ramping up all at once would be dangerous."

"Thank you."

"Tori will set an appointment a month from now. If you feel yourself regressing at any point, come straight here. We will adjust accordingly."

"The pharmacist will know?"

"You can go there now. Mr. Trencher, I strongly recommend you talk about these things with me or one of the other psychiatrists, or even a friend. The apocalypse has been hard on all of us. Therapy can help. Therapy works."

"I'll keep that in mind, doctor. See you in a month."

Chapter Five

The Defendants stood in line at the café to receive their fill of breakfast Soylent. They had an hour before trial would resume and more witnesses would be called.

Timothy was growing more comfortable, if not confident, after handling the timeline exhibit and his own testimony. The truth was on their side, and he felt it was getting across.

He got his meal replacement drink, which looked like a vanilla milkshake but tasted nothing like it. Soon after sitting, Robby approached.

"Hey man, got a minute?"

"Sure, what's up?"

"You are doing great, but I have one minor suggestion – ease off on Marcus."

"Why? How? He's at the root of everything."

"He is, don't get me wrong. But these people love him. He's part of their personal identities. If a stranger asked where they were from back in the day, they would say, 'Sherman, Indiana, Marcus Trencher's hometown.'"

"I don't know. I lived over there, and they were not happy with him."

Henry grimaced as he sat to join them.

"They'll still talk shit about Marcus amongst themselves," Robby said. "But you're the outsider. It's stupid, but that matters more to them."

"How do I work around it? He had people murdered. Hell, he shot Brad and that girl. He put us over there to mine coal. It's clear as day."

"Walk them up to the point but let them come to the conclusion," Henry said. "Robby is right, they'll get offended if you tell them what to think about Marcus. He's like friggin' Bobby Knight to them."

Robby stood and patted Timothy on the shoulder. "You're doing great. Just wanted to give you my read on the room."

"Thanks." Timothy chugged his shake and shuddered. "I'm going up to the room to shower. The hot water is a thousand times better over here."

He crossed the Gardens to the apartments reserved for them during the trial.

"Has anyone seen those soldiers that came over with Timothy?" Mariya asked. "They disappeared when the mob showed up."

"I've seen them," Kent said.

Kent the Computer Guy, as he was colloquially known on both sides of the bunker, was working overtime building out the network so the people could enjoy troves of digital entertainment on devices plundered from the storage tunnels.

"They are always out and about telling war stories. They seem popular."

* * *

"The prosecution calls Lieutenant Grant Maniego to the stand," Jacob said.

Grant emerged from the parted audience in full combat uniform, chin held high. He was sworn in as the crowd settled.

"Lieutenant Maniego, first of all, thank you for your service."

"It was my duty. God bless America."

"How did you end up down here? You're not from Sherman. Fill us in."

"I was part of a Special Operations unit, originally a SEAL team, but for the last year and a half, we became something else. We were tasked with maintaining secrecy."

"Secrecy of what, exactly?"

"The bunkers. The government told the public as late as they could, but these things took years to build. They knew of the asteroid a decade in advance. They wanted to keep it quiet to prevent anarchy.

"Toward the end, our unit worked exclusively for Senator Greg Granger. He briefed us that Marcus Trencher had overseen the construction of a bunker, but it was going to be seized from him and gifted to some East Coast elites."

The crowd grumbled.

"We did what we had to do. None of us would be here today if it were not for Marcus Trencher. It's been hard to listen to his name being dragged through the mud. That man is a hero every bit as our men in uniform."

Men in the audience called out in agreement. The judge tapped his shovel gavel.

"There was a coup attempt before we arrived that you helped prevent? You received a bid as a reward?"

"Correct."

"Where were you when the doors were opened?"

"Blaine and I were helping in the coal chamber, since Mr. Spencer and his colleague went AWOL. We heard the commotion and made our way up. The action had died down by the time we got there."

"No further questions."

The Defendants were stunned by the flagrant betrayal. Grant Maniego wrote himself and Blaine out of the crossover.

Timothy walked around the podium to get closer to Maniego.

"Can you tell the court what you did to combat the so-called coup?"

"A unit was going to take Mr. Trencher out, then engineers and elites were going to take the bunker. Senator Granger found out and volunteered us as the unit. We did what we had to, and he reported a collapse to cover it up. It was so late in the game that the government just took his word for it."

"What did you do to the engineers?"

"What we had to. Look, everyone here would be dead if we didn't. This was an end-of-the-world scenario. People who played by the rules are dead. These people are alive today because of actions we took, that Marcus Trencher took."

"Lieutenant, did you cross over with us?"

"No, I crossed when everyone else did."

"You didn't ride the elevator up to the surface with the Defendants, then melt into the crowd when you saw the danger they were in?"

"I've never met these people. I certainly haven't been to the surface."

He was a stone-cold liar. Timothy debated cutting his losses, but there was one more area to explore.

"What is your relationship with Ashley Cameron?"

"We help her out here and there, maintenance stuff."

"Did she know of the tunnel and the other side?"

"You would have to ask her."

"Good idea. No further questions."

Chapter Six

Lieutenant Grant Maniego's lies went over well with the audience. They had no confidence the jury felt any different. It was Timothy's turn to call witnesses.

"The defense calls Ashley Cameron to the witness stand," Timothy said.

Ashley wore loose fitting clothes and was borderline showing – right in the unsafe range to ask when she was due, in case she was not.

"Ms. Cameron, did you know Marcus Trencher and the Defendants were on the other side?"

"Yes, I knew."

"Was your role to keep us separated?"

"Yes, obviously. But what you think you know is wrong when it comes to why Mr. Trencher created the separation."

"Please explain."

"Mr. Trencher needed the coal mine after you leaked his unfinished reactor designs – which he was going to share once he perfected them. Your leak made it look like he was keeping it to himself, and that upset someone at the Pentagon. They refused allocation of fuel rods to our bunker."

"No, I leaked those plans because–"

"Your leak and the Pentagon's reaction..." Ashley interrupted, "forced Mr. Trencher to energy Plan B. If anyone wants to know why we need to mine coal, it is because of Mr. Spencer."

The audience was inclined to distrust Timothy, the outsider, but now they were armed with a reason.

"It doesn't end there," she continued. "They dropped Mr. Trencher's bunker bids down to fifteen before a faction made a push to seize the bunker entirely. Mr. Spencer here handed them the excuse."

Suddenly, he was the one on trial.

"I leaked those designs," Timothy said, voice straining, as the judge tapped his shovel gavel to quiet the crowd. "...I leaked those designs because Marcus was only going to take little over a dozen people down here. He was not interested in saving others if it meant sacrificing comfort. After I leaked those plans, the government scrutinized him and forced him to move all of you in!"

"Your leak only made it harder for him to save these people."

"Then why did he keep those doors closed, other than to not have to work in the mine or share with the rest of us?"

"He wanted to open them! But don't you get it? He had to keep us hidden. Some of the people that plotted to seize this bunker are in Bloomington. With the hole you blasted in the tunnel, you blew our cover. Your idiotic behavior debunked Senator Granger's collapse story."

Timothy laughed out of frustration. His focus on Marcus was backfiring.

"Marcus will have his own trial in the near future," Timothy said. "Let me redirect. Can you confirm that neither Henry Plyman nor Robby Reed, or any other Defendant, knew of the mining operation and all the people on this side?"

Ashley looked at Henry and Robby. "Before we came underground...no, they knew nothing."

There was a collective sigh of relief from the Defendants.

"No further questions."

* * *

Jacob the prosecutor smiled as he approached the witness, as if his whole case had not fallen apart.

"We have said it a thousand times already, but we are gathered here to determine *who-knew-what-when* regarding our presence on this half of the bunker. Ms. Cameron, I want to be clear on Mr. Spencer's last question – Henry Plyman and Robby Reed, along with all the others, had no prior knowledge of our existence before we moved in?"

"That is correct."

"What is important to know now is if they knew of our existence *after* we moved underground."

"Mr. Trencher and I did not communicate often, but the last time we did...he was deeply upset."

"What was he upset about?"

"He wanted to say to hell with keeping us hidden, that it was worth the risk to open both sides. We had no way of knowing if they were still digging the tunnel from Bloomington. He told me we would have warning and could hide everyone."

"What stopped him? The controls for those doors are in his bedroom after all."

"He wanted to respect the wishes of the *others*."

"Are you saying Mr. Trencher informed the others of our existence, held a vote on whether to open up, and found himself in the minority?"

"Yes, and it wasn't only a vote. They barred him from his own suite – he had no access to those controls. Not only did they all know, but they actively prevented Mr. Trencher from opening the doors."

The crowd erupted. What hope Timothy and the Defendants felt moments before vanished in the wake of a bold-faced lie.

Judge Culler banged his shovel gavel. "Order!"

"I've had enough," Robby said as he climbed from the bleachers.

The guards grabbed him.

"Mr. Reed, return to your seat at once."

"This kangaroo court bullshit isn't worth my time. I'm out of here."

He was apprehended by both arms. Two more guards joined.

He yelled toward Ashley, "You're going to get someone killed!" before being dragged away.

Judge Culler motioned to Jacob to proceed.

"It boils down to trust," Ashley continued, unflustered by Robby's outburst. "I trust Marcus Trencher. He had his reasons, and he has a plan. These people do not. They got in the way, and if left to their own devices, they could jeopardize our safety again with the threat we face from the powerful people down that tunnel."

"Thank you, Ms. Cameron," Jacob said. "One more question that has been brought up. I hardly care to ask, but is Mr. Trencher the father of your child?"

Ashley laughed. "I am flattered anyone would think I am his type! I mean, look at all the beautiful ladies he had to choose from."

Men catcalled and whistled at the mortified women.

"I am happy to clear this absurd rumor up. Lieutenant Maniego and I are together. Mr. Trencher and I were never a thing."

"No further questions," Jacob said.

Between Grant and Ashley's testimonies, Timothy could hardly count all the lies. He carried the burden of proof more than the prosecution.

"The witness is yours again, Mr. Spencer, for re-direct examination."

Timothy returned to the podium.

"When was your last communication with Marcus?"

"Around the time the bugs got out and attacked the crops. He *really* wanted to open the doors to help, but he made the mistake of putting it up for a vote."

"What proof do you have?"

"Your Honor," Jacob said from his bench. "A letter was found in Mr. Trencher's suite yesterday. We would like to submit it into evidence."

"Too late. Motion denied," the judge said.

Jacob tucked the paper away.

Timothy looked back and forth. "Oh, was that your proof? A forged letter? Do you or do you not have proof of this vote?"

"Marcus Trencher would never do what you accuse him of. He loves these people!"

The audience was moved to cheer.

"She has no proof of anything she has said. No further questions."

He sat down. The audience heckled him.

"Enough!" the judge said. "We will reconvene in an hour for closing statements and jury deliberation."

They were marched back through the connecting corridor. The chamber audience hurled insults and threats in their wake.

Robby waited at the end of the corridor.

"Did it get any better after I left?"

Henry put his hand on his shoulder.

"Nope. We should prepare for the worst."

Chapter Seven

Marcus slept five consecutive hours, a personal best during his life underground.

He took his first round of meds the night before and it made him drowsy. Upon waking, he took the ones that made him not drowsy. He had tasks to complete, no matter the brain fog, zaps, and headaches.

The first was his meeting with the council. A mishmash of academics and former government officials governed the Quarry. Odds were, a few knew what he knew.

He arrived on time carrying only a bunker-issued water bottle.

A cast of characters filed around the U-shaped table. Jim, the bunker architect and tour guide, informed Marcus of the council but failed to mention he was on it. He flashed a friendly smile and salute.

"Welcome, Mr. Trencher," a man near the middle said. "My name is Dr. Roger Cooley. I am the former Executive Vice President for University

Clinical Affairs at Indiana University. We will spare you the torture of going around the room, as we all have long, meaningless titles."

"Thank you for having me," Marcus said. "Everyone has been so kind."

"We never gave up on that train tunnel. Once we got the population moved in, not even a week passed before we resumed digging."

"And for that, I am truly grateful. We are excited to join the wider network of bunkers."

"On to business. First off, we have conflicting reports. We were told there was a collapse in your bunker, greatly limiting capacity. Then, days before impact, Guardsmen came through and claimed there were at least a thousand souls down there. Which is it?"

"There was no collapse. You will find approximately fourteen-hundred individuals in my bunker."

"Thank goodness. Is that at capacity?"

"Eighty-five percent. Room to grow."

"Similar percentage here, with a population of 18,000." He set his tablet down. "Our tunnel crew is not due back for a few more days. They have been instructed to quarantine to avoid that flu virus you warned us about."

"Are you in constant contact with the tunnel team?"

"No, the experts are on the machine, anyhow. We will run communication cables as soon as possible."

"And what about the power line?"

"Within a month or two. It is our highest priority. I can only imagine the quality-of-life boost that will provide when you shut that coal mine down."

"We'll declare it a holiday when it happens."

The council laughed politely. A woman to his left cleared her throat.

"We've heard about the trove of digital entertainment data you have to share," the woman said. "What else was designated to your bunker?"

"Fine art. I will gladly send all of it your way."

"Foodstuffs?"

"We can rotate what we grow to fill needs. We do have an artificial salmon run. It needs work, but it could be promising."

The council members gave each other approving nods. Anything to diversify their diet was worth pursuing.

Another member spoke up. "Are you looking to shift any population?"

"There might be a few that want a change in scenery. But after the mine shuts down, most will want to stay. We are open to exchange and can accept a few dozen guests at a time as part of a hospitality and tourism service."

"A coal-mining bunker doesn't strike me as a luxury resort," the member said.

"Our leisure space is as good as it gets. We could serve as a vacation destination." He read the council's indifference and thought a joke might help. "Or we can keep the mine open and turn it into a penal colony."

They laughed and he felt good about himself.

"We do have that lice-infested rapist from Louisville we need to get rid of," Dr. Cooley said.

The woman beside him rolled her eyes.

"Send him our way. We will take care of him," Marcus said. "Now, if you don't mind, I have a few questions of my own."

"Go on," Dr. Cooley said.

"What news of the surface? Our instrumentation got knocked out."

"Dr. Hart, want to take this one?"

"I'd call it a frozen hellscape," Dr. Hart said. "The temperature has been below freezing for some time, and recently dropped precipitously into the negatives. Safe to say the sun is not shining through the debris in our atmosphere."

"When are we heading up to check it out?"

"Couldn't if we wanted to," another member said. "Our vault doors have a two-decade timer to keep us locked in. The override requires a unanimous vote here – and in Carmel, and Louisville."

Marcus had no more questions. The council adjourned. Before any of the strangers could corner him for small talk, he went straight to Jim.

"Could point me to the IT department?"

"Tech is on eight. You'll find a bunch of your former employees there."

"I'd also like to get a blood test. Just an annual physical kind of thing."

"The folks in the research labs might be your best bet. They start on six and go all the way to the top. They are located over the farms."

"Those were not on the original blueprint."

"They were not, but by God, the government made sure Big Pharma had their place."

"Must be doing something important."

Jim rolled his eyes. "All they do is crank out ADHD meds to take while playing video games."

The other council members emptied out of the chamber, except one guy. There is always one patiently, eternally waiting to chat with the world-famous Marcus Trencher.

"Is all that stuff they were saying about the vault doors being time-locked for twenty years true?"

Jim nodded. "The hackers in IT haven't taken a stab at it, but the council has openly discussed it as an option. Sounds like we are better off down here for now though." He checked his watch. "Hate to run out on you, but the wife and I are cashing in our smoothie rations. They bring in bananas from Indianapolis!"

Jim's departure opened Marcus up for *the one guy*. It was someone close to his age, so at least an old-man lecture was unlikely. He took a deep breath, smiled, and waited for the man to waste his time.

"Mr. Trencher, my name is Adam Terry. Do you know a Mack Terry?"

"Sounds familiar."

"He was one of the engineers that built your bunker. My mom, too, Teresa. You all worked together the past nine years. He's there, right?"

Mack, Teresa, and Emma Terry were dead and buried behind a wall.

"Oh! Of course. I've called him MT for so long... He is doing great. When the train can get through, he will be the first one on it."

He sensed the man's disbelief. A threatening silence grew between them.

"Apologies, but I've got to be somewhere. Nice meeting you, Adam."

Adam paused before finally shaking his hand.

"See you around, Marcus Trencher."

* * *

He made a quick jaunt back to his room to retrieve the hardware he lugged down the tunnel in his duffel bag. It was his nuclear football, and the one thing that might get him out of the mess he made. If it still worked, it would land him in a bigger mess, but one he would much rather be in. Maybe even one he would thrive in.

For now, he was just happy that Timothy Spencer put a handle on it for easy carrying.

He found the IT department on eight. Server rooms and workstations filled the floorspace. It was the brain of the Quarry. He walked by a dark lab before realizing someone was inside.

A woman with blue, blonde, and pink hair was lit by a glowing trio of screens. Once he got closer, he was not so sure it was not a man with blue, blonde, and pink hair.

"Sorry to bother you," he said before realizing she had earbuds in.

"Holy shit, Marcus Trencher?" she said in a voice slightly more feminine than masculine. She removed her earbuds. "Where did you come from?"

"I came from another bunker. You do know they broke through in the tunnel a few days ago, right?"

52

"Had no idea," she said as she hit a series of keys. "Need the password to the cloud, or what?"

He lugged his rectangular case onto the table. It was encased in aluminum with a matte black finish, similar in size to an old desktop computer tower.

"I was hoping I could find someone to hack into this device."

She stood, taller than him, and took immediate interest in the mystery box. She grabbed the top corners and rotated it to look at the various ports.

"What is this? I'll have to rummage through some drawers to find a USB cord..."

"I'm sorry, I didn't catch your name."

"Genie." She extended her hand and gave a firm handshake. "Used to be Gene. Finally got the balls to transition right before they announced the world was ending." She opened a cabinet and pulled out a cable. "I know – it's surprising they brought someone like me down here, but I'm very good at what I do. Want to know who I worked for before all this went down?"

"Who?"

"You! At *Trencher Industries*. I was on Timothy Spencer's team."

"Were you now? Timothy is the one who wrote the code I want you to break."

"I might've talked myself up a bit. Timothy was a whiz. But I'll take a crack at it. God knows I have nothing better to do down here."

"Thank you and keep this between us. Don't want too many eyes on this thing." He let go of the handle for the first time. "You do look familiar. Did we ever meet at work?"

"You walked by my desk a thousand times, and I was a man at the time, but no, we never spoke. I was your typical quiet IT guy. I'm much more myself these days."

"I'm trying to be more myself these days, too. See if you can get a feel for the thing. I'll be back in an hour."

Chapter Eight

Judge Culler emerged from his chambers and the crowd hushed.

"We shall hear closing arguments. The prosecution will go first but may reserve time to respond to the defense's statement, as they carry the burden of proof."

Jacob the prosecutor made way to the karaoke machine. He paced with the microphone until the chamber was silent.

"What you have seen and heard during this trial has made it clear beyond a reasonable doubt that individuals on that side knew of our existence. They knew of our labor. They benefitted so greatly from it. They knew of our poor conditions. While we drank tasteless meal replacement shakes, they were thawing cuts of prime rib and drinking bottles of wine. They knew.

"We heard credible testimony from a decorated war hero and the woman trusted to administer our move in. The defense has only tried to blame Marcus Trencher. Yes, *the* Marcus Trencher, our literal savior! This, mind you, after they blocked him from opening the doors, and after they chased him down that tunnel.

"Some may have learned later than others. But they all knew. I understand that we are a forgiving community, but those that so clearly knew for so long deserve the full punishment, and that is banishment from this bunker."

Jacob abruptly turned and sat down.

Timothy took a deep breath, rubbed his sweaty palms on his pant legs, and stood.

"As I stated on day one, the Defendants did not know of our existence just as we did not know of theirs. Simple as that.

"I am as angry as any of you. It was not fair that they lived so comfortably while we suffered. But these people knew nothing. What I am asking us all to accept is that the man who saved us, Marcus Trencher, is also the man that enslaved us.

"Marcus Trencher went down that train tunnel. We can to! We can find him and make him answer. And we should do so before we lash out and punish innocent people.

"Lieutenant Maniego crossed over with us. He went to the surface. What you heard was a man preying on your love for Marcus Trencher. He told lie after lie and provided zero evidence.

"Ashley Cameron, the one person who did know of the other side, fabricated an absurd story to exploit your admiration for Marcus as well. What was it... Marcus needed to hide us, but then suddenly wanted to open the doors, only to be prevented? Again, not a shred of evidence.

"The burden of proof is on the prosecution, and they have not carried it. What we need to do now is work together to make this place as livable as possible for as many people as possible. The sooner we move on and take on that task, the better off we will be."

He sat back down, exhaled, and resumed wiping his palms on his pant legs. A minute passed before Jacob stood back up to use his remaining time.

"It's a good story, isn't it? A man from our side defending the people on the other side. Timothy Spencer would have us all believe he is the one that saved us, not Marcus Trencher. He even goes so far to say he saved us *from* Marcus Trencher! Is it not obvious that we are hearing the delusions of a jealous business partner who was fired from the company he played a minor part in starting?

"In the hours after he crossed over and kept the doors shut behind him, he colluded with these people to create an elaborate excuse for our enslavement. And he wants to call Lieutenant Maniego and Ashley Cameron's story absurd! Wouldn't be the first time an outsider thought everyone from Sherman, Indiana, was naïve!

"In closing, I trust the jurors will see through the lies and wild conspiracies. We must exile the slave masters that took our dignity and loved ones away from us! The prosecution rests."

The audience broke out in applause, which transitioned into shouting. They pushed the rope barrier forward.

"Order! I hereby charge the jury with..." the judge trailed off. "Ah, hell. Get them out of here!" He motioned for the guards to escort the Defendants out of the chamber. "...the jury shall deliber—...Order, *order!*"

They broke out into a panicky jog through the corridor. Members of the audience pursued.

As they crossed the threshold of the second door into the bunker proper, a harsh, metallic creaking joined the angry shouts echoing down the corridor.

For the first time since an angry mob crossed over and beat Henry Plyman to a pulp, the door closed behind them.

Chapter Nine

They crowded into an apartment above the Gardens. Timothy sat despondent at the end of a double bed. Adrenaline ran high as the jury deliberated their fate.

"I'm sorry, guys. I messed everything up."

"You have nothing to be sorry about," Robby said. "Their minds were made up."

Mercedes sat beside Timothy. "I'll never forget how you stood up for us."

His reputation was shot the moment he took on their defense. He knew it would be and was fine with it. After closing arguments, though, he felt his own life was in jeopardy. What would happen to his daughters if something happened to him?

"Let's be real," Brittney said. "Did any of us really expect a fair trial?"

"For a moment, yeah," Timothy said.

"I was brought up not to expect favorable outcomes from the law," Steve said. "I think it's best we all get out of here after this."

"Nora, Becky, and I, we were talking in the hospital," Audrey said. "We agreed, no matter the outcome, we are leaving."

"We came to the same conclusion," Mariya said, holding Henry's hand.

"My parents are in Bloomington," Henry said. "We wanted to be on the first train anyway."

"So, none of you...care?" Timothy said. "I didn't realize there was this consensus."

"We tried telling you a hundred times," Robby said.

"We should plead guilty and get it over with," Brittney said as she flipped her hair and left the room.

"I've just been so hyper-focused on winning," Timothy said. "Guess I'm in the same boat."

It was somehow cathartic to embrace the idea of exile. They wanted to leave Trencher's bunker.

Brittney peeked her head back in. "Brad and Becky made spaghetti. It's ready in the café."

"Hell yeah," Robby said, taking two steps to the door before catching himself. He turned back to ask Melonie if she wanted him to bring her some.

"Save me some. I'm not hungry yet."

She was balled up on the bed behind Timothy, dealing with a morning sickness that was beginning to stretch beyond noon.

"Timothy, you coming?" Steve said. "You gotta eat."

"I'll be down in a bit. Save me some, too."

After the spaghetti exodus, only Timothy and Melonie remained in the room.

He did not know Melonie and was not in the mood to begin to. He was more interested in a nap to slow his racing mind. He hopped over to the open bed.

"I have a question," Melonie said the moment he closed his eyes.

After a long internal sigh, he said, "Yeah?"

"Do you believe there was never really an asteroid?"

"I've barely given it any thought. I've been distracted with this trial and all."

"The reason I ask, is if there was no asteroid, wouldn't that mean your invention would still be working on the surface? That 'smart grid' thing you and Marcus made?"

Timothy's eyes were shut, and hands clasped over his chest in a posture of maximum disinterest – but her question was surprisingly interesting.

"Hmm... If there was no catastrophic impact, then yeah, I guess there wouldn't be any catastrophic impact on the grid."

"So all around the world, there are houses and buildings lit up and traffic lights working and stuff, but like, no people?"

"Power everywhere, but no people..." Timothy grappled with the possibility.

"It's driving me crazy! Why isn't the asteroid thing a bigger deal? Isn't that more important than this stupid trial?"

He sat up on the side of the bed to face her. She was on to something.

"Well, never mind," she said. "All the batteries are probably drained since the sun isn't shining on all the solar panels."

"There may be wind and hydro still feeding in..." He shook his head in disbelief. His mind was off to the races again.

"Can you, like, shift power where you want?"

"The smart grid did just that if customers opted in, but it wouldn't draw from units under a certain percentage. Only the users could manipulate that setting. Making them tamper-proof was a major selling point. So, no."

He stared blankly as a revelation washed over him. He bolted upright. He wanted to grab Melonie and kiss her forehead.

"I take that back. There is *one* way."

He sprinted out of the room.

* * *

Timothy took on an Olympic speed walk across the Gardens to the café. Melonie followed, bewildered.

"Someone's hungry," Brad said.

"Guys, Melonie is a freaking genius!"

"My Melonie? That Melonie?" Robby said.

She shrugged in the distance.

"I know what Marcus is going to do!" He accepted a plate of spaghetti and promptly set it down. "He wants to take over the grid on the surface."

"Didn't you two specifically design for that to be impossible?" Henry said. "For ten years every citizen in Russia was trying to hack that thing."

Timothy took a second to bask in Henry's cybersecurity praise.

"Marcus and I secretly created a way to take complete control over the original Midwest grid. We never used it, never told anyone. I forgot all about it until Melonie started asking questions."

"We're about to be sentenced to some bullshit," Robby said. "Why does this matter now?"

"If no asteroid ever blasted the infrastructure away, the grid is still intact."

There was a collective *ahh*.

"Okay, so long story short, when we were a startup getting some buzz, I got into a minor Twitter spat with this billionaire we were competing with – I'll give you one guess who. Two days later, the guy shipped us a package. Do you guys remember that company that tried to create a blood-testing machine that only needed a tiny drop of blood to run a whole bunch of tests?"

"Theros? *Than*-something? I saw a movie on it," Mercedes said.

"Yes, that one! Well, it bombed. Total fraud. The guy sent us an actual prototype of the machine with a note that said, *'Your little magic box is going to fail just like this one.'*

"Marcus and I decided we were going to make it work to get the guy back. We gave up after a quick Google search but decided to make our own thing out of it. We turned the defunct blood-testing machine into the only thing that can override the *Trencher Industries* smart grid."

"Not that I care, but that vulnerability would've wrecked us if anyone knew," Henry said.

"Let me explain! What made our invention so popular was that people could buy a home unit, link it up with a solar panel, and live off-grid. *Or* they could buy a unit, subscribe to our smart grid for a monthly fee, and the network would provide more stability. Say your home battery was running low because it was cloudy and you were charging two electric vehicles and running heat in the house, but your neighbors three houses down were out of town. The network shifted power to where it was needed from where it was not.

"My shining contribution was the blockchain controls and security. Nobody could mess with your power. At the time, hackers were breaking into smart home tech and terrorists were hitting big-time infrastructure, taking over pipelines and all sort of crazy stuff. But nobody could touch the blockchain encryption I rigged up. I mean, *nobody*.

"Anyway, we got this wild idea to order some DNA testing microchips. Marcus did all the engineering stuff, I wrote the software, and basically what it does, is the machine takes a sample of my blood and a sample of Marcus's blood and then, and *only then*, it would load up a pass key into a USB drive. This key could then be plugged in to one of our terminals, and with our hashed-DNA-encrypted-passwords, we could override the blockchain and commandeer the grid. Don't laugh, but we called it 'The Blood Key'."

"The blood key?" Mariya said.

"*Sick*," Brad said.

"God, you two were weird together," Robby said.

"Hold up," Steve said. "Remember what those soldiers said about hangars full of killer drones? They'd need the grid to charge up during their sweeps."

"Exactly!" Timothy said. "That's what I'm getting at! If all that stuff is true, Marcus could ruin everything for them."

"What's stopping him then?" Audrey asked.

"He needs my blood."

"You guys were *really* weird together," Robby said.

"We tested it once and then took a sledgehammer to the jump drive, sanitized the machine, reverted the controls, and never messed with it again. Marcus hid it away and we swore never to tell a soul. You guys are right about the trial – it doesn't matter. The blood key is what matters now."

Timothy noticed all eyes looking past him. A guard approached.

"Everyone up. Verdict is in."

Chapter Ten

Marcus found the research laboratories on the eighth floor a few turns away from IT where he left his magical machine with Genie the transgender computer programmer.

He tried to avoid human interaction by skimming the directory on the lobby wall, but the young male receptionist spoke up.

"Can I help you find something?"

Marcus forced a quick smile. "I was hoping to have blood work done."

"The general practitioners can do those."

Marcus's deadpan stare relayed no interest in that route.

"...Or, we do have the labs on ten. Right this way, sir."

He stepped into an elevator. The young man reached in and hit ten for him.

"I'll let them know you are coming," the receptionist said. "Um, I hate to ask, but are... are you Marcus Trencher?"

Marcus gave a sly smile as the doors closed.

He could see into two labs right out of the elevator. Researchers beyond the glass paid no mind. A young woman appeared from around a corner.

"Hello, sir? Craig said you were looking to have some blood work – oh, wow. It is you." She wore a white lab coat, hair pulled back in a simple ponytail.

"Hi, I'm Marcus. Yes, I wanted to have some blood drawn."

"Alice, pleasure to meet you. We can do that."

He followed her down a hall, making one left turn before entering an examination room on the right. She went straight to a drawer and unpackaged a syringe and vial.

"I need my blood in a 5-10cc purple-top tube."

"You know your stuff!" she said as she tied a rubber tourniquet around his bicep. "That's the first time I've had a patient request that."

She grabbed a tube with a purple top and showed him. His forearm offered a prominent vein.

"You shouldn't feel a thing."

He did not. He watched his blood fill the tube. Alice reached for another.

"That won't be necessary. One is fine."

"Are you sure? We won't be able to run a full panel."

"I'm certain. And I have another request – I need that tube. I don't need the test. I have my own machine."

"Um, yeah. It's all yours." She set the tube on a towel, untied the tourniquet, and applied a band-aid over the puncture. "Is phlebotomy a hobby of yours?"

"I procured my own machine after I found out people wanted my blood. A nurse thought I had genius DNA in my bloodstream, so she attempted to sell my blood to a CRISPR lab so she could get a magic potion to make her child do better in school."

"People are crazy! The gene-editing space got wild there for a minute. Heard a few stories like that about celebrities."

Marcus shook his head at the fabricated woman in his fabricated story.

"What are you researching in these labs?"

She went to the door, peeked out into the hall, and shut it.

"This might be rude, but I thought all the billionaires were in on it. We are producing an anti-aging therapy. It could add twenty years to the average lifespan, and that might be conservative. The telomere restoration is astonishing. Slows everything down." She lowered her voice even more to say, "Some of the researchers say it's already been around for a decade, but only for the super wealthy."

"I wasn't often invited in those circles, but I heard rumors."

"Please don't tell anyone I told you. I could get in major trouble."

He stood and grabbed his purple-top tube of blood off the counter. "Your secret is safe, so long as my health records are kept confidential."

Alice put her right hand up, "I swore a HIPAA-cratic oath!"

* * *

He returned to the IT department and found Genie. His machine was open and linked to a laptop.

"Any progress?"

"What is this thing? All I get is a message that says, 'Deposit blood now.'"

"Good, so it still boots up."

"I don't see a way around the prompt. There are these two circular ports up front, here and here, but I don't know what goes in them. I had to open it up. There are mechanical parts that physically move whatever goes in the ports. It looks like biotech. I think you *actually* deposit blood."

"That is correct," Marcus said.

"Could have saved me some time. Why'd you bring me a blood-testing machine?"

"It's not just any blood-testing machine. It is a key maker. It requires two samples of blood. The chips inside digitize DNA profiles of each sample, mashes them together, hashes it, encrypts it even more, and then loads it onto a jump drive that it spits out, here."

He pointed to a slot beneath the two blood-tube ports.

"That's messed up. I love it."

He pulled the purple-top tube of his own blood from his pocket.

"I have one half of the key here. I was hoping you could find a way around requiring the other half."

"You can't just put anyone's blood in there?"

"No. On the port to the right, you can see an 'MT' scratched above it. That is where my blood goes."

Genie looked closely. She looked at the left port that had a 'TS' above it.

"TS... Timothy Spencer?" Genie said. "You need Timothy's blood?"

"I do, unless you can find a way around it."

"If it recognizes the DNA profile, that means it already exists within the code to match against it." She shook her head. "That would be too easy. Timothy has that locked up tight, guaranteed."

She opened a program on her laptop.

"This will attempt a million password per...*oh shit.*"

Where there was a prompt asking for a deposit of blood, a message now read, "*If the current device is not unplugged in 10 seconds, the machine will self-destruct.*" The seconds ticked down.

Genie yanked the cord. The message changed to, "*Do not try that again.*"

"Timothy, you bastard. I don't see a way..."

"Understood."

She was right – Timothy would never have made it so easy.

"If this is a key, what is it to?"

"The grid."

"Oh," she said before it sunk in. "*Oh,* you mean *the* grid?"

"Yes, our un-hackable blockchain decentralized power grid can be commandeered using this key. You are the first person I've ever told."

"You could have cut power to whole cities."

"Whole states. You can see why we kept it secret."

"Definitely would have damaged the brand. So why mess with it now? There isn't even a grid to unlock anymore."

Marcus shrugged. "Maybe."

"What do you mean, *maybe*?"

"It was built to be resilient. There could be pockets of micro grids still intact."

"But it's an ice age up there with no sunlight."

Marcus feigned a laugh. "The key machine is just something fun to do. I've gone out of my mind with boredom down here."

Marcus grabbed the machine, side panel, and screws.

"Did Timothy make it? To a bunker, I mean. He was from Iowa, right?"

"Timothy is alive and well, but not in Iowa. He's in the bunker I just came from."

Chapter Eleven

Timothy and the Defendants returned to a sparsely populated chamber. Measures were put in place to reduce the audience size.

The mob that chased them after closing arguments were now roped off in the atrium. They still made their presence felt when they caught a glimpse of their arrival.

The door to the other side closed behind them.

Timothy's daughters were permitted in the chamber. Susan, their widowed neighbor, had been taking care of them during the trial.

Timothy knelt and hugged both his girls.

"Today is the last the day, I promise. I will spend all my time with you after this."

"We miss you, daddy!" Madeleine said.

Liza, his eldest, made a rare expression of affection. "Yeah, dad. We miss you."

He hugged Liza again. "I miss you, too. It's almost over. Are you feeling better? Are you getting enough real food?"

"Yeah, I feel better. I was for sure allergic to the soy drink."

"Yeah, I think you were."

The Judge's chamber door opened, and the jury filed out. Timothy looked at Susan. "I'll see you all later tonight. Bye girls. Love you."

Judge Culler emerged from beyond the drab green door and smiled at the near-empty chamber. No unruly audience to raise his blood pressure.

"The jury was instructed to deliberate and come to a verdict based on the facts of the case, and to do so for each individual." Judge Culler looked at the Defendants and then the jury. "Will the foreperson of the jury please stand."

A man with a goatee and a tucked-in sleeveless shirt stood from the jury box bleachers.

"Have you reached a verdict on which you all agree?"

"We have, Your Honor."

A bailiff fetched a piece of paper from the man and handed it to the judge. He read it, folded it, and handed it back.

"You may read the verdict."

The goateed juror cleared his throat.

"On the charges of conspiracy to enslave the people of our side, we find all the Defendants *kind of* guilty."

Judge Culler turned bright red. "Mike, there's no 'kind of' guilty. They either are or aren't! I just read that paper and that wasn't what it said."

"Your Honor, I can explain."

"Give it a shot."

"We agreed that all the women, and..." he looked at his paper, "Bradley Farris and Kent Grieve, they only *aided and abetted* the Defendants who knew

73

what was going on, and that was Henry Plyman and Robby Reed. Those two are 100% guilty. Not kind of."

Judge Culler had a hand over his face, rubbing his forehead. "By God, we're just going to have to work with this. So say you all?"

They jurors mumbled, "Yes, Your Honor."

"Alright then, this court will now proceed to sentencing."

There was grumbling in the archway where the mob waited.

"I sentence the 'kind of' guilty Defendants, to three months' probation. Stay and work in the bunker in assigned roles, be useful, help people, and we can move on.

"Henry Plyman and Robby Reed, I hereby sentence you to six months' labor in the mine. 70-hours weekly for the first 3 months, 60 hours weekly for the final 3 months. Everyone will be moved to apartments on this side of the bunker."

News of the sentencing made its way through the mob outside the chamber. Some began to boo.

"Your Honor," Timothy said. "I would like to request that the punishment be changed to banishment. There would be less mouths to feed, more resources for all remaining."

"I'll agree to that – *after* the guilty parties complete their labor sentences. Otherwise, they would only be fleeing jurisdiction."

It was not the instant train ticket to Bloomington they had hoped for, but all things considered, it was a favorable outcome.

Judge Culler grabbed the shovel gavel.

"The court is now adjourned."

Before the judge could bang the railing, a shot rang out in the atrium.

* * *

People screamed and scattered. With the door to the other side closed, everyone within the chamber could only shelter in place.

Five men armed with long guns entered, with more men following. Ashley Cameron, who had been missing from the day's hearing, arrived with them. Another shot was fired, this time in the chamber.

Judge Culler had the closest route to escape but chose not to take it.

"Put down those weapons at once! We will not have tyranny here!" he said, standing at the railing in front of his chamber door.

"Shut up, old man," the nearest terrorist said. It was Lieutenant Grant Maniego.

The other soldier, Blaine, following close behind. The others were recruits from the mine. They walked to the center of the chamber where Timothy and the prosecution, in the days prior, made arguments like civilized people. The Defendants hid beneath the bleachers.

"Don't try anything stupid," Grant said. "Come on out. Don't run, and you won't die."

None felt they had a choice. They made slow movements to their seats.

"Here's what's going to happen," Grant said. "That last part? We're going to do that over."

Grant jumped the railing in front of Judge Culler and struck him with the butt of his rifle. The judge fell back on the ramp, writhing in pain. A cut opened above his eye.

"All you fine ladies, the computer nerd, and the chef with the bullet wound – you will stay in this bunker and work. Henry Plyman, Robby Reed, you will work in the mines, just as the good judge said."

Grant took on a ponderous pose.

"Mr. Spencer, I believe you requested banishment? I shall grant this request!"

He leaned his rifle against the wall and picked up the judge's shovel gavel. He bashed it on the rail, sending a discordant ringing through the chamber.

"A grave crime was *just about* to go unpunished!" Grant pointed with the shovel. "Timothy Spencer murdered my friend, Corporal Samuel Caswell."

"He tried to kill me! He killed Rick Porter!" Timothy said.

Grant tossed the shovel aside and motioned to his lackeys. Two men grabbed Timothy.

Steve stood but quickly found himself at gunpoint.

"Full disclosure – my vote would be death," Grant said, strolling down the ramp. "Eye for an eye sort of thing. But I'll be generous and go with your banishment idea."

He called out another one of his men. "Get in there and open the doors."

The man went into the Judge's chambers and climbed the trapdoor ladder to Marcus's suite.

Grant went face-to-face with Timothy and stared him in the eyes before strutting to the center of the chamber.

"I hereby sentence Timothy Spencer to banishment – *to the surface!*"

"What? No! You can't!" Timothy looked to where he last saw his daughters.

He squirmed as the men dragged him toward the massive door slowly swinging open. They entered the corridor where his cries echoed.

His friends could only watch.

Bad guys had all the guns.

"Bring those two," Grant said, pointing to Henry and Robby. "I want them to watch."

Robby resisted. Henry was too tender to fight.

"You can't do this! My daughters are down here!" Timothy said. His legs gave out, but he was dragged. "I'll work in the mine. Let me see my daughters!"

His pleas were ignored. He was pressed onward and out of the corridor, into the bunker proper on the other side. Mariya, Steve, Audrey, Brad, and the others trailed under the supervision of Grant and Ashley's goons.

"This is insane, let him go!" Mariya shouted. "He doesn't deserve this!"

They moved past the hospital. Dr. Nora Weinstein, on duty watching Jenna Dothmayer, saw the passing commotion and stepped out.

"What is going on? What are you doing with him?" she hurried alongside. "Blaine? What is this?"

"Go away, Nora," Blaine said.

They forced Timothy, Henry, and Robby through the media room and then the decontamination chamber before the elevator. Mariya, Nora, and the others were shut out.

They stepped onto the elevator platform.

Henry's panic began to subside, critical thinking kicked in.

"Listen, Timothy," Henry said. "The elevator dome's man door faces *north*. Are you listening?"

Timothy asked again to see his daughters.

"Timothy, as soon as you step out, head west. That is *left*. There are houses three-hundred yards away. It's the closest shelter. You need to go straight there."

"Huh? Say again?"

"Listen to me! It's going to be freezing. Turn left as soon as you step out! Get to those houses as soon as possible!"

"Oh, okay," he said.

Grant was amused. "Better listen to your friend. Last we checked it was -29 degrees Fahrenheit. God only knows the wind chill."

Timothy snapped out of his malaise. He scanned the armed men. One had a knife out.

"Cut me. Put my blood in here," Timothy reached out to snatch Grant's canteen.

"Whoa! Somebody's lost their damn mind!"

Timothy locked eyes with Henry. "You *need* my blood..."

He was concerned about the blood key, of all things.

"No, you're going to find Marcus yourself. *Left, three-hundred yards.* Gather yourself there, and then...and then get to Bloomington. Look for a quarry."

The elevator came to a halt.

"This has been cute, but it's time," Grant said. He went to the man door, punched in the code he read off a scrap of paper, and the lock released.

The cold stole their breaths. Blinding light brought tears to their eyes. It was a whiteout. Grant shut the door.

"Whew! Now that is chilly!"

"You can't send him out in that!" Robby said.

The henchmen, including Blaine, looked down at their feet.

"Here, take this, it's Carhartt," one of the men in the back said, before placing the jacket in Timothy's hands. "Was wearing it when we came down."

"Dale?" Timothy recognized one of the few friends he made in the mine. "I can't take this. It's your favorite jacket."

"There are work gloves in the pockets. Take this, too." Dale removed his beanie and handed it to him.

"Who let Mr. Nice Guy up here?" Grant said.

The other men did not object to Dale's generosity. Grant sensed it.

"Fine. No, I like it. What fun is it if he falls over and dies 50 yards out?" He looked Timothy up and down. "Wearing all that, you should get at least 100 yards. Maybe 150!"

Henry looked to Robby, hoping for an assertion typical of him. Robby looked back, helpless. Someone had to do something. He had to do something.

"I'm going with him," Henry said, frightened by his own words.

"Dude, you can barely walk," Robby said.

"Tim doesn't know the area. He'll get lost out there."

"Guys, I'll be okay..." Timothy said.

Nobody believed him.

Robby shook his head. "Then I'm going, too."

"No, people need you down here. Melonie needs you." Blood rushed out of his head and around his body. "Find Marcus or get a message to him. He won't stand for this."

"I'll gladly let all three of you go. Less mouths to feed." Grant turned to the man beside him. "Give that one your gloves." He looked further down the line to another man. "That an overshirt? Give it over."

Grant shoved the items into Henry's aching midsection.

"I think you're out of luck, pal," Grant said to Robby. "Unless you think you can make it out there wearing that."

There was no chance and Robby knew it.

"At least take this," Robby said. "It's clean." He removed his t-shirt and helped Henry wrap it around his face.

"Alright, that's enough. Don't need you taking off your pants, too," Grant said. "Any departing words?"

Timothy turned to Robby and Dale. "Tell my daughters I love them and that I'll be back as soon as possible."

"Tell Mariya—" Henry shook his head. "Tell her, and everyone, we'll try to get to the bunker in Bloomington. We have to get Timothy there..."

"If it's too dangerous, just stay around Sherman," Robby said, tears falling. "I'll see you when I see you."

There was an impromptu moment of silence. Grant reached for Timothy's arm.

"Don't fucking touch me," Timothy said.

Grant tilted his head and gave his patented smirk. "Alright, then." He went to the door and again punched in the code.

Robby – close, tall, and peering – got a good look at it.

Grant opened the door to the biting cold. Robby recoiled from the blast of air.

Timothy took a deep breath and stepped into the white.

Henry looked back once, took his last breath of warm air, and departed.

* * *

A crowd gathered in the chamber. *What happened? Were those gunshots? What was the verdict? They went to the surface?*

In the corridor between the two sides, Grant and Blaine huddled around Ashley Cameron.

Men recruited to help overthrow the trial restrained Robby, who was shirtless.

The two soldiers nodded in the affirmative. Ashley walked up the ramp to her former suite, and more recently, Judge Culler's chambers. Frightened faces followed her ascent.

"We will be taking a more active role in governance moving forward," she said to the gathering crowd. "As we move into this multi-bunker phase, it is best that myself and my cohorts handle the delicate relationships to come."

"Where's Henry? What did you do with Timothy?" Mariya said.

Ashley looked down at her. "Timothy Spencer was banished to the surface for the murder of Corporal Samuel Caswell. Henry Plyman volunteered to go with Mr. Spencer."

Mariya cried out. Audrey and Becky held her up, then held her back.

Ashley looked out again to the greater crowd.

"Today we did what was necessary. Today – we got better."

Chapter Twelve

When the door shut behind Henry and Timothy, there was no time to feel sorry for themselves.

Timothy stumbled three steps ahead before turning right instead of left.

Henry could hardly blame him. Wind blasted in from the west. They had to walk into it.

"*Left!*" Henry shouted.

"*What?*"

Henry put both hands on Timothy's shoulders and yelled in his ear, "*Left!* I'll guide you! Keep your head down!"

Looking forward was fruitless. There was nothing but white. Piercing wind stabbed their skin and shot pain into their eyes. They were fifteen feet out and shocked.

Timothy was better dressed and in better physical condition. He became Henry's windshield. Henry put his hands on Timothy's back, leaning to steer him. They began their blind trek westward, the pair postured like a centaur.

The ground was snow-covered and sealed beneath a layer of ice. They hardly made footprints. Thirty yards out, they lost feeling in their toes.

Fifty yards out, they felt they might die.

The cold shut out unnecessary thought. The override was good – all logical parts of their minds had already given up – but before much longer, hypothermia would do them in regardless.

Henry stepped through a patch of shrubbery. He slipped and banged his knee on the ice. It was a silent event, despite his shouts, due to the deafening soundscape. Timothy separated, unknowingly. One step, two steps. After another, he would disappear.

Timothy put one foot in front of the other, head down, eyes squinting to see his blurry feet. He could only afford to think about himself, but a change registered. He felt less capable of pushing through the wind. He didn't know why.

Henry felt no pain from his fall. He was numb. But he did feel the panic. He scrambled to catch up to Timothy, who marched on machinelike.

He lunged forward, nearly tackling Timothy. He stabilized, put his hands back on Timothy's back, and pushed on.

Were they halfway? Three-quarters? There were no markers to let them know.

Both lost feeling in their feet up to their ankles, hands to their wrists. Ice formed on their eyelashes.

Only the tiniest blips of analysis breached the animal brain – they were on a gradual decline. They could not feel their feet, but some form of sensory feedback told them they were on a road surface beneath the snow and ice.

Timothy halted and stood upright. Henry didn't know or care why. He pushed his face into Timothy's Carhartt jacket and hid from the wind.

Timothy forced a blurry-eyed look ahead. Within ten feet, blighted and buried in snow, was the outline of landscaping – bushes, mounded up probably by mulch or rocks, and an unnatural rectangle. It was a sign.

Timothy pressed his eyes with the palms of his gloves to clear ice and tears. He looked again.

To his right, he saw another unnatural shape of straight lines. It was blueish-grey and stood from the ground to a higher point in the sky. It was a two-story home – the first near the entrance of the on-site housing development.

He turned to tell Henry. Henry fell off him.

Timothy tucked his frozen hands beneath Henry's armpits and lifted him. He buckled Henry's arms around his waist like a seat belt and dragged him toward the blue-grey house.

They crawled up the icy porch steps. Henry rolled over on his back. Timothy continued to the front door.

He could not open it. His hands were frozen. He clenched the knob in his forearms and willed one arm upward and the other down. His tears and snot froze as he pressed his weight against the door. His desperate gross motor movements rotated the knob further. It gave way, and he fell inside.

He crawled on his belly to get his feet through the doorway. It was still below freezing in the dormant house, but he was sheltered from the brutal winds.

The drastic increase in survival odds ushered in a thought: Henry was with him, but now he was not.

Timothy stood and slipped on the tile foyer, thanks to a layer of ice packed on the soles of his shoes. He skated out with his breath held. He wrapped his arms around Henry, again, and dragged him through the threshold, falling backwards indoors. Timothy kicked the door shut.

Henry was flexed, shaking, and breathing rapidly. A red blotch grew on his side. His wound had reopened during the trek.

Timothy was hardly better. Neither had warmth to share. Still, he moved closer and laid an arm across Henry's chest. He would get up and find a blanket in a minute. He just needed to rest a second.

He closed his eyes.

He found himself in his home back in Iowa on a sunny morning, inexplicably lying in the foyer with his wife, Shelley. It made sense there, in the dream. His two daughters played in the living room. It was a warm feeling. Shelley stood and walked into the hall.

His arm dropped and he rolled over. He opened his eyes and the dream ended.

Henry stood above him, looking ahead in a sleepwalk state. He shook off his gloves and remove his cap. His fingers were too numb to unbutton his shirt, but he tried. He stumbled forward and fumbled his frozen hands at the button on his frozen jeans. He was trying to strip.

Timothy wanted to speak, and say, *"Hey, don't do that,"* but he couldn't muster the words. He looked on with curiosity.

Henry lurched another step forward and leaned against a wall at the edge of the foyer.

A series of chirps and clicks came from all over the house. Timothy thought his ears were popping. Then, a great electronic *whirr* sounded. The house came alive.

Life was detected, and the smart home had work to do. Lights turned on and the sound of air came through vents, somewhere.

He felt a surge of hope. Henry continued into the hall, noticing none of it.

"Hen...Henry. Power's...on," Timothy said. He stood and caught up to him. "Henry...there's..."

They found a vent in the hall at floor level. Even if the air coming through was merely freezing, it was still warmer than the ambient temperature.

Timothy let Henry down in front of the vent. It blew the warmest air they had ever felt.

Timothy removed his gloves and Carhartt jacket. He corralled as much warmth as possible. They crowded close as if it were a holiday fireplace. There could have been a real fireplace the next room over, they hadn't checked, but they would not move until thawed.

How much power remained in the *Trencher Industries* home battery unit was unknown, but it was enough to give them a fighting chance.

"Hang in there, Henry. It's getting warmer."

Chapter Thirteen

Robby broke out in a feverish sweat, still shirtless after shedding it so Henry had something to shield his face from the cold. Melonie sat by his side in their newly assigned apartment down the hall from Timothy's former place.

"You did all you could," Melonie said. "And Henry was right. We need you. Me, the baby, everybody."

"You didn't feel the cold like I did. It was ten times worse than when we went up. I don't know..." he stopped and took a deep breath. "I don't know if Henry and Timothy could've made it to those houses. It was that brutal."

Melonie rubbed his back. "We are going to believe they made it, okay?"

Robby broke into sobs. He didn't know if he would ever see Henry again.

There was a cursory knock at their door, as it was opened immediately. Robby bottled his emotions.

"Sorry to barge in," Steve said, half his body in the hall. "They are gathering us all up."

"What for?" Melonie asked.

"Some post-trial bullshit. Pardon my language."

Robby rubbed the tears from his eyes. He pulled a grey t-shirt from a bag and rolled it on over his sticky body.

In the hall, Steve stopped Robby. "They made it, man. Believe it. Timothy, Henry, they are tough dudes."

Steve led them around the corner to where everyone was gathered. Some stood and leaned against the wall, others sat. Robby and Melonie were the last to arrive.

A woman stood at the front. It was Robby's eighth-grade homeroom teacher, Ms. Brynn, who he absolutely tortured.

"*Shit,*" Robby said under his breath.

"Mr. Reed, glad you could join us," Ms. Brynn said.

He gave an awkward wave, reminded of the record-breaking tardiness he racked up in eighth grade.

"My name is Natalie Brynn, and I've been assigned to keep tabs and make sure you are attending your assigned duties each day. Other than some dietary restrictions, and restrictions on travel to the other side of the bunker, you will mostly be free in your non-working hours.

"I will come to you or your supervisor, so no need to track me down. At the end of each day, I will turn in the attendance sheet to...oh, what's her name..." she flipped a page on her clipboard. "Ashley Cameron."

Brad raised his good arm. "Who gave her authority over us? Or anyone else for that matter?"

"A council was formed to create more structure and accountability in the bunker. The miners got three seats. A security department was formed. They get a seat, as do the farmers and food service workers. With that tunnel connecting us to Bloomington and other bunkers, the council elected Ms. Cameron to represent us in whatever negotiations might take place. Interbunker relations, they called it."

There was a silent air of defeat.

She lowered her clipboard. "Look, I'm sorry about your friends. I taught Henry in school. He was a wonderful kid. I sincerely hope he is okay up there, I really do. Same for your other friend.

"If you show up and do your time, I'll be your strongest advocate. Not all of us were bent on revenge. Work with me, I'll work with you, and we can make the best of the situation. If there are no further questions, I'll pass around the assignments, and you will start tomorrow."

She handed out a thin stack of paper copies. Some lingered to discuss their assignments, others shambled back to their new barebone apartments.

Robby approached his former teacher.

"Mr. Reed, good to see you are alive and well."

"Wouldn't say I am well but thank you. I, uh, want to apologize for how I acted in your class."

She laughed. "Don't worry about it. I had one or two worse than you in the following fifteen years."

"It's just that you were really nice, and I drew penises on like every surface, and I disrupted every class..."

"Really, it's okay. You grew up. The world ended. All is forgiven."

He sighed in relief as some weight of middle school regret was lifted. "Why aren't you teaching down here? Not enough kids?"

"There are plenty, but there are also enough other teachers. Plus, the basic science I planned to teach wasn't Biblical enough..." She stopped herself.

"Sorry to hear. You were an all-time favorite, even though I tortured you. You'll make a great parole officer."

She thanked him. He gave another awkward wave and they parted.

"That was good of you," Melonie said.

"I wanted to apologize for the time I brought up her divorce and made her cry in front of the class, but I chickened out."

Melonie hit him on the arm, then hooked into it as they walked back to the room.

Robby laid down on his flimsy cot. His mind wandered back to the days he made Henry laugh during class. Henry, the good kid that he was, tried desperately not to. Robby was successful enough to get them separated to opposite corners of the classroom, which only amplified his shenanigans.

Marcus was an after-school friend – he had already moved on to high school and college courses. Henry and Robby were inseparable during those years.

Henry left for college then worked overseas for Marcus's company. They drifted apart. Despite the end of the world being what brought them back together, Robby enjoyed the renaissance of their friendship.

Now he was gone. Up on the frozen surface. Maybe alive, maybe dead.

* * *

Down the hall, others gathered in Brad and Becky Farris's room to discuss their work roles. Some had it better than others.

"These people are out of their minds if they think I'm doing maid service," Brittney said. "I've seen them in the halls. They have the little hotel maid carts, and they gather linens and stuff. It's disgusting."

"What did you write on the index card they had us fill out?" Audrey asked.

"When they asked what skills we had? I wrote *'Fuck off'* on it."

"Becky and I are glorified cafeteria workers," Brad said. "Minus, I guess, any level of glory."

"They have me in the hospital all day," Audrey said. "Lot of sick people here."

"I wrote a bunch of techno-jargon about the water treatment plant," Mercedes said. "It worked, I guess."

"They put my ass back to shoveling coal," Steve said. "Hopefully Robby can take Timothy's spot and work with me."

"I wonder how he is doing," Audrey said. "He looked like he was in shock."

"He got another dose of survivor's guilt," Steve said. "Not to say Henry and Timothy are not surviving up there – they got to be."

Before another word could be said, Mariya flew into the room with the assignment paper in hand.

"Those racist bastards put me in the nail salon! It's because I'm Asian!" Her face was flushed red. "I've never even had a pedicure before!"

"Did you tell them to 'fuck off' on your index card?" Brittney asked.

"What? No, I wrote I was a veterinarian, graduated from UC-Davis."

They laughed, mostly at Brittney and their inside joke, but Mariya was in a more precarious emotional state. Her anger crashed to sadness.

"I want my Henry back," Mariya said. "I can't do this without him!"

"Oh girl, it's okay. Come here." Brittney hugged her as she broke down.

"...He left me here."

* * *

Jenna Dothmayer was wheeled out of the infirmary for the first time since she was put there unconscious and clinging to life after being struck by a bullet fired from Marcus Trencher's gun. She would walk again someday – the bullet did not hit her spine – but she was wheelchair-bound for the foreseeable future.

Dr. Nora Weinstein pushed her through the door into the open space. Nora had been by Jenna's bedside since she was called upon to help. She saved Jenna's life.

Still, they had not held a conversation.

Nora witnessed little of the trial, but she did see the outcome. Timothy Spencer, the man that saved

93

her in more ways than one, was dragged to the surface and made an outcast. She didn't understand – he was the guy that broke through and exposed the lie they were all living in. Why was he punished?

Jenna was more alert than usual. Nora could see that she wanted to say something. She leaned down to listen.

Jenna said, in a raspy whisper, *"Who are you? Who are all these people?"*

Milling about were dozens of bunker denizens from the other side. She had been so sedated and sequestered that she had not seen a single person she did not know, other than Nora. Only now could she muster the words to ask.

"My name is Nora. I am a doctor. A lot has happened since you've been in recovery." She set Jenna up with a wide view of the bunker proper and stepped around the wheelchair. "First of all, do you remember what happened to you?"

Jenna nodded.

"Shortly after, that giant door over there opened. There were over a thousand people living on the other side. There is a whole separate half of this bunker. That is where I came from."

Jenna looked to the open door.

"I don't know exactly why we were kept over there, except that the people mined coal and ran a power station, which provided electricity for the entire bunker. That reactor on this side was a mock-up. The real power came from slave labor."

Tears fell from Jenna's eyes.

"Enough of that. Let's check those bandages."

Before they got back in, Ashley Cameron and her entourage of henchmen emerged from the corridor and marched by. Some of the men did a doubletake of Jenna. Even after a week of teetering on the edge of death, she was still beautiful.

"Here, this section of wall was designed to be taken down," Ashley said fifteen yards left of the infirmary. The train tunnel was beyond it. "Knock out enough to get a vehicle through. I want to meet the tunnel crew tomorrow morning."

Two men took off toward the Gardens and the storage tunnels. The others turned their attention to the wall, immediately making markings on it.

Ashley passed by, again without speaking. Grant and Blaine stopped.

"You two should be ashamed of yourselves," Nora said.

Blaine looked as though he was.

"You know, Nora, they have whole barrels of bourbon over in the pantry," Grant said. "Much better than that powdered alcohol you were hooked on. How about we I grab a drink. Smooth things over."

"You disgust me."

Grant put his hands up and grinned. "Alright, then. See you around, Nora. Maybe next time you'll be more polite and introduce me to your friend."

He winked at Jenna and departed back to the other side. Blaine looked on apologetically. Nora wheeled Jenna back into the infirmary.

"I hope the tunnel collapses on them tomorrow," Nora said.

Chapter Fourteen

Marcus met Jim for breakfast in the diner on four.

"Tomorrow's the big day," Jim said. "The tunnel crew comes back."

"Are they are finished?"

"I'm sure the walls are done. The machine takes care of that as it goes. They have gaps where they'll have to lay rail, but running cable shouldn't take long."

Marcus sipped his small coffee, a once-a-month luxury for adult-aged citizens of the Quarry. A robot delivered their veggie omelets.

"When does the next train come in?"

"What is today? Shoot, I bet it's down there now."

Marcus nearly choked. "What time does it depart?"

"Not until tomorrow. They'll spend all night loading and performing maintenance. It'll take off around the same time the tunnel crew returns."

Marcus wanted out before the crew returned. If they brought back news of his crimes, he would be arrested and charged with attempted murder, or murder, of whoever he shot. He could hardly recall. Was it Brad, the chef from Louisville?

Nice guy. He hoped he was okay.

Memory surfaced of his other victim, Jenna Dothmayer. Jenna the Geneticist. He recalled their date at the height of his paranoia, and he felt shame all over again. She tried to get him to open up. In his state, he thought she was digging for information.

She never asked how he and Senator Granger secured the bunker, or about the bodies walled up on the other side – she didn't know about the other side. She didn't ask about the global holocaust underway. There was no indication she was about to ask for the blood key.

The image of her falling in the gardens made him shudder.

"Think you could talk the council into letting me on that train?"

"Shucks, you just got here," Jim said before cracking a smile. "I can do that, no problem."

"What can you tell me about Adam Terry? He approached me after the council meeting."

"Serious fellow for someone so young. He was in the Army Corp of Engineers. Jumped all around the U.S. on bunker projects. His parents were well-connected contractors, also engineers. Real Right-Wingers. Why do you ask?"

"I found him off-putting. Thought I'd see if you knew what his deal was."

Marcus put his napkin on his plate, triggering a robot to come clear the table. They walked to the concourse outside the café.

"I'll line that train ticket up for you," Jim said, patting his belly. "Any plans the rest of the day? Up for some racquetball after the food digests?"

"Thanks, but no thanks. I need to visit some folks before I leave."

* * *

Marcus searched the directory kiosk and committed a room number to memory.

As a guest in the Quarry, his temporary quarters were only a few doors deep in the Stacks. The apartment he was looking for was on the top level, and a whole half-mile in.

It was a nightmarish trek past repetitive doors and light fixtures under a seven-foot ceiling. More food-delivery robots zoomed by than people. Side hallways had aggressive signage warning of dead ends. The main hall looped around, eventually. The Quarry had admirable public spaces, but the Stacks were atrocious.

He pressed on and found the apartment, knocked, and waited.

Cheryl Plyman, whom he would only ever refer to as Mrs. Plyman, answered. Her hands went to her mouth as she screamed with excitement.

"Marcus!" She hugged him before yelling at Mr. Plyman.

Mr. Plyman was wearing a virtual-reality headset in the living-room-slash-bedroom. He also sported haptic feedback gloves and a vest.

Mrs. Plyman pushed his headset up. Mr. Plyman stood baffled by the sudden return to real life.

"Marcus, my boy! You're here!" He shook him with old-man strength.

Seconds passed before they looked past him, hoping to see Henry.

"I don't want to get your hopes up. Henry is still back at the bunker. The tunnel machine broke through a few days back and I'm the first visitor."

They were more relieved than dismayed. In the chaos of the last days on the surface, there was no certainty.

"He is doing great. I think he is love with that girl..."

"Mariya? We really liked her, didn't we Harold?"

"Yes, wonderful gal," Mr. Plyman said.

"Please, have a seat. I'll put on some tea."

They had a queen-sized bed, loveseat, and their very own blue light faux window. It had a limestone ledge in front of it. Marcus propped himself up there.

Mr. Plyman carefully placed the headset on a hook. He was famously averse to modern technology. Henry and Robby had long-running jokes about it growing up.

"What is with these headsets? I have one in my room," Marcus said.

"You haven't tried it yet?" Mr. Plyman asked. "It's the *Metaverse*! There are whole virtual worlds to explore. I was a skeptic, but it's fantastic."

Marcus was never a gamer, but he was aware of the virtual-worlds explosion in the years prior to life underground. He pathologically avoided them.

The VR revolution was a legitimate free market event, but the timing was impeccable for the technology to finally breakthrough right before mankind moved underground. The Quarry had 18,000 inhabitants, yet public spaces were rarely more than lightly populated. People were placated in the Metaverse.

"Doesn't it give you a headache after a while?"

Mr. Plyman shook his head. "Quite the contrary! There are places I can go that clear my mind. You can listen to soothing music that gets in-tuned with your brain waves. It's magic. Plus, it only weighs about as much as a ball cap. And not to sound grim, but it gives a lot of people a reason to keep going."

"He is on that thing all doggone day," Mrs. Plyman said, bringing Marcus a cup of tea. "I have to wrestle it away when I want to meet the ladies for cards."

"Honey, I think cards come second to the storming of Normandy Beach, June 6th, 1944," he said, winking at Marcus.

"Harold, you've stormed that darn beach with your buddies every night for weeks! The war's over!"

"We requested another headset, but we were put on a wait list."

"You can have mine," Marcus said.

"The admins wouldn't like that," Mr. Plyman said. "They track that kind of thing. Serial numbers, I think. There was a black-market headset scandal a few months back."

Marcus took a sip of tea. "I apologize for not stopping by sooner. I was in quarantine, then the council kept yanking me around. I wanted to visit first thing but got caught up in all that."

"No worries, we're just happy everyone is okay," Mr. Plyman said. "Henry will get here when gets here."

"It could be a while. They haven't laid all the rails to connect the tracks."

"Understood. Plenty to do in the Metaverse to keep us occupied. We've met folks that live in the Indianapolis and Louisville bunkers."

"Speaking of Indianapolis, I am hopping on a train there tomorrow."

"Why not use the headset? It is almost as good as face-to-face. Maybe even better."

"I'm old-fashioned, I guess."

"Nobody is more old-fashioned than us. Why do you need to go all the way to Indy?"

"Politicking, interbunker trade deals, stuff like that. I prefer to do it in person."

He contemplated what he could tell them. What would disappoint them? What would endanger them?

"Actually, that's not entirely true. I also just need the space."

"We don't make judgements. You know that. What happened?"

"I've begun to address a medication issue, but there were external forces, too. Right at the end, before going underground, they were going to kill me and steal my bunker, after all the work..."

"Hold on. Who are *they*?"

"I don't know. Someone in the government? Senator Granger sent soldiers and they killed all the engineers. They lived on site all those years. They were in on the plan to take it. Granger reported that part of the bunker collapsed, as a cover up."

"We had no idea," Mrs. Plyman said.

"I couldn't tell anyone – not even after we got underground. Now that our bunkers are connected, there are people here waiting to see their friends and family come down that tunnel. One has already asked me. I couldn't tell him."

"It's not right that anyone could swoop in and steal your bunker, let alone murder you," Mr. Plyman said. "Is there anything we can do to help?"

"Just tell Henry where I am. Nobody else, though. It's best you don't tell anyone about our association."

"I may have mentioned you to the ladies at card club," Mrs. Plyman said.

Marcus laughed. "I don't think that will be a problem." He looked at Mr. Plyman. "How about you. Did you tell your war buddies about me in the Metaverse?"

"No time to gossip when Nazis are shooting at you."

Mrs. Plyman rolled her eyes.

"One other thing. The bunker was bigger than I let on. They only gave me fifteen bids to work with, and the government was going to use the rest of the space with whoever they chose."

"How much bigger are we talking?"

"There was space for approximately 1,400. The government thought they lost that capacity. It was so late, they never sent anyone to check firsthand."

"Please tell me you didn't leave it vacant," Mrs. Plyman said.

"We moved 1,400 people down a few days after you left for Bloomington. Almost all are from Sherman County. It was as many as we could fit and still feed."

"That is fantastic! You're a hero!"

"They probably don't think so. If I am one, I am the worst hero ever."

"How so?"

"We've had to run a coal plant, which required mining coal. The bunker consists of two halves connected by a single corridor. I shut that corridor. We lived on one half, while the 1,400 lived on the other. Guess which side did all the mining."

Mrs. Plyman tried to comprehend. "But...why?"

"Those 1,400 people are off the books. I had to hide them. But someone from the other side broke through the train tunnel, and now everybody knows. I had to flee. Tomorrow the tunnel crew comes back. They are going to come for me. I'm not safe here."

"Are you going to live like a man on the run?"

"For now. But I will redeem myself. When I return, I'll have more than an apology. I will have a key to their freedom."

"Freedom? What kind of freedom?"

"It's best you don't know. Just...Henry is fine."

He moved to the door.

"Marcus Trencher," Mrs. Plyman said with authority. "You are not leaving without giving me another hug."

He turned around and obliged.

"If you get into any trouble, you come right back here, okay?"

Mrs. Plyman let go, and Mr. Plyman gave him a firm handshake.

"Go do what you need to do."

"I'm going to fix all of this. I promise."

Chapter Fifteen

Robby arrived at the mine for his orientation at 5am. His assignment to work with Steve in the coal chamber was nixed. The powers that be wanted him to receive the full mining experience.

Half-asleep, he caught a helmet to the chest. He picked his gloves off the ground.

Guess it's going to be like that.

"My, my, how the tables have turned," said Billy Manus, the village idiot of Sherman. "I'm about to put you to work. Something I know you ain't used to. I'm the mine supervisor this shift."

"Who'd you have to blow to get that?"

The men cracked up. They had no love for Robby, but they did love laughing at the born loser, Manus.

"You better watch your mouth," Manus said, stepping up to Robby, six inches shorter and physically inferior in every way. "I'll put a hole in you like I did your pal, Henry."

"I'd like to see you try. I'll beat your ass like I did in Dan-O's bar."

"I slipped! You got lucky!"

Robby sighed. He set a personal goal not to fight on his first day. It was 5:05am.

"Whatever, boss. Can we get on with training?"

"Ronnie C., Jeff, you two give him the tour, then put him on the south wall in the room-and-pillars."

He followed the men through hanging plastic, into the mine. Neither of his tour guides said a word until they reached the first collection of equipment. There was a conveyor, a roof bolter, longwall shearer. They made one special stop.

"This is where that guy blew a hole into the train tunnel," Ronnie C. said.

"Has anyone gone down it yet?"

"It's 25 miles to where they broke through. A guy came from that way a few days back. Didn't have much to say. He thought we all had the flu."

"They knocked a wall out at our end last night to get vehicles in," Jeff said.

They stepped through into the train tunnel. A trio of vehicles approached from the west. They were the golf carts he used to race before he sunk one into the swimming pool. Familiar faced rolled by.

Blaine drove the lead cart, Grant Maniego the middle. Ashley Cameron sat on the passenger side. She looked straight ahead as they passed. A third cart was loaded with extra batteries and was driven by a new lackey.

"Looks like they are sending an envoy."

"Don't get comfortable with those people," Robby said. "They don't care about you or any of us."

They backtracked to the room-and-pillar section of the mine. Jeff handed Robby a pickaxe.

"It ain't rocket science," Ronny C. said. "Chip away, fill the cart. There are shovels lying all over. Push the cart to the chute when it's full and dump it."

"Just one question," Jeff said. "You really didn't know we were over here? Even when we had the explosion?"

"We had no idea. We figured it was a tremor."

The men left without another word.

Robby tapped the wall and coal flaked off. There was no one around to crack the whip. He took a few easy swings. With twelve hours ahead of him, he wasn't about to exert himself.

Two teenage boys approached with immaturity echoing before them. He was alone for all of five minutes.

"Whoa, there's a dude down here!"

"Bro, it's one of the guys from the other side."

Robby turned around. "I'm not deaf, kiddos."

"*Kiddos*, hah! He talks like he's from the 90's!"

"It's not even 6am. Tone it down a bit?"

There were more giggles, but they did start to work. The ping of pickaxes was preferable to their inane banter.

Coal accumulated at the bottom of the wall. The heap was getting in the way, making Robby reach further for his strikes. He found a shovel leaning on a nearby pillar. The teenagers grabbed their own and all three started shoveling the coal into the cart between them.

Robby turned for a shovelful and received a shower of coal down his back, which was damp with clammy morning sweat. The boys snickered.

Robby steeled himself. *No fighting.*

Then, he was hit with a second hailstorm.

"Alright, fuckers. Shovels down."

"What? Relax, bro."

"I'll relax after I beat both your asses."

He stood in the open ready to fight the scrawny teenagers.

"We were just joking."

The flash of anger came and went. It was approximately 7am and he was ready to fight his second and third individuals of the day. Something had to change.

"Look, I just lost one of my best friends. A week ago, my other best friend left, and I don't know if I'll ever see either of them again." He pointed at one of the boys. "Imagine he died yesterday. Would you be in the mood to have some little shit tossing coal down your back?"

The boys shrugged.

"My name is Robby. What's yours?"

"Hunter."

"Braxton."

"We're all stuck down here. Let's try not to piss each other off."

They ambled back to work.

"Who were your friends?" Hunter asked.

"Henry Plyman and Marcus Trencher. Ever heard of them?"

"No way! Everybody knows who they are. They were billionaires."

"Want to hear a crazy story about Marcus Trencher?" Braxton asked.

Robby looked forward to the amusement.

"Before we were brought down here, my dad's phone kept ringing, even though he had already closed the garage. He finally answered and it was Marcus Trencher. He told my dad he would get our family bunker bids if we did a job for him."

"Did he need his Ferrari fixed?"

"No, man, even better. He had us show up at one of those big warehouses north of town. It was full of vehicles and fuel and stuff. He wanted us to winterize everything, put chains on the tires. He even had those military vehicles with tank tracks instead of back tires. It was pretty sweet."

Robby listened without input. He found the kid believable, despite not knowing of this venture. Marcus didn't tell him everything.

"He told my dad that if the asteroid isn't as bad as people say, it won't destroy everything, it'll just block out the sun with all the dirt and ash in the sky. He wanted to have the right kind of vehicles to drive in the snow."

"Dang! That guy really was a genius."

"In like five years, I'm going to go up to the surface and go straight there."

Robby thought about Henry and Timothy. Marcus's cache of winterized vehicles would be useful to them, if they knew about it, if they were alive.

He wanted to escape to the surface the moment the door shut behind them. A teenager's bullshit story was enough to bring the urge back.

He could do it. He saw the code to the door and memorized it. He was watched, but not closely. The soldiers and Ashley Cameron were traveling down the tunnel at that very moment, as if he didn't need more temptation.

He had a girlfriend. He had a baby on the way. He had to stay. There were obligations.

Still, he was curious.

"Are you talking about the warehouse near the railroad? Where they did manufacturing in the early days?"

"I never knew what it was growing up. It was just a big warehouse when I was there."

"The company outgrew it. What auto shop did your dad run? I wrecked a few vehicles in my day."

"Durham's, down near the Little League fields."

"Ah, I took mine to the south end. Is your dad down here?"

The teenager, Braxton, hesitated on his next strike to the wall of coal. "He was, but...he died in the mine explosion."

"Damn. Sorry for your loss."

They continued to work and eased toward casual conversation about growing up in Sherman, Indiana. Robby saw his younger self in them. It was probably why he wanted to fight them within the first half hour of meeting.

A whistle blew, indicating lunch time.

* * *

Robby was anxious to see what was on the menu. He was starving.

He watched the men in front of him walk away with garden salads. He saw tomatoes, cucumber, and a drizzle of ranch dressing.

Brad was behind the counter prepping vegetables. He gave Robby a nod.

When he reached the front, the lunch lady did a double take. She put the salad bowl away and grabbed an aluminum cup instead.

"Oh, c'mon."

"The council said only Soylent for you."

She pressed a lever for a serving of powder and another for water, then put the cup under a milkshake mixer. She slid it under the window.

"Thanks. I love this stuff."

He chugged two gulps of the chalky liquid and walked off before the lunch lady could see him gag.

The cafeteria was mostly empty. His new teenage friends ran off to sit with girls their age. He scanned for a place to sit like a high schooler.

He spotted one familiar face.

Audrey Bruni perked up. He took a seat across from her. He sipped his disgusting Soylent. She took a bite of salad.

"How is your first day in the mine?"

"Terrible. Are you going to eat those tomatoes?"

"Um, no. Never liked them."

Robby reached in and grabbed the two quarter slices, throwing one in his mouth immediately. Juice dribbled down his chin.

"How is your forearm feeling?"

He had almost totally forgotten about the burn he received while retrieving a pan from the oven weeks prior. The event somehow led to him and Audrey being alone in the infirmary, which led to more, which he deeply regretted.

"The pain is gone, but I have a shiny scar."

He put it his arm on the table turned palm up.

She grabbed his hand, pretending to look the burn over with medical expertise. She wasn't fooling him. She wanted to touch him to see if sparks flew — the same kind of sparks from the infirmary.

"...so, are we just not going to talk about us?"

Robby took his arm back.

"Look...it was a mistake. I've got to stick with Melonie. I really like her. I mean, I might even love her. We're having a baby."

"There are different kinds of love. We can have something."

"I'm not going to sneak around on my pregnant girlfriend. You've got to move on."

Tears formed in the corners of her eyes.

Brad Farris approached in his chef's apron, oblivious to their drama.

"No sling, I see," Robby said. "Ready for some tennis?"

"Just about. Audrey and the wife patched me up good. I come bearing gifts."

Brad revealed eight cucumber medallions.

"It ain't much, but it's all I could sneak by that crazy lunch lady on short notice."

"Thanks, I'll take what I can get."

"That's probably ten whole calories. Don't spend them all in one place."

"I don't think I have a choice there."

An electronic tone tolled the end of lunch.

"Back at it. See you guys later."

He bolted for the exit. He'd rather pick coal than face Audrey and her feelings for him.

He wanted out. He wanted out of all of it.

Chapter Sixteen

Henry and Timothy survived their first night on the frozen surface thanks to the smart home detecting their presence and springing to life. It warmed to fifty-six degrees Fahrenheit that evening, and sixty-six by the morning.

They thawed as best they could, body and mind. Timothy was eager to tackle the next step in their survival, and to get back to his daughters. Henry struggled to sleep with such intense pain in his side. Trekking across the arctic Indiana landscape did a number on him. He kept to the couch under blankets and comforters.

Timothy began another pass through the house to take inventory of what they had at hand. The previous search was a purely blankets-and-pillows expedition.

He stepped into the garage and the first thing he saw was his breath. There were garden tools, toys, and little else. In a cardboard box by the door, he found a pair of single-pane swimming goggles tangled in a croquet set.

His returned to the kitchen and opened the refrigerator.

There were a dozen eggs cracked by the cold, rotten tomatoes, and broccoli, all frozen solid. He grabbed two rock hard bottled waters. The freezer was stocked with frostbit pizzas, fish fillets, and a rainbow of popsicles.

He closed the door and examined the family photo under a magnet – mother, father, military son, and a teenaged daughter. He put it in a drawer.

The pantry was stocked with peanut butter, coffee pods, and a case of bottled water, among canned and boxed goods. He grabbed granola bars and joined Henry in the living room. The electronic fireplace was on full blast.

He handed Henry a water. "This one's starting to melt. You should be able to get a few sips."

"Thanks. I just realized how dry my mouth is."

Timothy took notice of Henry's pallor.

"You don't look so hot. Are you feeling okay?"

Henry pushed his blankets off his upper body. The dark red spot on his shirt, over his ribs beneath his right arm, had grown.

"You should have said something."

Timothy grabbed a towel from the bathroom. In the hall closet, he found a fully stocked first-aid kit.

"You're in luck," he said, flashing the kit. "This isn't one of those cheap ones, either."

Henry rolled his shirt up, peeling it from the wound. The puncture where Billy Manus planted a pickaxe had popped half its stitches.

"Damn," Timothy said with a dry towel in hand. "Let's clean that up."

"Try the sink," Henry said.

"I'm sure the pipes are frozen."

"It's well water out here. I bet they dug straight under the house."

Timothy gave it a shot. The pipes shuddered for several seconds, but out came running water. He soaked the towel.

He took a second to decipher whether his tingling hands were deceiving him. Maybe the sensation was brought about by frostbite, but he was certain symptoms of frostbite didn't feel so good.

"Hey, I'm getting warm water!"

He returned to find Henry nodding off.

"Huh? Did you say warm water?"

"Unless my hands are messed up. Here," Timothy said, handing him the towel.

"Definitely warm. The pipes must run down to the bunker. These houses are right above the water treatment plant. Marcus thought fifty steps ahead."

Henry was overcome by a wave of pain. Feverish sweat began to bead on his forehead.

"Enough about the water." Timothy wiped blood from around the wound. "This might sting."

He applied an iodine tincture around the wound and used the towel to spread it around.

Henry bent away. The muscles between his ribs flexed and forced the air from his lungs. The open wound, unraveling stitches, and ring of nasty brown iodine made for an unpleasant sight. Timothy grabbed tweezers from the kit.

"I'd be lying if I said it was about to get easier."

The nylon suture was easy to find, but he had no clue what to do with it. He plucked at the string nearest the intact stitches, pulling the skin together. Henry grimaced.

"See if the deeper layer of stitches took," Henry said.

Timothy squinted as he investigated the gash. He saw a layer of flesh with fresh scarring deeper in the wound.

"It looks closed up, but I don't see any stitches."

"They dissolved. As long as that part didn't open up, I should be fine."

The yawning epidermal layer didn't look fine to Timothy. He saw tiny holes where the string was once stitched through, but he couldn't loop the suture through any of them.

"Hang in there. New plan."

He pulled a large compress pad from the kit and pinched the wound closed before applying the bandage to hold it.

Henry arched his back in pain.

"Sit up, sit up."

Timothy wrapped gauze around his ribs and the opposite shoulder. He taped the end of the wrap and guided Henry back down. He bit open a sample-sized packet of Ibuprofen.

Henry swallowed the tablets and drank all that was unfrozen from his bottled water. He closed his eyes to face the pain in a state of unconsciousness.

Timothy moved back, unsure of what else he should do. He placed a granola bar and another bottle of water next to the couch.

"I'll let you rest. I'm going to look around."

He peered through the porch window. Visibility remained poor, but he could see out to the sign at the front of the housing development. Beyond that, the ground and sky blended in a hazy gray. It wasn't a windblown whiteout as it was during their harrowing march, but it was only moderately better.

He skipped the basement on his previous house tour, figuring there was nothing there to generate warmth. He was not wrong, but he did find a utility room with a familiar apparatus on the wall – a *Trencher Industries* battery panel. He zoomed through the user interface that he designed.

The house had a day's worth of power at the current usage rate. The grid around the house could chip in another half-day before hitting lending limits. A fraction of power fed in from a residential wind turbine. It wasn't much, but it would contribute a kilowatt hour or two per day.

Timothy walked upstairs to the master bedroom. He stripped covers off the bed the previous night. He was back to raid the closet. The next time he set foot outdoors, he wanted to be dressed for the occasion.

His eyes lit up at the sight of faux fur. He grabbed at the thick olive-green material beneath it. It was a high-end winter coat with a fur-lined hood. He hugged it as if a loved one were in it.

He pulled the remaining clothes out in armfuls and threw them on the bed.

He plucked a pair of worn-out boots from the closet floor. They were a size too big, which was ideal. After three layers of socks, they would fit snug.

He shook off revisiting visions of the dead bodies he found in the wall. The people who lived in that house were almost certainly among the corpses. He had to get used to it if he was going to survive on the surface. He was about to borrow a lot of things from the dead.

The second closet was stocked with women's clothes. He took a scarf. He opened a plastic bin of photo albums. He didn't need to see those.

The next bedroom belonged to a girl. He thought of his own daughters for the millionth time since waking. He wanted to leave it alone but felt it prudent to do a cursory search.

He gravitated toward a bookshelf with heavy college textbooks stacked on top. The shelves were filled with young adult novels. Between the youthful literature and the advanced engineering textbooks, the MIT sticker and pop star posters, it was hard to approximate the girl's age.

He opened the nightstand drawer and found a notebook with a sparkling cover. EMMA was spelled out in sequins. He picked it up to look for something useful beneath, but still mindlessly flipped through the pages. They were filled.

September 19, 2022

> *Mom and dad told me we are moving for their jobs. I told my friends we were moving to Colorado, then dad told me it was really Indiana. wtf? I've been crying all day! I will miss Zoey and Alicia the most!!! I don't know why we have to go all the sudden. Mom and dad told me sorry it was top secret AND THEY TOOK MY PHONE! OMG*

October 23, 2022

> *I hate it here! IT'S THE MIDDLE OF NOWHERE! I hate online school. I can't even talk to my old friends. We live next to mom*

and dad's construction site. It's underground and they won't tell me what it is. They act scared and it gives me anxiety. There are other kids here, but they are younger. Adam is going to college and the military. He is annoying but I will miss him.

Timothy was enthralled by the historical record. He skipped to the last entry.

January 5th, 2030

Dear Diary,

Sorry it's been a few years. I was so happy they let me escape to college that I ran off without you. I re-read my past entries – cringe! I loved MIT, but I missed my parents and my brother. I even missed this place. It's boring, but way more peaceful than the real world. It was a strange childhood in this isolated village of engineers, but there were good times.

Tomorrow I FINALLY get to see the bunker firsthand. I've waited so long for this. I'll be underground for the next several days, but not permanently (yet!).

The public will be informed soon. I can't help but feel guilty that I get to survive when so many will die. My parents say we were chosen, and that we deserve it and earned it. I don't know. Nothing is fair. They've grown more extreme in their beliefs. They are clueless about Adam. They'll never know.

I'll be back to write about my first impressions of the bunker!

P.S. Marcus Trencher, my idol and my biggest childhood crush ever, will be there to meet everyone!

P.S.S. Dad says Marcus Trencher won't live in the same bunker as us. He probably has a swankier one somewhere else. Darn it!

There were no more entries.

Timothy kept the diary and retrieved the winter coat, boots, and a couple shirts from the master bedroom. He went back downstairs to find Henry flipping through blue-screen channels on the living room television.

"Anything on?"

"Nope. Every channel looks like this."

"It was worth a shot." Timothy turned it off. "Better conserve what power we have. Meter downstairs says we only have another day or so."

"Any power feeding in?"

"A small wind turbine. Not enough, but it's keeping this micro grid from dying."

Henry saw the button-up shirt in Timothy's hand and reached his good arm out for it.

"There are two dozen smaller houses past this one, basically cabins," Henry said, with one arm through a sleeve. "At the end of the drive, there's an apartment complex. I drove back there once, and Marcus got on me about it. Didn't want me interacting with the workers, but it had already been vacated."

Timothy tossed the diary on Henry's blanket. "Check that out. There was a couple of engineers living here with their daughter. She kept a diary."

Henry winced as he put his other arm through the sleeve. After pain subsided, he looked at the bedazzled notebook, then at Timothy.

"What are we going to do? What's our plan?"

Timothy went to the window. Outside looked as hostile as it did a half hour earlier. He wanted to get back to his daughters. He wanted to get to Marcus.

"We have to get you back on your feet before anything else."

"It could be weeks. My legs are almost as bad as my side." Henry pulled a pant leg up to show the colorful bruising and scab on his shin. "If you want to start the journey to Bloomington any time soon, it might have to be without me."

Chapter Seventeen

Marcus packed his bag with a change of clothes, medication, and the blood key. On a whim, he grabbed the virtual-reality headset on the way out.

The train was scheduled to depart at 2pm. He planned to be on the platform an hour early.

He stopped at an automated canteen outside the Stacks for a quick meal. *SoyBar* glowed in fancy lettering above a touchscreen and window. No signage could make it taste any better.

He tapped the flavorless option and choked it down with a cocktail of medication, chasing it with the last drops from his water bottle. He deposited the aluminum cup in the repository and received thanks from the cartoon cup on the screen.

"Sammy the Soyshake likes to show his gratitude for letting him assault your taste buds," a man said behind him.

Marcus struggled to peel his chalky tongue from the roof of his mouth.

"Here, this thing is a water fountain, too."

The outgoing fellow took his empty water bottle, tapped the screen, and out came precious water.

"Thanks. That stuff is like liquid chalk."

"Got that right, but there is nothing cheaper on the ration menu. If you suffer through six Soylent meals a week you can earn an extra cup of coffee at the café down on five. You know, like a Starbucks Rewards program."

"I would kill for Starbucks."

"I'd settle for charging station coffee, or even gas station sludge." He reached out his hand and they shook. "Name's Bhaskar. Marcus Trencher, right? Pleasure."

Bhaskar wore navy blue coveralls and hauled his own duffel bag, much like the one Marcus had over his shoulder.

"Heading back to your bunker with us today?"

"Ah, you're on the tunnel crew. No, I won't be returning yet. I'm going the other direction."

"Louisville or Indy? Louisville royally botched the transition underground. Mobs showed up because every local knew the Mega Caverns. It's in the middle of the city – worse kept secret. They ended up gunning down crowds. Could you imagine having to shoot a bunch of innocent people to protect your bunker?"

Marcus could, all too well.

"I'm going to Indy. I hadn't heard that about Louisville. That's awful."

"I've been on the I-65 tunnel since the start. All the crews talk when we connect."

They were about to meet up and chat about their latest connection. All their pals would learn about the innocent people Marcus Trencher shot and the innocent people he enslaved.

Bhaskar checked his watch.

"I better start running through the checklists. The crew should arrive right around your departure. Did you want me to deliver any messages? We don't have the cables hooked up yet."

"Actually, I might."

* * *

Marcus entered a much busier IT department than what he found the previous visit. Genie saw him and pulled her headphones down. There were other programmers working at the stations nearby. All wore headphones, a few had full headsets on.

"I wanted to see if you thought of any solutions to the problem we discussed," he said, resting his duffel bag on the desk, the bulky blood key outlined in the canvas material.

"Honey, it's *all* I've thought about."

Marcus felt a spark of hope. "And?"

"...And I think the program Timothy wrote will function exactly as he intended. No way around it."

He slouched.

Genie swiveled in her chair to face him squarely.

"If you want that box to spit out a key, I suggest you resolve your issues with Timothy and get him to donate some blood."

"It's complicated."

"You want to know what is complicated? A sex change, right before the goddamn apocalypse, and nobody knows how to adjustment your hormone medicine, and..." she stopped and took a deep breath. "What I'm trying to say is, you are both being hard-headed. The world ended, and so should your silly little grudge."

"Tell Timothy that if you see him. He might be on his way. I'm leaving for Indy."

Genie glared. "Are you shopping for a second opinion? Now I'm offended!"

"No, I have to meet with people. Organize trade deals and whatnot."

"Not a soul in Indianapolis will crack that code. You're wasting your time."

"Look, I need to get away. I'm not safe here. While I'm in Indy, I might need to communicate with you. What is the best way to go about it?"

"The Metaverse. We hacked the hell out of it to protect privacy rather than invade it. Don't mess with the interbunker email. People can read that."

"Got it. That reminds me..." He reached into his bag and pulled out the VR headset from his room. "Any way you can wipe this so a couple friends of mine can use two in their room? They said these things were serialized or something."

Genie laughed. "Sure, give me a room number and I'll take care of it."

Marcus wrote the Plyman's room number down on a sticky note.

"Thank you for that, and everything."

"Yeah, yeah. If I see Timothy, I'll talk sense into him. Life is too short to fight with friends."

* * *

He found an insular stairwell outside of IT and descended one floor, emerging before the Offices of

Mental Health Services. He wanted to top off his prescriptions.

With the initial ramp up of his medication going well, he thought maybe he could level up a few milligrams. The receptionist greeted him.

"Is Dr. Cline with a patient? I wanted to update her on how I'm doing."

"She can see you now."

He put on a good mood before entering.

"I wanted to let you know, so far so good."

"Glad to hear," Dr. Cline said. "It's only been a few days, so we will keep monitoring."

"About that. I'm leaving for Indianapolis and I'm not sure how long I'll be. Could I refill my prescription, or go ahead and get the next level of dosage? I'll finish the lower milligram pills first, of course."

"Have their pharmacist reach out, I'll send what they require. They have everything we do and more."

"I'd prefer my file not be sent along. Privacy isn't what it used to be."

"We will work something out if the time comes." She removed her glasses. "Have you given therapy any more thought? Getting to the root causes of your struggles will be every bit as beneficial as the medication."

"I have a train to catch. Maybe later."

He slung his bag over his shoulder and left before Dr. Cline could say more. He asked for and received two pieces of paper and a pen from the receptionist. He flew into the department hall where he bumped into a man.

He started an automatic apology. The victim of his rushing about was Adam Terry.

"Sorry, I wasn't looking where I was going. It's Adam, right?"

"Taking advantage of our Mental Health Services, I see," Adam said. "Mental health is so important these days, especially down here."

"I needed a minor prescription. Apologies again, but I need to get going..."

"Worried about the train? It doesn't depart for another hour-and-a-half," he said, extending his arm to lean against the wall, blocking half the narrow hall. "I'm curious, what do you hope to accomplish in Indy? You know you can set up video calls, right? We even have email integration between bunkers."

"I am old-fashioned. I'll be back in a couple days. Now, if you'll excuse me."

Adam didn't move.

"Thought you'd like to know I am heading the other direction – to your bunker. Can't wait to surprise my parents and sister."

Marcus's stomach dropped. He forced a smile.

"Tell your parents I'm working on a few trade deals. Hopefully I come back with some apples or bananas. We don't have the best fruit options there."

"I haven't seen them since well before impact. My sister returned from college, got a nice call, and haven't heard from them since. Then I heard rumors about a collapse. So, yeah, I can't wait to see them."

"Things got crazy in those last days. But, hey, the tunnel broke through and it's all good. Now, if you don't mind..." Marcus leaned to move around him.

Adam stared him down with untrusting eyes.

"I look forward to seeing your bunker. My parents sacrificed everything to build it."

* * *

Marcus restrained the panic long enough to round a corner and find an empty public restroom. He splashed water on his face at the sink and began wringing his hands under the faucet. He broke out of the loop by slamming his fist on the counter.

Hunched over, he locked eyes with his reflection in the mirror.

"Murderer."

Murderer? He didn't kill Adam Terry's family. The soldiers Senator Granger sent pulled the triggers. And if they didn't – they were going to kill him and steal his bunker. Kill or be killed.

Whether he killed Jenna Dothmayer or Brad Farris was a fair question. Another bullet could have hit someone else. Maybe he was a murderer.

Adam Terry was about to find out, possibly before stepping off the Quarry train platform. The returning tunnel crew might deliver the news first. *Marcus Trencher went mad! He is a murderer! Read all about it!*

He fumbled through his bag for the right prescription bottle. He was ready for higher dosage. He needed it. He halved a pill, tossed one part back in the bottle and swallowed the other.

The door to the restroom opened. A man backed in with a cleaning cart, propping the door open with it before noticing Marcus.

"*Jesus*, scared the hell out of me," the janitor said. The familiar expression of recognition lit up the man's face. "Hold up, ain't you Marcus Trencher? I used to work for you! Got certified to install your rigs back in the day! I got a hell of a deal on my own. The savings paid for itself in no time. Smartest thing I ever done."

"Happy to hear. That's what it was all about."

"I wouldn't be here if it weren't for you, in a roundabout way. Got hired at the university to do maintenance on their campus grid – panels, turbines, battery arrays. When the end-of-the-world went down, they took me and my family here. Not bad for a bunch of townies."

"Townies?"

"It's how those liberals at the university referred to us locals. Term used to be *cutters* back when there were more quarries." He took a mop and plunged it in a bucket. "Anyways, now I clean toilets, but my family's alive, so hell, I can't complain."

* * *

Marcus made his way to the train platform more at peace with his fleeing. The townie janitor snapped him out of his spiraling. Dr. Cline would call it effective talk therapy.

The ground level swarmed with activity. Teenagers walked in clusters around the track. The fitness facilities were filled with motivated people working out to upbeat music. Golfers lined up in pairs behind the tee box for a closest-to-the-pin tournament. He kept his head down and descended the subway-styled stairs.

The train platform was also abuzz. The last three cars of his Indianapolis-bound train peeked out from the east tunnel beneath the championship banners. Workers were loading watermelons in the last passenger car.

He scanned to his right, to the west, and could not tell if the tunnel-digging crew had returned yet. Food, supplies, and giant reams of cable were loaded on pickup trucks and trailers.

He found a bench close to the train. If everything was on schedule, he still had forty-five minutes before departure. He took out paper and pen and propped his bag on his lap. He contemplated the messages he wanted to send.

The task was complicated by the need to be discreet. He was going to hand them off to someone he barely knew, and with no envelope. He started the first letter:

> *Sorry for the mess I left. I will make it up to everyone. We will be in touch when the communication cables are laid. It's best I stay away, but I need you to help get Timothy to me.*
>
> *Tell Timothy: We are blood brothers, remember? I have the key. Come to Bloomington, find Genie. We need to meet.*

He folded the paper three ways and wrote, "To: Henry Plyman, Timothy Spencer, or Robby Reed."

He addressed the second letter to Ashley Cameron:

See to hospitality of Adam Terry. His parents were engineers during bunker construction. Be careful.

Provide update as soon as comm lines established. Am I wanted? Send Timothy Spencer to me. I need him.

He looked for Bhaskar, the crewman he met that morning. There were several men and women in the same uniform. When he got up to seek him out, there was a commotion at the west tunnel.

A woman in coveralls said, "We got a visual on headlights. They'll be here in five."

Marcus spotted Bhaskar. He called out and cut off a worker to get to him.

"Bhaskar, I have a few letters, if you don't mind."

"Sure thing, Mr. Trencher."

Marcus passed him two neatly folded squares.

"Hand them directly to who I addressed them to. Ashley Cameron will read the other letter if you give it to her, so don't. Ask around and they should get you to one of these guys."

"Henry Plyman and Timothy Spencer? I might recognize them."

"You might. Robby is the other. Tall guy, dark hair. Goofy. Best I can describe him."

Bhaskar put the notes in his pocket. Marcus walked back to the other end of the platform, dodging Adam Terry along the way. A young man dragging luggage passed by.

"Excuse me, when can I board?"

"Ah, Mr. Trencher. The car in front of you is for patients headed to Indy for treatment. Let me get them on, and then I'll open the last car for you."

Before he could object, the attendant was already in the second-from-last car tucking the luggage away. On the opposite platform, a sickly old man was wheeled to the railcar from the quarantine area. Had to be a politician or old money. A younger, but equally ill woman followed.

Cheers broke out to his right. The tunnel crew had arrived. Would his arrest not be the first order of business?

The sick and elderly were situated, and the attendant returned.

"Apologies, Mr. Trencher. You have the caboose to yourself. Well, except for all the watermelons."

"That's fine. I just want to board now."

"Sorry, I don't know why they closed it..." The nervous kid squeezed a button on his radio. "Please open the caboose again. Our final passenger is boarding, over."

To his right, the returning crew were climbing to the platform with the help of their replacements. There were high fives and laughter.

"I-I'll take care of this right away, sir." The attendant ran down the east tunnel.

On the other end, the jubilation died down.

"*Did you guys go all the way to the other bunker?*" a man asked.

"*Folks came to us on golf carts this morning. A lady gave me a letter to deliver to Marcus Trencher, that billionaire.*"

"*He's around here. I just saw him.*"

Marcus looked straight ahead, trying to telepathically open the railcar doors.

"*There he is, over there.*"

In his peripheral vision, the man approached. The door finally opened.

"Mr. Trencher, I have a letter for you. Sir?"

Marcus ignored him and stepped in.

"Do you not hear—" The man sprinted up to the closing door. "Some pregnant woman wanted me to give this letter to you."

He tossed the letter to his feet inside the railcar.

Pregnant woman?

The door closed between them.

He took a seat amongst the watermelons. They filled the cabin minus his one seat. He stared at the letter on the ground with burning desire to both read and not read it.

Compressed air released, and the train lurched forward. A watermelon rolled from its precarious perch and cracked on the floor.

A voice came over an intercom speaker: "Welcome aboard the Bunker Express. It'll be slow going until we exit the east tunnel at the Columbus Junction. We pick up speed after the turn north. Our first stop in the Indianapolis network is approximately ninety minutes away."

He picked the letter up from the cabin floor. It was from Ashley Cameron.

His eyes darted back-and-forth over the lines. It was brief – but changed everything. He turned the page over to check for more. He ran to the intercom button.

"Stop the train, I need to go back."

There was a long silence.

"Mr. Trencher, sorry, we can't do that. We need to get these patients to Indy."

It was an unreasonable request, but he suddenly couldn't wait to get home.

The voice returned. "We'll arrive in Speedway shortly, if you would like to get off there."

"Excellent. I think I will."

Marcus cackled and stomped the cracked watermelon on the ground. He plunged his hand into the watermelon flesh and ripped out a heart-sized chunk and bit into it.

The people in his bunker not only forgave him – Ashley assured him – they wanted him back.

Chapter Eighteen

Robby stumbled out of the mine like a zombie. He was finishing day four with fifty hours under his belt. Aches and pains were adding up.

A quarter of the way around the atrium, a newly installed display panel caught his eye. The people were making great use of Kent the Computer Guy.

It shuffled through two public service announcements on food rationing and hygiene, and then a Bible verse. The last slide got his attention:

"Let's Celebrate! To commemorate the train tunnel connection, enjoy a night of music, food, and drinks in the Gardens! Tomorrow evening, 7-11pm. **Reduced staff 2nd shift in the mine. See your supervisor."

He had no desire to attend, but if it shaved time off his shift, he was all for it.

Ashley Cameron approached from the corridor, leading a tour for the first visitors from Bloomington.

"This chamber is used for gatherings," Ashley said. "Children put on a school play here last week."

She continued toward the entryway Robby stood
in and gave him an icy glare.

"...And through here is our living quarters. We
have fourteen floors with apartments radiating from
the atrium at the center. They are modest, but with
the leisure space we just came from, I'd say our
quality of life is as good as it gets."

"Howdy, y'all!" Robby said, covered in coal and
waving like an idiot. "Hope y'all enjoy your stay!"

The visitors in coveralls smiled. The other man
kept a stern face. Ashley scowled and kept the tour
moving.

Robby took the elevator to the top floor and
headed straight for the showers.

He grabbed a towel from the cart between the
men's and women's areas. Susan the widow kept it
stocked. She also looked after Timothy's daughters.

A shower was running on the men's side. It was
odd. Steve and Brad worked different shifts, and Kent
was on a different floor. He was too tired to call out
his arrival. He stripped in the entryway.

Upon rounding the corner, he was greeted by a
full view of Audrey Bruni. Her hands were in her hair.

"You've got to be—" Robby said under his breath
as he retreated.

The women had their own side. He had a pretty
good idea of why she was in the men's showers at that
particular moment. He couldn't simply go to the
women's side. What if the old lady Susan walked in,
or Timothy's daughters?

He was covered in coal. He couldn't *not* shower.
Screw it. I don't want her. She needs to see that.

136

He walked back in. Audrey faced him with a mischievous grin. She said nothing, hid nothing. He struggled to recall his elaborate plan.

Ignore her. That always works.

He kept his face beneath the shower head and rubbed hard water around his skin. He had no soap. He turned to wash the filth off his back. His eyes were shut, but he imagined what he was missing.

After an eternal ten seconds, he tried to steal a glance – and got caught. He turned back to the showerhead and scrubbed his face.

"Here, I had the soap," Audrey said, suddenly beside him.

He flinched before snatching at the bar of soap. It dropped and glided across the shower floor.

"I'll get it."

The soap slid and spun, and naked, wet Audrey moved to retrieve it. Before he could avert his gaze, she bent to grab the soap.

"C'mon, you need to leave," he said.

"You don't want me to."

Instead of handing him the soap, she pressed her body against his. His left arm was trapped between her breasts and their bodies. He froze. What was he to do? Even a slight nudge on such a slick floor could lead to disaster.

She lathered his back and whispered, "Nobody knows I'm here. This could be our time together."

"I told you—"

"Oh, I can see what you are telling me."

She slid her left hand to his lower abdomen, keeping her body on his, and her right arm moving the soap on his back.

"We can't—"

"We have to stay quiet," she said, reaching further. "Sound travels through these...*pipes*."

He lost his ability to speak. She made it harder to stop.

He grabbed the cheap galvanized pipe to the shower head and secured his footing. She moved in front of him. He lifted and pressed her against the wall – and failed his idiotic plan to resist her.

* * *

"Hey, babe. Work any better today?"

Melonie went through the trouble of getting up to kiss him.

"Same old thing," Robby said. He tossed his dirty clothes in the corner. He put his hand on her belly before holding her in a swaying hug. "How was your day?"

"It was good. Everyone is so nice! I styled some hair, and the old ladies loved it. When my feet started hurting, they let me sit down and help Mariya."

"How is Mariya holding up?"

"She hates it. She really misses Henry."

"Yeah, me too."

"I don't think anyone likes their new job, except me. Oh! Did you hear about the celebration?"

"Yeah, I might get off early from the mine."

"The others are meeting in twenty minutes to discuss whether we should go. You haven't hung out with anyone in four days." She propped herself up on her side so he could see her and stroked his chest. "Please?"

He let out a dramatic sigh that made her giggle.

"Fine, I'll go. Just for you."

"You did hear me say the meeting's not for another twenty minutes, right..."

She moved her strokes down to his abdomen and pecked him on the cheek.

He considered it. He was still wildly attracted to her. But the guilt and exhaustion were too much.

"I'm sorry, babe. Maybe tomorrow night."

She took the rejection in good spirit.

"Alright, then...my *coal miner baby daddy*," she smothered him with teasing kisses before laying her head on his chest.

He stared at the ceiling and caressed her hair. Tears pooled in his eyes.

The time passed silently until a knock at the door. Steve's distinct voice carried through. "We're meeting down the hall, lovebirds."

He sat up, turned to the side of the bed, and rubbed his eyes. He circled the bed and helped Melonie up. They walked out holding hands.

* * *

There were too many to gather in a single room, so they filled the T-intersection of the hall. Kent graced them with his presence, and Dr. Nora Weinstein came to visit with baby Ben in tow.

Brittney, the bunker's newest maid, had the floor.

"These people's rooms are *fucking disgusting*."

She pinched her fingers together and bobbed her head for emphasis.

"Get this – I'm cleaning some slob's room and I pick up one of those aluminum cups from the cafeteria and its full of brown stuff. I don't even know what it is, so I sniff it. It was *chewing tobacco*! I didn't even know that shit existed anymore. These rednecks found a crate of it in the storage tunnels!"

"Marcus brought down tobacco?" Robby asked.

"Shut up, Robby. So, then I start gagging, and this slob was watching me the whole time like some perv, and he laughs while I'm dry heaving. Finally, I threw up, and guess who had to clean that up?"

They laughed and gave her a round of applause.

"Okay, we can start the meeting."

Robby's smile faded when Audrey arrived. Her hair was still damp. He looked away.

Brad Farris stood to address the group.

"I'll make this quick. They are holding a celebration tomorrow night because of the tunnel connection. Becky and I will be there because they are making us prepare finger foods."

"Don't you mean *hors d'oeuvres*?" Kent said.

"Not for these assholes," Brad said.

Becky hit him on his good arm.

"They want me to bartend, too. They are hauling one of the bourbon barrels down for the night."

"If that's not a recipe for disaster..." Steve said.

"Right. I haven't received word if the rest of you are even invited, but if you are, we need to discuss whether you should attend."

"Hell no," Mercedes said. "Bad idea."

"I'm with her," Robby said. "These people liquored up? No bueno."

"They don't hate all of us," Audrey said. "Those of us working in the hospital are appreciated, for the most part."

"If you want to go, go. But if we are putting it up for a vote, I vote no. I'll see you guys later. I need to get some sleep."

Chapter Nineteen

Timothy wore an undershirt, overshirt, sweatshirt, Dale's Carhartt jacket, and the new heavy winter coat with the fur-lined hood. Swimming goggles rested on his forehead.

He also put on a pair of women's yoga pants beneath his jeans and sweatpants.

Henry chuckled, which hurt his side, but gave Timothy props for the smart crossdressing.

"What? They are just like runner's leggings."

"I'm messing with you," Henry said, smiling through his pain. "When you get to the dome, try 5-0-4-4-7 on the keypad. It was what we used while transporting stuff down in the final days."

Henry wrote it on a page from the girl's diary.

"I wiped all the lock codes after I crossed over. Ashley reset them, but I'll try."

He put his gloves, scarf, and goggles on and took a garden hoe from the garage to use as a walking stick. He gave Henry a nod before stepping out the front door.

What little exposed skin he showed, the cold found. Visibility was double what it was the previous day, and for the first leg of the journey, he had the leisure of the wind at his back.

The road was blanketed in snow, but it was apparent where it was. He crossed and climbed a minor ascent. Minutes into his brisk walk, he could see the outline of the concrete dome over the elevator.

At the door, he punched in Henry's code.

No luck.

It was reinforced as well as any military bunker. Both the man door and cargo door were solid steel. Without the code, there would be no breaking in.

Warmth left his body, but he felt comfortable. He walked to the east side of the dome, out of the wind.

A scattering of pillbox structures with conical hats billowed steam. One had an uprooted tree next to it. Beyond the collection of vents, a pipe spouted black smoke. He oriented himself to the bunker below. It was the coal plant's smokestack.

He climbed to the rim of a steep drop off down to a half-drained lake. The water level was flat with ice and snow. He retreated and spotted a beige construction site trailer camouflaged by the snow stuck to its side.

Shelter from the wind was the first thing of value he found inside. He took two neon mesh vests from hooks on the wall and put them in his pockets. A docking station with a pair of two-way radios sat on a desk. He grabbed the whole apparatus.

Outside the blurry plastic window, he made out two unnatural forms. He took a deep breath, put his goggles on, and stepped back out.

Two vehicles, encased in ice, sat in separate mounds of drifted snow. The closest was a topless, combustion engine Jeep.

He brushed snow off the other, discovering a top-of-the-line SUV. Timothy, an electric-vehicle aficionado a lifetime ago, knew the make and model. It was the first-to-market with a solid-state battery.

The door was frozen shut. He took the garden hoe and chipped away. It felt criminal to damage such a brilliant piece of engineering, but it was the post-apocalypse, he was freezing, and the vehicle probably belonged to Marcus.

He removed the ice and some of the paint. He pulled at the door and felt it give. He wedged the garden hoe in and leverage his weight. The door popped open. Ice crackled and echoed like a gunshot.

He said a prayer and pressed the ignition button. Electronics clicked on, and the engine roared to life.

He banged on the driver's wheel and yelled, "*Whoo!*"

He blasted the heat until he could clear the windshield. Self-driving mode was unavailable, not that he would have trusted it. He backed up, turned, and drove where it looked like there was a road.

He fishtailed a slope but gained traction at the bottom. He drove parallel to the fence, passing by the gatehouse leading out of the site.

After another successful right turn, he saw the house to his left. He pulled into the driveway and sprinted inside.

"Henry, we have a vehicle!"

Chapter Twenty

The day's shift blurred with all the others. Robby and his teenage sidekicks chipped away at the walls, filled carts, and dumped coal into chutes.

"I heard some of the guys talking," Braxton said. "We're getting out at six for the tunnel celebration."

"What time is it now?" Hunter said.

"Ten till."

Robby didn't want to get his hopes up, but ten minutes later, the whistle blew.

"What did I tell you, bro!"

"Let's get out of here. You coming, old man?"

At the mine entrance, Billy Manus stood beside Natalie Brynn, the teacher-turned-parole-officer.

"Hi, Ms. Brynn," Braxton and Hunter said in unison as they passed.

Robby greeted her the same and tried to pass Manus without confrontation.

"Where do you think you're going?" Manus said.

"Spare me the power trip."

"I was about to let you go, but since you want to get smart...I need you to clean the stations. Should take about an hour. I better not see you a minute sooner."

"I'll go ahead and mark it down toward your time," Ms. Brynn said.

Robby put his helmet on and tipped it to Ms. Brynn before turning back into the mine. He passed stragglers on their way out.

He wandered to the room-and-pillar and straight tunnel intersection. Neither direction appealed to him. One thing was certain – he wasn't going to do what Manus told him to do. Instead, artistic inspiration struck.

He found a pick and observed the rounded corner like a blank canvas.

He outlined an oval that topped out seven feet from the ground. He chiseled away until a nose formed, then eyes, then a mouth. He backed up to get a view, made his next chisel, and backed up again.

The final product wasn't his best work, but the art energized him. The stone face looked Mayan. He grinded coal into the pupil of each eye to make them pitch black. The finishing touch.

He walked up the straight corridor to kill time. His plan was to pass through the hole Timothy blasted into the train tunnel, double back and come out on the other side of the bunker.

At the train tunnel, he tried to imagine how Timothy felt when he first discovered it. He turned left and heard faint music. A couple hundred yards down, he stumbled upon an empty train station. He climbed the platform and noticed a hall.

The passage was narrow, unlit, and musky. He turned his headlamp on.

He came across a series of rooms. Each had a cot and toilet, like jail cells. He wiped the dust off the print on the closest door. Stenciled on it was 'Quarantine 3'.

At the end of the hall and to the left, steps led back to the tunnel. The door to his right required a security code.

He punched in the code he committed to memory when the Grant shoved Henry and Timothy out into the cold. It worked.

Lights clicked on and illuminated a familiar room, though he didn't recall the door he came through. There was usually a cabinet hiding it.

The quarantine room had a wide path leading to the media room where Marcus first informed the others what they had been chosen for. During the last days, they drove pallets from the elevator across the bunker and into the supply tunnels.

He opened a wardrobe and found the "space suit" Marcus wore when he went to the surface. There were two more in the next. Henry and Timothy could have used those, he thought.

He peered through the elevator's grated door. Maybe he should ride up and prop the surface door open? Timothy and Henry could sneak back down.

Before he could dismiss or act on the urge, the wide door to the media room began to slide open. A voice in mid-conversation came through.

He fumbled the keypad code and had to abandon the effort. He scrambled across the room and dove into the wardrobe, pulling it closed behind him.

"...This is our quarantine area for when interbunker travel picks up. The train platform you saw earlier connects to this room," a voice said, now in the room. "But the main attraction is the elevator to the surface."

Robby recognized the voice as the soldier that turned on them, Grant Maniego.

"Is your elevator not time-sealed?" the other man said. "We can't open our vault doors for another twenty years."

"Nope. Do you want to see it? The surface?"

"This is egregiously out of compliance. Look, I appreciate the tour, but I need to see my parents now. I don't want some sappy serviceman-reuniting-with-family spectacle at the celebration."

"I get it," Maniego said with a laugh. "Alright, you are ex-military, I'm ex-military – I'll level with you. Marcus Trencher caught wind of the plan to assassinate him and take his bunker. I don't know if your parents were in on it, but they were certainly victims of it backfiring."

"What are you saying?"

"I'm saying your parents and all the other engineers that were going to live in this bunker – instead of Marcus Trencher and the people he chose – are no longer with us."

"What did you do? Who gave you the ri— whoa, whoa..."

Robby, from his dark confines, suspected a weapon had been pulled.

"Relax, I don't want to take the life of a veteran."

Robby heard the elevator doors opening.

"I'll give you a fighting chance. It's cold up there, I think you know that. The last two guys we sent up said there were houses about a half-klick away. Maybe you'll make it."

"People will know I'm gone. I'm on the Council!"

"Get on or I make a mess right here."

The elevator doors closed, and the platform began to rise. Robby crawled out from the wardrobe and fled the room. He flew into the train tunnel and jogged toward the lights and music, emerging in the bunker proper.

Jenna Dothmayer sat out front of the hospital in her wheelchair, watching people mill about the carnival atmosphere.

"Hey, Jenna. How are you feeling?" His eyes scanned the crowd.

"I took a few steps today." She noticed he was distracted and spared him details of her physical therapy. "You look like you've seen a ghost."

"That G.I. Joe prick just booted a guy to the surface."

"I saw them go through that door," she said, nodding toward the media room. "I didn't recognize either of them."

"One was visiting from the bunker down the tunnel. He expected to find his family living here, but they were murdered...by the other guy. Have you seen anyone else around?"

"Melonie wasn't feeling well. You just missed Audrey, Brittney, and Mariya. Becky brought me food but had to go."

"Great, it was good seeing you." He took a step to leave her side but stopped. "Do you want to come along? I can push you."

"Please! I haven't been thirty feet from this stupid hospital in forever."

He wheeled her toward the gardens. Country music blared, and a light show flashed on the dome above. Almost the entire bunker population migrated over for the celebration. It was peaceful, but early.

Ten rows of happy people line-danced to a classic country song on the grasses.

"Thank Baby Jesus, after most of the world population was wiped out, we preserved this culture."

"Oh, hush," Jenna said. "Let them have fun."

In the sea of line dancers, Steve stood out like a sore thumb. He was bigger, taller, and darker than everyone, and somehow scored a cowboy hat. People around him loved it. Maybe the party really was an opportunity to assimilate.

There was a time he would have jumped right in, hellbent on being the center of attention. But now, he was tired, pessimistic, and covered in coal.

A line led through the café to get tiny portions of food prepared by Brad and Becky. People lined up at a freshly tapped bourbon barrel.

A small man with a *not from around here* look hovered nearby.

"Hello, I was wondering if one of you happened to know a Henry Plyman, Timothy Spencer, or Robby Reed? The last guy I asked told me to go eff myself."

"I'm Robby Reed. Who is asking?"

"Name's Bhaskar. I'm on the tunnel crew from Bloomington. Marcus Trencher gave me this letter to deliver." He handed a folded paper to Robby.

"Marcus is alive? How is he?"

"Definitely alive and seemed fine to me. He was headed to Indianapolis."

"Thank you, Bhaskar." He nodded toward the crowd. "My advice – call it a night before they start drinking."

Bhaskar bowed then wandered toward the café. Robby squinted at the letter.

"Are you okay here? I need to go where I can read this."

Jenna waved him off. He walked through the corridor to the other side. For once, it was quieter and better lit. He read Marcus's letter.

> *"...Tell Timothy: We are blood brothers, remember? I have the key..."*

They didn't part on good terms, and Marcus left a mess, but Robby was relieved knowing he was alive. And if anyone could lead an effort to bring back Henry, it was Marcus.

As for the blood key, it would have been of interest to Timothy, but Timothy was on the surface.

He stood in the chamber, still in his coal-caked clothes, with no desire to stick around for the festivities. Not even for a swig of bourbon. If anything, it made him want to get to his room as soon as possible. But an annoying sense of duty made him return to the gardens. People passed with cups filled with bourbon.

Jenna was not where he left her. He spotted Kent holding a tablet device. He was swarmed by people requesting songs.

He found Brad slammed at the makeshift bar next to the café.

"Brad, where is everyone?"

"I don't know but get them the hell out of here!" Brad yelled over the music. He ladled bourbon into an aluminum cup for the next person in line. "I'm walking away. They can serve themselves. It's already out of hand."

The man Brad served swilled the entire contents of his cup without moving. "Don't get cheap on me now!" he said, waving the cup for a refill.

"No, sir. Back of the line!"

He found Steve near the café. He was not concerned for his safety. There was bound to be a few racists down there, but there would have to be a half dozen to mess with someone Steve's size.

"We need to round everyone up and get them upstairs."

"You read my mind," Steve said. "The ladies are on the other side of the gazebo."

They found Audrey, Brittney, and Mariya talking with three younger men.

When they got closer, Robby recognized them. Todd and Craig were flunkies he sold vape pens to in high school. The other was Dale, a good ole boy everyone liked.

"Hey, it's time to head up," Robby said.

Brittney booed him. All three were inebriated.

"Yep, time to go," Steve said as he steadied Mariya.

"C'mon Rob, let the pretty ladies stay," Dale said. "We're having a good time."

"Not everyone here is as trustworthy as you, Dale. It's best they call it a night."

Audrey hugged Robby. "You want to take me upstairs?"

"No- I mean, yes, but...*damnit.*"

Steve got Mariya moving in the right direction. Robby took Audrey on his right arm. Brittney staggered between them.

Brad and Becky vacated the café. It was a free-for-all at the bourbon barrel. Blood-alcohol levels were rising by the second. Drunk people presented obstacles across the gardens, especially for the girls who were stumbling drunk themselves.

They made it to the bunker proper where it was less chaotic.

"Did any of you see Jenna?"

"Um, I bet she went to her bed in the hospital," Audrey said. She swerved in front of Robby to face Brittney and Mariya. "Oh my God, did I tell you she gets to move upstairs this week?"

Robby hesitated before the corridor to the other side. He wanted to check on Jenna, but it would turn into a spectacle. They kept moving.

By the time they emerged on the other side, Audrey was missing a shoe and Mariya was having a meltdown.

"I miss Henry! I love him so much."

Robby and Steve herded them across the trial chamber. It took trying, but they made it to the atrium, and, finally, the elevators.

"I'll go back and find her shoe. I'll be right up."

"You're good. I got it from here," Steve said.

The last thing he wanted to do was search for a shoe, least of all for Audrey, but a shoe down there was not easy to replace. He figured he could also check on Jenna to ease his mind.

Before he left the atrium, he heard a sharp-but-distant scream.

He looked back. The elevator dinged, already on its way up. He froze and listened. A muffled cry turned his attention to the mine.

He sprinted through the hanging plastic.

He found a wheelchair lying on its side.

Chapter Twenty-One

Another desperate cry rang down the mine. An aggressive male voice responded. Robby sprinted to the intersection where the stone face he had carved looked on. His footfalls alerted the assailant – or assailants. Grotesque shadows crept across the walls. He grabbed a pickaxe.

"What the fuck is going on here?"

He found the soldier Blaine sitting against the wall. Jenna Dothmayer, clothes tattered, was sprawled out behind him.

"Give me the girl. This is over."

Blaine shimmied his body up the wall.

"I know you run with that asshole Grant, but I thought you were one of the good ones."

Blaine laughed. "I'm not good. I've never been good." He pulled out a combat knife.

Robby gripped his pickaxe.

"The last good thing I ever did was blow a hole in that tunnel. All I was ever good for was blowing shit up. But I'm still no good."

"Give me the girl. That would be a start."

"Did you know I shot all those people? We buried them in the wall. They made me slit Jared's throat. He was my friend."

Blaine stumbled toward him, knife in hand, glean in his eye.

"Stay back."

Robby cocked his pickaxe.

Blaine took another step.

"Sorry about your lady friend. I don't know what I was..."

"Just put the knife down, man."

Blaine's shoulders relaxed. He sobbed two rapid breaths.

"I'm sorry for everything I ever did. Tell Maniego I'll see him in hell."

Blaine put the knife to his own throat and slashed across.

"No!"

A crimson curtain fell from the gash. He gasped, gurgled, and collapsed to the ground.

Robby cursed while his mind caught up. He dove to Blaine's side and covered the wound. Blood pumped through his fingers. He added his other hand. It was hopeless. He watched the light go out in Blaine's eyes.

He pulled his hands back and wiped the blood on his shirt and pant legs. He kicked away from the twitching body until his back hit the wall.

Jenna Dothmayer groaned in pain.

He crawled to her. He didn't know what damage had been done. He steadied her head and neck and turned her over. She bled from her scalp.

"Jenna, can you hear me?"

She blinked at him. She was breathing.

"I need to go get help, okay? I'll be right—"

He stopped to listen. Laughter echoed down the tunnel.

He inhaled to yell for help, but something told him the men headed their way might not be the helpful type. He grabbed the bloody knife beside Blaine's body.

"Blaine! Bro, what are you doing? Let's get back to the party. Don't tell me you have the wheelchair chick back here."

It was the last voice Robby wanted to hear.

Grant Maniego rounded the corner, along with a new lackey. Both were distracted by the stone face Robby had carved into the wall.

"When did this get here?" the sidekick asked.

Grant did not answer. He saw the body. Blood coagulated with dirt in a widening pool.

Blaine was dead.

"What did you do?" Grant said, anger trembling in his voice.

"He did it to himself, I swear."

"Nobody slits their own throat. You killed him!"

"I heard her scream, and I came to see, and he started talking about how he had done bad things, and...I swear, man."

Grant and his sidekick shifted side-by-side, blocking the tunnel.

He could flee into the room-and-pillar section where he worked, but it was a dead end. He could fit into a coal chute, but if he survived the journey down, he would be no better off. He needed to get by them.

"I'll ask again. Why did you kill my friend?"

157

"I didn't. I told you..."

"Why do you have his knife? You're covered in his blood. Why the fuck did you kill my friend?"

"Look, she needs help. Let's get her taken care of and we can get someone down here to investigate."

Grant stared down at Blaine's pale white face. Robby reached to the wall and grabbed his pickaxe.

"Let me through. He assaulted her and killed himself. Let's not make this worse."

They closed in. Grant unsheathed his own combat knife.

Robby was sober. They were not. But there were two, and sober or not, Grant was trained on how to fight with a knife.

"You're not leaving this mine."

He held the pickaxe in his dominant left hand, knife in his right. Grant got within six feet. He took a controlled swing with the pickaxe. The other man stood back, next to Blaine's body.

Robby held the pickaxe high, as if awaiting a lob to come down in a game of tennis. With his right hand, he clicked on his headlamp to blind them. He swung down from overhead and launched the pickaxe.

It struck Grant square and bounced away. It did not stick into his flesh, but it put him on the defensive. The other man tripped backwards over Blaine's body. Grant recovered, lunged, and slashed Robby's left thigh.

Robby clipped the wall but kept forward momentum. His helmet tumbled off, sending wild light around them.

Grant angled to block the tunnel to the main entrance. Robby turned right.

He had enough adrenaline to run through a wall. Yet, he started to slow. He discovered the slash in his pants and the bright red slit in his left leg. Seeing it did not register any pain, but he could not correct the involuntary limp.

He nearly missed his turn into the train tunnel but skidded on his good leg and came back around. Grant and the other man were thirty yards back – a comfortable lead if he were not hurt, or if it were a game of football. But he was hurt, and the men pursuing were out to kill, not tackle.

He approached the train platform. If he continued straight, he could make it to the bunker proper. He could hear the country music and see the lights. Grant wouldn't stab him with so many people around, would he?

He didn't trust the notion, and he didn't trust his leg. He dove onto the waist-high train platform and crawled forward, leaving a bright smear of blood.

He ducked into the hall off the platform.

Grant yelled, "He's up here!"

It was pitch black but straight. He passed the quarantine cells and knew he was close to the end. He felt to his right and found the door into the quarantine chamber. The silhouettes of Grant and his lackey closed in.

He felt the keypad like braille and visualized the orientation. Was it like the number pad on a computer keyboard, or a phone? He picked one and entered the digits as the footfalls grew louder.

A tiny green light flashed, and the lock released. He burst through and slammed the door behind him. A body thumped into it from the other side.

"Go around! He's trapped!"

He slid a tall grey cabinet in front of the door. Grant could force his way through, but not if Robby held it in place. But with the other man headed to the other door – one he could not block – he could only delay the inevitable.

He leaned against the aluminum cabinet and absorbed blows. He looked across the room at the wardrobe he hid in earlier. There was only one option.

He pressed the elevator button and sprinted to the wardrobe. He grabbed a space suit and helmet, opened the next compartment, and grabbed one more suit, minus the helmet.

He slammed into the cabinet one last time before stepping onto the elevator platform. The media room door began to open. As the elevator doors shut, Grant knocked the cabinet clear.

The platform began the ascent. He laid on his back and stared into the lights high above. He felt dizzy.

At some point he closed his eyes. He pumped a lot of blood through his legs, and one had a gash in it. He awoke when the platform came to a halt.

He shimmied into the space suit and crawled off to the stationary platform. Any moment, Grant would hail the elevator back down.

He entered the code, put his helmet on, and stepped out into the cold.

The midnight sky was blanketed by blue-black clouds. The snow glowed in contrast. It was silent and otherworldly. To get a sense of the cold, and to hear his surroundings, he removed his helmet.

His breath was stolen, and the air stung his skin. Five seconds was more than enough. Before he put the helmet back on, he heard something other than the wind. Then, heard it again.

It was a shout – someone making what primal noise he or she could muster out there.

A man was hugging a billowing steam vent to his right, surviving off the heat. It could only be the man Grant threw out earlier in the night.

He trampled through a snowdrift to get to him.

The man was drenched where facing the steam and iced over where he was not.

"I'm going to put this suit on you!"

The man was rigid and shaking, but he got one pant leg on. Robby felt like he broke the man's leg to get the other. He threaded an arm into a sleeve but did not have the patience to do the other. He zipped him up and pulled him off the vent.

He dragged him to the elevator dome. He didn't want to hand him back to Grant, but the guy was almost dead.

He punched the code in at the door. It did not open. He tried again, and again. It did not work.

He put the man's arm over his shoulder. They marched west past the dome. Within fifty feet, he was dragging him over the banks of snow.

They reached the crest of a hill.

In the distance, there stood a house with a porch light on.

161

Book II

Chapter Twenty-Two

Timothy, toothbrush in mouth, stubbed his toe on a pile of supplies looted from the other houses in the development.

"*Ouch*! I didn't get to all of them, but I think it's going to be slim pickings further back," Timothy said, stopping by the kitchen sink to spit toothpaste. "The last two cabins were empty."

"The workers were sent away after the major construction phase," Henry said. "You won't find much—"

There was a stomp and shuffle on the porch.

"Did you hear that?"

Something slammed into the front door. A desperate animal trying to escape the cold?

The door flew open, and two astronaut-like figures burst through. The one on the right fell forward, bouncing his helmeted head on the floor.

The other, Robby Reed, collapsed to his knees.

"Robby?" Henry jumped up, ignoring the pain in his side.

"This guy...I don't know if he's still alive," Robby said, out of breath.

"I'll fill the bath," Timothy said.

Robby removed the man's helmet. Henry dropped a blanket on the stranger and draped another over Robby. Timothy sprinted back in and pulled the blanket off.

"Get his wet clothes off while the tub fills."

The man's shirt and pants beneath the thermal suit were frozen stiff. There was no point in stripping him further. Timothy dragged him to the bathroom, stepped into the quarter-filled tub, and hoisted the stranger in. Timothy had no idea who he was.

In the living room, Robby bearhugged Henry, who cried out in pain. Robby also winced, as the pain in his leg started to awaken as adrenaline subsided.

"I didn't know if you two were going to make it through that blizzard," Robby said.

"I took it about as well as that guy," Henry said. "Who is he, anyway? And what the hell are you doing up here?"

"Mind if I sit by that fireplace first?" Robby said, stripping out of his suit.

"Make yourself at home." Henry noticed the blood covering Robby's shirt and pants. "Man, are you okay? Are you bleeding?"

"My leg, but most of it isn't mine." He let out a grim laugh. "It's a lot cooler when they say that in the movies."

He hobbled to a chair close to the fireplace. Henry brought him a wet towel and the first-aid kit.

"They held a celebration for the tunnel breakthrough and decided it was worth bringing down a bourbon barrel," Robby said, his blood-flecked hands outreached to the electronic flame.

"People got wasted. Blaine, that sidekick of Grant's, dragged Jenna into the mines and assaulted her. I was passing by and heard her scream, so I ran in and confronted the guy and...the dude slit his own throat right in front of me."

He took off his blood-soaked shirt. Timothy stepped into the doorway to the hall.

"Jenna was beaten up pretty bad, so I was about to get help, but Grant and some groupie of his came looking for Blaine. They thought I killed him. I ran, Grant slashed my leg, and they chased me. The elevator was my only choice."

"This *just* happened?" Timothy said. He ducked around the corner to make sure the guy hadn't slid under water and came back. "Who is this guy, anyway?"

"He's from the Bloomington bunker. I don't know who he is, but Grant threw him outside an hour or two before I got chased out. I found him hugging a steam vent. He was half-frozen when I got to him."

"What did he do to deserve that?" Timothy asked. "Are they trying to start a war with the other bunker?"

"I was in the wrong place more than once tonight. I overheard that his parents were engineers that helped Marcus build the bunker."

"He expected to find his parents living there," Henry said.

Timothy ran into the kitchen and opened a drawer. He returned with a photograph and handed it to Henry.

"I knew he looked familiar. This was on the fridge. That's him."

Henry glanced at the photograph and handed it to Robby.

"His parents lived in this house during bunker construction," Timothy said. "He had a little sister, too."

"We won't have to break the news to him. Grant was kind enough to tell him he gunned his family down before he shoved him out into the cold."

Robby felt Marcus's letter in his pocket.

"By the way, Marcus is alive. He sent a letter. He apologized for the mess he left, which is a minor miracle, but he also had a message for you, Timothy."

Timothy took it and sped through it.

"...*We are blood brothers, remember? I have the key,*" Timothy read aloud. "Holy shit, he has the blood key! I knew it!"

The hypothermic man in the bathtub groaned. Timothy tossed the note by Henry and ducked out again.

"Do you remember if the code to get out of the elevator dome was the same to get back in?" Henry asked. "Unless they're guarding it, we could sneak back down. We could even get to Bloomington that way."

"I tried it. I was going to dump that guy back in because I didn't think he'd make it. But the code didn't work."

* * *

Robby patched the laceration on his leg and filled them in on bunker happenings in the days following their exile. Mariya missed Henry. Timothy's daughters were taken in by Susan. Robby confessed his affair with Audrey.

The stranger Robby rescued hobbled down the stairs wrapped in a blanket. He stopped at the edge of the living room. They stopped their conversation.

"Thank you for saving me."

"Glad you made it. I'm Timothy Spencer, and this is Henry Plyman, and the guy that found you is Robby Reed. Come in, take a seat."

"Adam Terry."

Timothy struggled to restrain a barrage of questions. Instead, Adam Terry started.

"You were a project manager at *Trencher Industries*, and you co-founded the company," he said to Henry and Timothy. He turned to Robby, "Clearly, you knew him as well."

Timothy looked at Henry and Robby. "That is correct."

"Can any of you tell me why Marcus Trencher had my parents murdered?"

Chapter Twenty-Three

Marcus stepped off the train at the Speedway Bunker expecting a short layover before catching a ride back to Bloomington. The train would make stops beneath Indianapolis, and Carmel at the end of the line, before doubling back to pick him up, or so he thought.

A nervous attendant stood before him.

"Two weeks? What do you mean two weeks?" Marcus ran a hand through his hair. "This is unacceptable!"

"Well sir, we unload food, medicine, and other goods here at Speedway, then we take the sick people to the Meridian hospital bunker under the city. We make deliveries and pick up garbage in Carmel and bring it back. Then the train sits a day or two, for maintenance."

"That doesn't add up to two weeks."

"The train does about the same in Louisville before returning to Bloomington."

"This is preposterous. Is there a vehicle I can take? I can't sit here for two weeks."

"I just unload bags. You'll have to ask someone higher up," the attendant said. "But, um, it was an honor to meet you."

Marcus said *yeah, yeah* and waved the kid off.

The conductor approached. "I apologize, Mr. Trencher, but we can't alter the schedule. We will be departing shortly, though." The conductor looked around before leaning in. "I think you'll find accommodations in Carmel to be much nicer."

Marcus looked over the conductor's shoulder at the men and women unloading the rail cars. Two workers approached to take the watermelons out of the caboose.

"I'll stay," Marcus said out of spite. "But I would like to arrange a vehicle to get me back to Bloomington sooner."

"I'll put in the request right away," the conductor said, before again leaning in. "Are you sure you want to stay here? Carmel is *very* nice."

"I'll be fine here."

The conductor acquiesced. "Hop on if you change your mind."

He was left alone on the platform. A man and a teenage boy began unloading the watermelons from the caboose into laundry hampers.

"Yo, want to help with these melons? This looks like some racist-ass shit, you just standing there watching," the man said to Marcus.

Nobody had spoken to him like that in his life.

"Oh, sorry. Sure."

The man burst out laughing.

"Dawg, I was just playing! We got this."

"I don't mind," Marcus said, stepping in and grabbing a watermelon.

"Aight, then. We'll start a line. Stand here and pass along."

They emptied the car of the last watermelon, save for the one crushed on the floor. The boy wandered off. The man whistled and gestured down the platform, signaling they were finished.

"You getting back on?"

"I was hoping to stay. If you'll have me."

"My man! Took you for a Carmelite!" He offered his hand, and they shook. "Push one of these hampers and follow me. My name's Taveon. That scrawny boy that ran off was my son, Trevion. We'll be happy to have you."

Marcus introduced himself.

"Shoot, I know who you are. You're a damn American hero!"

"I don't know about all that."

"The first thing I did when I came home from overseas was buy my momma one of your battery units. We had a cookout to celebrate and everything. Brought her electric bill down to nothing."

They wheeled the melon-filled hampers through a wide sectional door off the platform. New lights, sounds, and smells hit Marcus all at once, but it was the enormous space that awed him.

"Welcome to Speedway," Taveon said.

The underground warehouse was so vast, he could not see the end of it. Six-level racks interspersed with support pillars stood in rows, leaving an aisle down the center and egress on each side. The lots were filled with pallets of food, supplies, medicine, and myriad more. Forklifts whisked the latest delivery deep into the warehouse. He pondered if there were weather effects in such an environment.

"Leave the melons. C'mon, I'll show you around."

They got into a golf cart and drove onto what amounted to a paved road along the right side of the warehouse.

"I'll spare you the safety training," Taveon said, stopping to check both ways at an intersection. "High velocity stuff like food is kept up front, closest to the train tunnel. The rare stuff is kept in storage way the hell back in the dark. We have tons of medicine and medical devices in the middle. The dangerous shit we keep locked up. Hell, we lock up a lot of things. Sneakerheads started raiding the shoe racks, so we had to fence that up."

They drove by a sensor that sent a plastic doorway coiling to the top. Cold air blew through the hanging strips of plastic.

"That's one of our coolers. It's chilly, but it ain't nothing compared to the freezers. We store medicine and vaccines in those, and food."

They drove by two more cold storage chambers. Each were the size of a city block.

"How is all this stuff tracked?"

"Warehouse management system. Barcodes and shit," Taveon said, stopping the cart and pointing. "See that machine on the side of them racks? They do the picking and put-away. We – as in us humans – unload the trains and drive it to the end of the aisles. The rest is automated. We mostly do maintenance."

"Did you work in logistics before you came down here?"

SHANE NOBLE

"Yessir. Automation and AI didn't replace us all. I played ball overseas and worked in a warehouse in Plainfield when I came home. Shit pay, but I'll be damned if it didn't end up saving my life."

"I assumed you were famous, or knew a U.S. senator," Marcus said.

"Oh, you have jokes! Nah, man. Right before stuff went down, military brass came through our warehouse and said we were moving everything into a bunker, and everything in every *other* warehouse in the park. Then that turned into *everything coming into the airport*. We didn't have an option, but hey, they kept their word and let us live down here."

"I take it we're not directly beneath the Indianapolis Speedway?"

"Nah, I don't know why they messed up the name so bad. We're under the airport in Plainfield. They dug a shaft from the 500 infield to drop one of those tunnel-boring machines a few years back, though."

They continued through the endless warehouse. He found Taveon easy to talk to, even for him.

"I promise we ain't going back there," Taveon said, motioning to the dark expanse beyond. "We're headed to the farm."

They took a right, and after a set of automatic doors, entered yet another massive space. This time, instead of racks, there were animal pens full of livestock.

Taveon pulled up to a potbellied man in overalls. "Farmer John, what's good?"

"Hey, Mister Taveon. Come to milk the cows? The one over yonder with the horns could use your supple touch."

Taveon laughed with a dash of exaggeration. "John, you know I'm from the hood! I'll leave that one to you and your 4-H pals. Y'all the experts!"

They passed by chickens, cows, and pigs. Taveon did his best to explain the agriculture program of the bunker. The animal population was kept in equilibrium. The primary purpose of the farm was to collect tissue samples for the lab-grown meat plant in Louisville. Dairy and traditional meat processing came secondary.

"The farmers were a little scared of us black and brown folks over in the warehouses at first, but now we have our own trade pact. It's crazy how good we get along. We get them whatever they want, and we eat chicken, bacon, and burgers more than them stuck up folks in Carmel."

"So, storage, disposal, and food are all done in Speedway. There's a hospital somewhere beneath Indianapolis..."

"Yeah, Meridian."

"Okay, Meridian – the hospital, they take care of sick people. And then there's Carmel. What do they do there?"

Taveon slammed on the brakes.

"You want to know what they do up in Carmel? They have golf carts like this, and they drive around roundabouts all day, and not shit-else."

"They drive around...roundabouts all day?"

Taveon held a serious face for as long as he could. The joke dawned on Marcus.

They burst out laughing.

173

Chapter Twenty-Four

Henry was awakened by Timothy rummaging through supplies. Robby dozed off in the recliner.

The previous night ended on an uncomfortable note when Adam Terry questioned them about the death of his parents. They gave him varying degrees of non-answers.

"Where's our guest?" Henry asked, sitting up.

"Upstairs," Timothy said. "He was looking through family photo albums this morning, and I gave him his sister's journal."

"I feel for the guy. He lost his family."

Robby rustled awake. His obnoxious yawn was interrupted by pain shooting through his leg.

"Before he comes down, let's get on the same page about the asteroid," Timothy said. "I say we play dumb. We don't know what he knows."

A board creaked at the top step. Adam came down and gave them a curt nod.

"Good morning. Grab a granola bar and join us. We need to discuss our next moves."

"How are you holding up?" Henry asked.

"Achy, but better," Adam said.

"Here's the deal," Timothy said. "Power will start cutting out today, and this house won't hold heat for long. I cleared ice off another wind turbine on the house across the way, but we're getting nowhere near replacement levels."

"What are our options?" Henry asked.

"We have the EV in the garage. Its batteries are down to a percent, just like the house. We can either drain the EV and power the house for another few hours, or we drain the house into the EV to give it enough juice to get us into town."

"That's a no-brainer," Robby said. "Plug her in. Let's head to town."

"If this micro grid held as much power as it did, the town of Sherman will have plenty," Henry said.

"It is encouraging," Timothy said. "At town-level density, I doubt there's even been an outage."

Adam cleared his throat. "We go to the nearby town, charge the vehicle. Then what?"

"We head to Bloomington and find the bunker. I don't know how we get in, but we'll have to figure it out when we get there."

"The vault doors are sealed for twenty years," Adam said. "People inside can't even open it without a whole bunch of keys. And like the concrete dome out there, nothing short of a bunker-buster missile would get through."

Timothy's mind raced. How was he going to get back to his daughters?

"...but you guys are in luck. The Quarry door happened to be my contribution as an engineer on the project. My parents consulted, but it was my designs."

175

"What are you saying?"

"I'm saying, I can get you into the Quarry bunker from the surface."

"I'm glad I peeled you off that vent," Robby said.

* * *

They gathered supplies from Timothy's pile of loot and loaded it into the electric SUV charging in the garage. When the power cut off, it was time to depart.

"I'm driving," Robby said.

Timothy opened the garage door. Lazy snowflakes fell from the blighted sky. Robby backed out and slid from the driveway to the road. Timothy penguin-walked out and got in the back with Adam.

"Full disclosure, I lost my license awhile back," Robby said. "But I gained valuable experience in dangerous conditions right beforehand."

Robby crept to the gatehouse and drove through the flimsy red-and-white reflective arm. They were off bunker grounds for the first time since the day they went underground.

Deep drifts built up along the fence from the snow blown across the fields. Henry, Timothy, and Adam's faces were glued to the window. At one point in their lives nothing could have been more boring than the flat Indiana landscape. Now, they were enamored.

Robby maneuvered the minor dips and hills with strategic acceleration, as well as the snow and ice. Henry was careful not to compliment him. Timothy was not.

"Like a pro," Timothy said after they climbed the steepest incline yet.

"Got that right," Robby said, fishtailing down the other side.

Henry, Timothy, and Adam did a collective, *"Whoa, whoa, whoa!"* to Robby's satisfaction.

They passed the first house a mile-and-a-half from the bunker site, a rundown trailer abandoned well before the end of the world. Nicer homes followed.

"It looks like an ordinary day over winter break," Henry said. "I feel like we're going to pass someone waving at us even though we don't know them."

"It looks pretty, but it's a balmy -29 degrees out," Robby said, tapping on the temperature display.

"What if we run into someone?" Timothy said. "We should find weapons."

Robby laughed. "Pick a house, any house, and you should walk out with an arsenal."

"Where should we go?" Henry asked. "My parent's house will be powered."

"I want to stop by the *Trencher Industries* plant north of town first," Robby said. "I got a tip that Marcus stashed winterized vehicles there."

"He never said anything to me about that...which is normal. Who tipped you off?"

"A teenager named Braxton."

With Robby's adept winter driving, they crossed an icy bridge, skirted a fallen tree, and conquered the railroad tracks where idle trains once caused country traffic jams.

Robby pulled into a sawmill and cut through to the warehouse on the other side. The black *Trencher*

Industries logo high on the side showed through a sheet of ice.

Timothy grabbed bolt cutters. They bundled up and stepped out. The wind picked up. They jogged to the entrance, cursing the cold.

Robby tried the door handle. Locked.

He grabbed the bolt cutters out of Timothy's hand and stepped over a skeletal bush in the landscaping. There were no bolts to cut. He swung at a windowpane, shattering it.

"Stay here. I'll climb in and open the door."

He avoided the shards of glass still in the frame and stepped gingerly on the ones on the ground. He turned the simple lock and let the others in. The next door, into the actual warehouse space, was electronic.

"Henry, what was the code out at the bunker before it got changed?"

"5-0-4-4-7."

Robby entered the code and got the green light. It was too dark inside to make out what all was there, but they smelled fuel.

Timothy opened an electrical box and flipped a switch. Dim lights clicked on and gradually grew brighter.

"Whoa, that idiot kid was right," Robby said.

The warehouse was full of heavy-duty pickups with chains on the tires, military grade Humvees, tractors, and snowmobiles. The big stuff required fuel, the rest electric. All were optimized for winter.

"Hey, check this one out," Henry said. "It's got tank tracks for back tires."

"Hell yeah, we're taking that one," Robby said.

"We each take one," Timothy said. "Any engine trouble or one of us slides off, we have backups."

"Henry, you take the half-track. I get the Cybertruck," Robby said. He ran off like a toddler to check out his new toy.

Adam opted for an electric Humvee. Timothy went for an SUV of the same make and model as the one they drove there, except with chains on the tires. The keys were placed on the dash of every vehicle. Batteries drained while in storage, but there was enough juice to get them to their next destination.

Robby lifted a garage door. With a little valet work, they got all four vehicles out, plus a snowmobile trailer. Robby closed the door and ran to his Cybertruck.

Adam stood at the open door of his Humvee, looking up into the bright, blank sky. He was focused on – as far as Robby could tell – nothing.

"You okay, pal?" Robby asked, following his gaze into the white void above.

Adam shook out of his sky stare. "Yeah, I'm good. Let's go."

Henry led the convoy toward downtown Sherman, Indiana.

Chapter Twenty-Five

Mariya comforted Melonie, all the while not over her own missing man, Henry. Robby never returned to his room the night of the tunnel celebration.

"Maybe he went back and drank after we left," Brittney said. "He knows people here. He'll turn up."

Mercedes wanted to say she told them the party was a bad idea but held back.

"He went to search for Audrey's shoe," Steve said. "I've already spoke to people this morning. Nobody saw him drinking in the gardens."

Melonie cried in Mariya's arms.

"Sorry, Melonie," Steve said. "I don't mean to alarm, but it ain't adding up."

Becky and Audrey entered the room together.

"Something bad happened last night," Audrey said. "They wouldn't let us in to the hospital this morning, so Dr. Nora met us outside. Jenna was attacked. She had lacerations on her tongue and her fingers were broke."

"Someone wanted to keep her quiet," Mercedes said. "Lord have mercy, we need to get up out this place."

"I need to help Brad with the lunchtime rush," Becky said. "I'll listen to everyone coming down the line."

"It's best if we're all out and about," Steve said. "We won't learn anything staying up here. Mariya, Melonie, I'll walk you to the salon. Maybe the women will have gossip."

"We have company," Brittney said at the door.

Ashley Cameron and Lieutenant Grant Maniego, along with two muscular men, entered uninvited.

"We've investigated an incident that occurred in the early morning hours," Ashley said with her hands folded in front of her. "At some point during the celebrations, Jenna Dothmayer was abducted and taken into the mine. She was assaulted and has suffered serious injury. She is being transported to Bloomington for better medical care."

"Who attacked her?" Mariya asked.

"It has been confirmed by multiple eyewitnesses that Robby Reed pushed Jenna Dothmayer, in her wheelchair, into the mine, and—"

"Robby would never do that!" Melonie said.

The others expressed vehement disagreement.

"It is believed he had too much to drink and preyed upon Ms. Dothmayer, whom he was seen with earlier in the night."

"Where is he? What did you do to him?" Melonie asked.

"Major Blaine McCammon must have heard screams from the mine and went to investigate. Mr. Reed murdered him, presumably, to cover the crime he was committing."

"Not a soul in this room believes Robby murdered that man, or laid a finger on Jenna," Steve said. "Did you arrest him? Tell us where he is!"

"He's on the surface," Grant said, breaking his silence. "He murdered Blaine, tried to rape that girl in the wheelchair, and escaped to the elevator."

"You lying son of a..."

The two muscular men restrained Steve.

"We have a solution," Ashley said. "We had a visitor from Bloomington that was tall and slender with dark hair, much like Mr. Reed. We did a tour, people saw him. This man also had, shall we say, an *unfortunate* accident last night. As far as anyone is concerned, he assaulted Ms. Dothmayer – not Mr. Reed. If anyone asks about Mr. Reed's whereabouts, he simply missed his friends, stole the door codes, and went to the surface to search for them. I think it is a fair compromise."

"Look, miss," Steve said. "You don't want us here. We don't want to be here. Let us lead a search party. After that, send us down that train tunnel to the next bunker. You'll never hear from us again."

"We need to handle the delicate matter of notifying Bloomington of their representative's crime and subsequent death," Ashley said. "Afterwards, perhaps we can discuss placement, or search parties. Now if you'll excuse us."

Ashley and the men turned to exit.

"How do you think Marcus is going to react when he finds out you sent his closest friends to the surface?" Mariya said.

Ashley stopped at the door. She felt Marcus's letter in her inner coat pocket.

She interpreted Marcus's request to "be careful" with Adam Terry as instruction to get rid of him, a task she delegated to Grant.

His request to keep Timothy Spencer alive was not one she understood. She and Grant did the opposite, which she omitted from her response. But he would appreciate the initiative. Timothy was a nuisance and a traitor.

She turned and cleared her throat.

"I've not heard from Mr. Trencher. I'll certainly let you know when we do."

Chapter Twenty-Six

Marcus swallowed a cocktail of medication before stepping out of his room. He merged into a stream of people headed to work, or breakfast, in the glorified warehouse that was the Speedway bunker.

He looked back to see who followed him and kept distance to avoid conversation. The interior design left much to be desired. Like the Stacks in the Quarry, it looked like a hotel with no carpet or décor. If they sank a Soviet-styled apartment underground, it'd probably be about as nice.

He had little right to judge. The other side of his own bunker was left in similar, unfinished fashion.

They filed into a cafeteria where he was hit with the aroma of his all-time favorites: bacon, sausage, pancakes, and eggs. A coffee station topped it off.

"Good morning, my man," Taveon said, patting him on the shoulder. "I'd like you to properly meet my son, Trevion."

"Nice to meet you," the gangly teenager said. "Did you invent the *Monolith*? We had one at our house."

"Yes, I did," Marcus said, distracted by the delightful food ahead.

"Wow, you must be rich."

"Boy, be polite," Taveon said.

They grabbed trays and shuffled along. The aluminum basins of breakfast food were bountiful. "Do you eat this well every morning? I may never want to leave."

"I told you our farmer friends take care of us."

Marcus got a sausage patty, a slice of bacon, a half-cup of buttery eggs, and a pancake with syrup.

"That's real butter. They churn it over there like the Amish. But no, this ain't typical. Today is special."

"I don't even know what day it is."

"One year ago today was the day of impact, my man. We were forced down three damn weeks early, but yeah, today was the day."

Marcus went *ohhh*. Time flies.

He filled a coffee mug at the drink station. He added a dash of heavy cream and waited for Taveon and Trevion to claim a table.

"If you do go up to Carmel, don't tell them how good our food is. They do lab-grown meat up there. We don't need them doing their stupid-ass audits and deciding to take our bacon."

"They think we're their slaves," Trevion said. He looked at his disapproving father. "What? It's true. We work all day and send them stuff, and they don't do anything."

"I might be here for a few days, I'd like to help," Marcus said. "Maybe I could learn to drive one of those forklifts."

"You, a billionaire genius, want to become forklift-certified?" Taveon laughed. "Nah, man. Think you could tutor young Trevion on his algebra? That AI teacher ain't teaching him shit."

"It's not my fault! I don't even know what questions to ask it!" Trevion said. "Why do I even go to school? I'm just going to work in this freaking warehouse until I die."

"Because, son, the Hunter family ain't a bunch of illiterates. Your mom and I got degrees and so will you, even if I have to climb to the surface to enroll your skinny butt."

"Colleges don't even exist anymore," Trevion said, laughing at his dad's education spiel. "The asteroid obliterated them to nothing."

"I know that, boy. It's called *hyperbole*. Is your English robot not teaching you either?"

Trevion laughed even harder.

"I'm not a great teacher," Marcus said.

"You've got to be better than that cartoon in the computer," Taveon said, getting up from the table. "Spend the morning with him, see what he sees, and offer pointers on solving that stuff."

He raised his eyebrows and pointed at Trevion.

"Take advantage, Tre. It's not every day you get a genius to teach you something."

* * *

Marcus and Trevion walked to the bunker library. It was full of shelves with real books.

They passed second-shift workers on desktop computers. Others sat and read in chairs and sofas.

Trevion led the way to a square room with tiny cameras mounted on the walls.

"I go back here to a study booth for my classes."

Marcus expected Trevion to pull a textbook from his bag. Instead, a headset.

"You can borrow the set on the wall. You won't need the vest."

"No books or paper or pencils?"

"Huh? I mean, not real ones. It's virtual learning. Log on, and I'll invite you to Algebra Island."

Marcus couldn't believe he got dragged into tutoring a kid, but he needed to learn the Metaverse. He slid the haptic gloves over his hands and put the headset on.

"Where are you?"

"I don't know. Some setup menu."

"What! You don't already have an avatar?"

"No, I've never been to the Metaverse."

"Seriously? You could've bought whatever you wanted and played any game and purchased the best armor and weapons!"

"I bought whatever I wanted in real life."

"But could you kill Nazi zombies or fly to another planet?"

Marcus conceded. An option floating in front of him that he intuitively used his hands to select. A screen appeared, showing a live third-person point-of-view of the room.

"This is spooky."

Instructions told him to put his arms out, turn, and to take the headset off and spin around. When he put it back on, there was a recognizable model of himself. Next to it, a cartoonish version.

"What do most people choose? The realistic avatar, or the animated one?"

"Only creeps and grownups go realistic. Skip the rest. You can finish your profile later."

The menus disintegrated and the room transformed into a mountaintop lodge overlooking a stunning vista.

"Wow, this is neat," Marcus said. He walked to the window to get a better view – *actually* walked.

Red flashed around his periphery and the virtual world disappeared as the headset lens went translucent, but not in time. He collided with the real wall.

Trevion lifted his to see the commotion. His jaw dropped.

"Did you *really* just do that?" Trevion said, putting his headset back on. "...Millennial noobs. Just stand still. I'll send the invite."

Marcus accepted the invite and shot out of his mountain lodge, through the clouds. A second later, he descended upon an island in the sea.

"You can skip the travel animation. Put your hands together in front of you."

He touched his hands and zoomed down to Algebra Island. He saw another avatar that looked like Trevion, except with fox ears and a tail.

"What's with the animal features?"

"Most animals are dead. Me and my friends like to keep their memory alive."

Trevion conjured the problem he was stuck on.

Marcus knew the answer in a millisecond. He blurted it out.

"How did you get that so fast?"

"I don't know. That's just...what it is."

"I'm messing up a step...and robo-bitch over there can't tell me which."

Marcus peered at the feminine robot hovering at the edge of their island jungle classroom. He didn't feel it was his place to discipline Trevion for calling it a name. He looked back at the problem. *Steps?* In his brain, there was only one step: *solve.*

For once, he slowed down and thought about his thinking. He walked Trevion through the problem. After two more, Trevion managed one start-to-finish on his own. He found teaching oddly gratifying.

For fun, Marcus did a speed run through Trevion's practice work.

"That's insane!" Trevion said. "We better stop before the algorithm makes my assignments harder."

"Alright, enough math," Marcus said. "Can you tell me how to contact someone?"

"Just ask. You can say, like, 'Call Trevion Hunter,' or whoever and you'll find them, or at least get a short list. You can add the bunker name, too. I have friends from Louisville, Bloomington, Carmel, Lexington, Cincinnati..."

"Got it. I'll give it a shot."

"I've got to go do my Language Arts in the library. I have to read a real book."

Trevion left to re-enter the real world. Marcus called out to the virtual one.

"Metaverse? Find Genie, from Bloomington."

Contacting Genie... displayed in the top right of his vision.

A centaur with a rainbow-colored tail appeared before him. The upper body looked *something* like the Genie he knew.

"Identify yourself, anonymous troll!"

"Genie, is that you? You're a centaur."

"Marcus? Sorry, your profile is blank," she said. "And yes, a *sexy transsexual centaur*, to be exact. Watch this—"

Genie's avatar whinnied and bucked in a bizarre, glitchy animation.

"Wow...Anyway, I'm stuck in Speedway and need to arrange a ride to my bunker."

"Honey, I don't have a vehicle. Ask the Council."

"I don't trust them. I think I was being pursued when I left."

"Let me work my connections. I'll hook someone up with a virtual yacht in an exchange of favors."

She winked out of existence.

"Metaverse, find Harold Plyman."

Marcus accepted an invite. He teleported to a muddy field of tanks and tents. An army man stood before him.

"Marcus, is that you? You joined up!" Mr. Plyman said.

Planes zoomed overhead. His avatar switched to the realistic scan – a prerequisite for the war game.

"Where are we?"

"Caen, France, July, 1944! We'll push those Nazi bastards back across the Rhine in no time!"

Marcus heard other live voices, including a high-pitched squeal of what had to be a ten-year-old. "Is there somewhere private we could speak?"

"Sure thing," Mr. Plyman said. They warped to a military tent.

"Have you heard from Henry?"

"Not yet. Rumor amongst the troops is that the cable should be online any day. We can hardly wait to see him."

"Any other news in Bloomington?"

"Men knocked on our door looking for you. They didn't say you were in any kind of trouble, but I didn't get a friendly impression. We told them we thought you were still in the Quarry. I don't think they knew you had left."

The door to the study room opened. He lifted the headset to see Trevion before returning to Metaverse World War II.

"Thanks, Mr. Plyman, I'll let you get back to battle."

"Sure you don't want to join? We could go liberate Paris."

"Maybe later."

Chapter Twenty-Seven

The smart grid in the city of Sherman was wholly intact. Even the traffic lights still worked.

"I knew it was resilient when we created the thing, but this blows my mind," Timothy said, pacing the living room of Henry's childhood home. "It's the post-apocalypse and all the houses have electricity."

A strand of blinking lights outlined a porch across the street.

"Those Christmas lights are freaking me out," Robby said. "How many homes could the Sherman grid support right now?"

"Sustainably? Two hundred, no problem. Maybe double that. Those wind turbines add up."

"Sherman might be an outlier since every home has a unit," Henry said. "Even the trailer park had solar panels. But what were we up to before the end of the world, domestically? 40-percent of U.S. homes on our grids?"

"Add all the commercial and municipal arrays, and six more months' worth of residential installations in 2030 before the world shut down – it was well past 50-percent," Timothy said. "I think most of North America still has power. Probably never lost it."

Rooftop solar panels wired to *Trencher Monolith* home battery units became the dominant energy source. Yet, even with no sunlight, the grid was functional. With no people, minimal usage, and 1-in-20 homes with wind turbines on their roofs, the grid was alive and well.

"I'm every bit as impressed as you all are," Adam Terry said. "But it is -30-degrees out. We need to be traveling more than house-sitting."

Robby made a face behind Adam.

"Of course," Timothy said. "We do need to start planning this trip."

Henry tossed a 2003 Rand McNally road atlas on the coffee table. "Bloomington is approximately sixty miles from here."

"Nice find!" Robby said. "Your dad's distrust of GPS finally pays off."

Henry flipped past the states in alphabetical order to Indiana.

"You're the Hoosiers," Timothy said, scooting forward to see the map. "What is our route?"

"Our straightest shot is State Road 54," Henry said, tracing his finger from Sherman, Indiana, east to Bloomington. He handed Adam Terry a pen. "Mind marking where that quarry is?"

Adam drew a careful square south of Bloomington city limits.

"What kind of road are we talking here?"

"Two-lanes, rural. Straight as an arrow but starts to get hilly further east." Henry pointed at dots along the route. "There are small towns along the way where we can charge the vehicles. This is an old map, and somewhere in here there is a newer road that might be an option closer to Bloomington. Intestate-69, I think."

"Nice," Robby said.

"What are we looking at? Two days' travel, tops?" Timothy asked.

"If all goes well, even 10 miles-an-hour gets us there this evening," Henry said.

* * *

They departed in a four-vehicle convoy. Henry led, followed by the non-Hoosiers Timothy and Adam. Robby took up the rear and pulled the snowmobile trailer. He and Henry were given the two-way radios.

Henry's vehicle created deep tracks to follow. It didn't take long before Robby began to swerve in and out of them. Henry had yet to eclipse 12-miles-per-hour.

"Fine, I'll speed up." Henry kicked it up to 15-miles-per-hour.

They passed Dan O's Bar and Grill south of town, and a half-mile later, turned east onto State Road 54. Fat snowflakes fell from the sky.

Henry leaned forward, chin over the steering wheel. He didn't expect the degree of difficulty in discerning the road boundaries. He slowed back to 10-miles-per-hour.

Snow blanketed the landscape. Fences, ditches, and road signs got him to the outskirts of Sherman, but soon enough, markers became fewer and farther between. Ditches were flattened by snowdrifts, concealing their true drop-offs. Trees and power lines offered little guidance when it came to whether he was in a lane, on a shoulder, or off the side of the road.

The one thing going for him was that the road was perfectly straight.

The temperature display showed a drop of four degrees since departure. It was -36-degrees Fahrenheit in July. The light snowfall grew heavier.

Within another mile, it got downright ugly. The snow slanted. Wind whipped across the road.

Henry recognized an overpass ahead and contemplated stopping beneath it. He powered on, not wanting to hear from Robby. On the other side, tree lines closed in on each side of the road, narrowing the guesswork. They reached the edge of a small town on the Sherman-Greene County line.

He pulled into a ransacked Casey's Gas & Charging Station next to a burned-down church and looted Dollar General. Henry took a deep breath and jumped out.

"It's getting nasty!" Henry said, putting his head in Timothy's window. "We might want to setup camp here and see what the weather does."

Timothy squinted at his windshield, as if he hadn't noticed.

"It's not *great*, but we just started. How far is the next town?"

"Another seven or eight miles."

"Let's knock out this stretch to the next town and call it a day. Pull over if it gets to be too much."

Henry wanted to protest more, but he was standing in -40-degrees. He bit his lip and ran back to his vehicle.

He pulled back onto the road, across the wind and against his instincts.

Chapter Twenty-Eight

Marcus cut day two's algebra lessons short with young Trevion. He was battling a major headache. He blamed the Metaverse headset, but he knew it was because he increased his medication that morning. He was tired of slow walking his regiment.

After a midday nap, he forced himself out of his room. The amphetamine did not perk him up as much as he would have liked, but he knew better than to take another. One increase in dosage at a time.

He hoped to get an update on whether transportation back to Bloomington was arranged, or if the train was back from Carmel.

The warehouse was bustling with activity – a good sign. He kept to the yellow tape path. Before he could open the man door to the train platform, Taveon zoomed up on his forklift.

"Yo, my man. Hold up a sec."

"Hey, Taveon. Is the train back?" Marcus said, reaching to push the door open.

"*Hold up.*" Taveon hopped off the forklift. "It's here, but some suits from Carmel showed up with it. They ain't doing their normal audit."

Marcus stepped back from the door.

"They was asking if we'd seen you. They never said your name, but they were describing you, like we was all stupid."

"I requested a ride back to Bloomington. Are you sure they're not looking for me to let me know whether they could accommodate?"

"They wasn't being nice about this shit. Nobody snitched because we all got that feeling, but someone will eventually."

"Where should I go?"

"They've been popping in and out, so let's get you the hell away from here. Get on the golf cart and follow me."

Taveon led Marcus deep into the warehouse where the automated lights had not been triggered in some time. They passed the corridor to the farms and traveled another hundred yards.

"Let's chill here a minute."

"Sorry, I don't know who these people are."

"They said you're wanted for murder."

"Murder? I've never killed anyone. I've not even been to the Carmel bunker."

He was not certain he did not murder Jenna Dothmayer and whoever else he shot before he left his bunker, but he assumed they were alive. Ashley Cameron's letter said all was forgiven. Everyone wanted him back. He could not imagine word traveled that fast about his mental breakdown.

"I believe you, I do, but you gotta have some idea of what these people want. If I'm about to help you evade authorities, I need to know what's up."

He weighed what revelations were warranted.

"Taveon, I have the key to the world. I didn't think anyone knew about it."

"What do you mean?"

"When we first met, you told me you bought one of my battery units for your mother. Do you remember the options when you got it installed?"

"We were first on the block, so we only had one option since no other units were close enough to initiate a grid," Taveon said. "I had to run to Home Depot and drop another couple hundred dollars for a solar panel. After a few neighbors got units, we qualified as a subscription grid. What's this got to do with anything?"

"I have the key to control all of those units, whether they subscribed to the grid or not."

"Do you remember an asteroid wiped it all out? This place rumbled for days. What's it matter if your grid ain't there, and we're all down here?"

Marcus did not answer.

"Are you saying everything wasn't destroyed?"

"It is my belief that we will resurface sooner than anyone thought. When we do, I will control the power grid. People want to take that from me."

"Why don't they just ask nicely? Someone liked you enough to give you a whole-ass bunker."

"And they tried to kill me and take it at the last moment. These are not the type of people interested in sharing. They want absolute control of when and how mankind re-emerges from these bunkers. If I get up there and commandeer the grid, they'll have to negotiate with me."

"Who are these people?"

Marcus walked to one of the racks. Automated lights above were dim but growing brighter. "Come here. Check this out."

He pointed to the base of a support beam.

"See how this goes into the floor rather than bolted to it with steel angle plates? I bet if I reach in here, I can find...got it."

He plucked a wire out of a notch.

"What is that?"

"An antenna. It leads down to a machine at the base of the beam. I'd be willing to bet there are machines at the end of every aisle. They are programmed to talk to each other and know when to go off."

"Go off and do what?"

"You said this place shook for days after impact, right? It wasn't from an asteroid. It was these machines. I bet they made noise and shook, but not enough to knock the goods down. Jackhammer motors, if I were to guess.

"Every bunker has stabilization systems. They were simply programmed to create rumbling rather than counteract it. What I'm getting at is, we were never hit with an asteroid. All that shaking was special effects."

Taveon shook his head in disbelief.

"The whole thing is a lie. We're down here so they can depopulate the earth, block out the sun, and build up the ice caps. They want to reverse all the environmental damage and get rid of the people nobody knows what to do with."

"Man...you, you, you billionaires like to fuck with people, right? You're fucking with me, man."

"People want me dead because I could interfere. So, when scary people show up looking for me, I have to assume they are in on this."

Taveon walked to the next aisle and plucked an antenna wire from the base.

"I don't even want to know who 'they' is. This some *Illuminati* shit."

"Unfortunately, I don't know who they are, but I do know they want me dead."

"What now? You say you need to get back to your bunker? Why the hell you leave in the first place?"

"I had a personal matter I had to distance myself from..." Marcus sighed. "If I can get back, my old business partner can assist in taking control of the grid. God knows what will happen after that, but I think we will be a step closer to resurfacing."

"I might see the light of day again?"

"You might even get to enroll Trevion in college."

Chapter Twenty-Nine

Henry hunched over the steering wheel of his half-track vehicle, squinting as he looked out at a full-blown blizzard.

He also sulked, having failed to realize picking the vehicle with the best traction automatically volunteered him to drive lead.

"How are you doing up there?" Robby said over the two-way radio.

"Can't see a thing," Henry said. "I'm about to call it. We need to pick a place and wait this storm out."

Roadside grass, crushed beneath the snow, created a lip he used as a guide. The subtle undulation was fading fast under the fresh-and-falling snow. His eyes watered from intense focus.

"The closer we get, the more houses will have power," Robby said. "You should be coming up on a bend any minute."

"You drive this way often?"

"Dated a girl around here. Biggest mistake ever."

"Why the hell am I driving lead?"

"Those tank tracks are keeping us all on the road. Good choice."

The road peeled south. A vague memory of the turn resurfaced in his brain. He had not traveled through the area in a decade.

An inch of additional snow had accumulated since the county line, but he noticed ridges of snow off the edges – higher than the subtle lip created by uncut grasses – giving him an approximation of where the road led.

The new angle was not so much crosswind. Visibility improved. He kept his eyes on the ridges that guided him like lights on an airstrip.

His appreciation for the ridges turned to suspicion.

"Are you seeing the snow piled up on the sides? I think this road has been plowed."

His eyes bounced to each side. He grew more convinced. There were no fresh tire tracks, but the uniform mounds of snow were unnatural. He surmised the road had been plowed after a previous snowfall, some indeterminate time ago.

"You might be on to something."

They came across signs of power – landscaping bulbs glowing beneath the snow and motion lights triggered by the wind. A streetlight created an icy halo above a church parking lot.

Henry notched his speed up to nine miles per hour. They passed fewer homes and more business properties. The road bent back, due east.

A red building with a neon light caught his eye. *Jo Etta's Pizza Villa*. If the world was ending, why not leave the sign on?

"Coming up on your left. I'll take it from here."

Robby flashed his lights and made the pass. *Have at it*, Henry said to himself, happy to hand over the reins.

Robby's Cybertruck flew by as they approached a railroad crossing. His snowmobile trailer fishtailed up the incline. Atop the tracks, he tapped the brakes, pulsing out bright red light. He swerved hard to the right before disappearing on the other side.

Henry was not in the mood for Robby's antics. He reached for the radio to tell him as much – before being blinded by headlights bouncing over the tracks. A truck slid toward him before correcting and narrowly passing in the other lane.

It was a snowplow.

"*What the f—*"

He eclipsed the tracks to find Robby's glowing taillights straight ahead. The road veered left.

Robby had jumped the curb and slammed into a municipal sign with two brick bases. The snowmobile trailer was bent askew.

Henry jumped out into the hostile cold. Timothy and Adam pulled up behind him. Robby flung his door open, hitting the left base of the sign again. The shell of ice encasing the sign shattered and hailed down on him.

"I freaking hate this town," Robby said.

The sign read: **You'll Like Linton**

Chapter Thirty

Taveon led Marcus through the living quarters, stopping to peek around each corner before crossing.

"Make it quick," Taveon said.

Marcus retrieved his blood key and belongings. They hustled down to Taveon's room.

Authorities avoided the Speedway bunker living quarters. The only time Taveon could recall agents venturing into the apartments was when a trash collector was accused of stealing an autographed Zach Edey jersey during a stop in Carmel.

"They searched my room, even though I wasn't a trash collector, or no Boilermaker." Taveon opened the door to his apartment. "But I do know the guy who stole it. He wears it during our pickup games."

"What are you doing back here?" his wife said.

"I want you to meet someone," Taveon said. "This is the second most famous Hoosier ever, right behind Larry Legend – *the* Marcus Trencher. And Mr. Trencher, this is my wife, Leslie. She's a vet tech on the farm half."

"Pleasure to meet you."

Trevion walked in and plucked his earbuds out.

"Tre, you know those suits that came down from Carmel? They're looking for Mr. Trencher, and we need to help get him back to his bunker."

Trevion shrugged and said, "Okay."

"It's too far to walk, and it's too far to drive a cart or forklift. Our emergency vehicle never got back to us after a guy drove himself to Meridian with a broken arm. Unless you jack that SUV the agents drove down in, that pretty much leaves the train. It departs in about an hour."

"How am I going to get on?"

"I have an idea," Trevion said. "I have a friend in Louisville. I met...her...in the Metaverse. Her and her dad unload trains like us, so I started hiding stuff for her to find, just for fun."

"*Her?*" his mother said. "Is she your *girlfriend*?"

"How many cute girls unload trains, Trevion?" Taveon said. "That's probably some bald ass man!"

"She's just a friend! Ugh, I knew I shouldn't have said anything..."

"Sorry—" Marcus put an arm out to stop Trevion from storming out, "Let's hear him out."

Trevion glared at his parents who glared back. They stood arms crossed, unsure if they were going to be upset or proud.

"You know those pallets full of Vitamin D tablets we always ship out? It's not hard to make a hollow space that a person can fit in."

"Fitting and sitting there for hours are two different things," Marcus said.

"Once the train starts rolling, you could climb out," Taveon said. "This could work."

They went to the warehouse where Taveon retrieved a pallet of 200 neatly stacked cases of Vitamin D tablets. He and Trevion hastily hollowed it.

"Alright, climb in," Taveon said.

Marcus did so, liking the plan less once inside.

"We'll put this cardboard slip over the top, then a top layer. I cut breathing holes. Once you get moving, get your fingers in there and pull it down."

"I'll get on the Metaverse and give my friend a head's up. Her name is Jayla."

"And if it's some guy named Jay, whoop his ass for me," Taveon said.

Marcus crouched into the cavity, which became pitch black with the slip overhead. He jostled about as the forklift lifted the pallet. They were on the move.

Taveon warned when it was time to stay quiet.

"Yo, we got one more," Taveon said. "Vitamin D tablets for the pasty folks down in Louisville."

"Not on the manifest," a voice said.

"Them Kentuckians are always requesting stuff last minute."

"Set it down."

Marcus absorbed the landing. He heard the crinkle of the plastic wrap and felt the wall pushing in. Someone was leaning into it. He braced the wall.

They began picking off boxes. Beams of light shot through the breathing holes. His tell-tale heart pounded.

"Ah, shoot! Y'all the guys from Carmel, right?" Taveon said. "Someone said you was looking for

Marcus Trencher? I saw him when we unloaded the train a couple days back."

The removal of cases ceased.

"We released a description that may or may not match that of Marcus Trencher," a man said. "...I swear I saw you when we announced it earlier."

"Nah, I must've been back in the warehouse. Lot of brothers here."

"Can you tell us where Mr. Trencher went after you saw him?"

"Sure, I was right next to him unloading watermelons. He told the conductor he wanted to stay. When the guy walked away, he took one look around the platform and got back on the train. He made some excuse, said he needed to fill a prescription. Have y'all checked Meridian? Ain't no billionaire staying in Speedway, my man."

Cases were tossed back on the pallet. The breathing hole light beams disappeared.

"Right," the man said. "Good to go."

The pallet was picked up again, driven a few yards, lifted higher, and set down.

He was on the train.

Taveon yelled, "All aboard!" In a softer voice, he said, "Sorry for the race bullshit. Had to get them off our backs. See you when I see you, my friend."

* * *

Marcus felt the train move and gave it a few minutes. He felt for the breathing holes, poked his fingers through, and tore the cardboard down. Boxes caved into the cavity. He climbed through like a zombie from the grave.

Clearance was no concern. The top of the tunnel was five feet overhead. Still, it was a tight gauge. Engineers cut safety lanes, side tunnels, and reduced the diameter so tunnel-boring machines could get further faster during construction.

He enjoyed the earthy breeze and the hypnotic lights. Near the Columbus Exchange, the tunnel skirted the edge of a vast cavern along the eastern side. It was filled with thousands of heavy-duty machines – tractors, backhoes, combines – a cache waiting to rebuild the world.

He caught a fleeting glimpse of the tunnel back to Bloomington. The train barreled past.

He was Louisville bound.

Chapter Thirty-One

Robby left the Cybertruck lodged beneath the "You'll Like Linton" sign and jumped in with Henry. Timothy and Adam followed, as did the stranger in the snowplow.

"He wants us to stop," Robby said.

They flew past a Beer Cave, fire station, and police department. The snowplow gained on them, flashing his lights in the other lane.

"Who knows what kind of lunatic this could be," Henry said.

"Yeah, we are in Linton...Dude, look out!" Robby said, pointing ahead.

The road was barricaded between two brick buildings. Henry grinded the half-track to a halt.

"*Shit*. Do I ram it?"

"I would, but that *probably* means you shouldn't." Robby rubbernecked to look back. "Stay here. I'll talk to the guy."

"We don't have any guns."

Robby took the black two-way radio from his pocket. "Looks close enough."

They idled before the barricade. The snowplow pulled into an empty lot before the building on the barricade's right flank. The driver got out.

Robby jumped out. "Stop right there!"

The snowplow driver put his hands up. "I'm unarmed and alone! It's just me!"

The snowplowman unwound his scarf to show his face. He sported a patchy teenage mustache. Not tall, not big. He was bundled in winter wear like Ralphie's little brother from *A Christmas Story*.

Robby kept his guard up but felt more threatened by the cold than the kid.

"I can get you to a warm place, and I have food. This is a bad storm!"

"If you lead us into a trap, we have grenades and machine guns."

"I won't, I promise! Follow me!"

Robby stopped to tell Adam and Timothy. Neither protested. He jumped back in with Henry.

"Follow him. It's just a kid."

"What if he leads us into an ambush?"

"Just keep your eyes peeled."

* * *

They circumvented the barricade a block over with the snowplow clearing the way. Following a stranger in strange times put Henry on edge.

"Relax, I'm 80 percent sure the kid is harmless," Robby said. "He didn't even have a weapon."

"There were probably snipers on the roofs."

"It's way too cold to be up on any roofs."

211

They drove through Linton and the slanting snowstorm bombarding it. There were more indicators of power in the grid – traffic lights, business signs.

"You keep calling him a kid. Is he that young?"

"Snow was blasting me in the face, but yeah. Twentyish at best."

The snowplow driver used his left turn signal. Robby remarked on how thoughtful the gesture was. They entered a lot preceding a sign that read: *The Park Inn – A pleasant surprise.*

"I remember this place," Henry said, pointing at a snow-covered Gulf War tank. "We went to a concert in that park once."

"Freshman year. I drank Mad Dog and threw up everywhere."

The snowplow pulled up beneath a port-cochere – by far the fanciest feature of the Park Inn. The kid ran to the lobby door and beckoned them to follow.

"He does look young," Henry said.

There were no shadowy figures lurking on the balconies. The park was eerie and empty. Robby got out first and signaled it safe.

"This place warms up fast," the kid said, hurrying in and out of an office behind the front desk. "I turn the heat down when I know I'll be out for a few hours."

They filed in and silently scrutinized the kid. He removed his scarf, hat, gloves, and winter coat, leaving them wondering if there was going to be anything left if he removed his blue-and-red high school hoodie.

"Sorry about the wreck. I wasn't expecting anyone coming across the tracks. I always turn around at the liquor store and push some snow back in that lot and—"

"Kid," Robby interrupted, "first things first. What is your name?"

"Oh. Um, Cameron. Cameron Ayers."

"Don't worry about the truck, Cameron. I've wrecked more vehicles than I can remember. My name is Robby, this is Henry, Timothy, and Adam. You said you're alone. Was that, like, all-around?"

"I'm the only person in Linton, unless someone is really good at hiding."

"What are you doing here?" Timothy said.

"Um, I live here? I've always lived here. Well, not the motel, but around town. Sometimes I stay at different houses."

"No, Cameron – I don't mean this motel, or this town...I guess I should ask, '*How* are you here?'"

"Oh! You're talking about the end of the world, right?"

Timothy bobbed his head *yes, obviously.*

Cameron exhaled, paused, then said, "The world...*didn't end.*"

Timothy stared at him in awe. Robby covered his mouth. Henry, seeing Robby, had to do the same. Even Adam twitched a smile.

"I'm not kidding! The President and people on TV said an asteroid was going to hit on July 23rd, 2030. It didn't happen! You guys were underground, right?"

"We were, but how do you explain the weather?" Timothy said, playing ignorant for Adam more than

213

the kid. "It's summer, yet it's colder than the worst winter. There must be ash in the atmosphere."

"I'm not a scientist," Cameron said, "but from the TikTok videos I used to watch on the world ending, the ash would've already come down. That's all snow out there."

"It's clear *something* happened."

"I watched the sky that night – and the next, and the next – I never saw an asteroid. I've thought about this a lot, and maybe the magnetic poles of the planet flipped and so the seasons did, too. You know when it's summer in Indiana, it's winter in Australia, but now, maybe it's backwards? Or maybe an asteroid did strike where I couldn't see it and splashed in the ocean and the water went so high it froze in the upper atmosphere, and now it's coming down."

"I'm no scientist either, but those are reasonable guesses," Henry said. "We only resurfaced a few days ago. When did it first start getting cold?"

"I'll walk you through everything. Somehow, everybody in Linton got bunker bids. Even old people, and my mom who was on disability, and drugs. A month before impact, the National Guard rolled through to transport everyone. They loaded people onto cattle cars at the railroad tracks. It reminded me of that thing with the Jews, but the opposite, I guess.

"I didn't get on. Volunteers did a sweep door-to-door for a couple hours, but all you had to do was hide. It wasn't that hard."

"Why didn't you go?"

"Two reasons, and they contradict each other, so I don't know if it'll make sense, but first...it just didn't

214

feel right. People believed they were emptying the old folks' home to take up space in a bunker? C'mon. I worked at a gas station. The government thought I was worth saving? Yeah, right."

"It was a lottery, from my understanding."

"And everyone in Linton-freaking-Indiana won? Know what I think *really* happened? They loaded everyone up on that train and killed them."

"That's dark," Henry said.

And entirely accurate, he thought.

"What was your other reason?" Robby asked.

"Like I said, it's a contradiction, but I accepted that I was going to die when they announced the asteroid. If I'm being honest, I was okay with it.

"I didn't have much going for me. I don't know my dad. I lived in a trailer with my mom. After she received her bunker bid she partied with all the other junkies in town, OD'd, and died. She OD'd the night the asteroid was announced, too, but got Narcanned that time."

He became flustered and buried his face in his arm on the front desk counter.

"Sorry for your loss," Henry said. "It's okay, you don't have to—"

His head popped back up. "It's ironic, right? I was ready for the asteroid to put me out of my misery, but now I'm happier than I've ever been! I eat better than when I was poor. Isn't that crazy? I don't know what will happen when I run low, but for now, I love it. I found oat milk and name brand cereal at the grocery store manager's house. The other day, I went to Taco Bell and made a quesadilla!

"I go around and take whatever I want. I found a bunch of video games and a huge TV. I could never afford stuff like that. Best of all, I don't work fifty hours a week to scrape by."

"Work does suck," Robby said.

"I do work now, like snowplowing and looting, but that's kind of fun. But to answer your question, it didn't get cold until last winter, but then it just stayed, and got colder and colder. I swear it was a clear day, then all of the sudden the weirdest clouds formed and then it was completely overcast in a couple hours."

"You spoke of other people," Adam said, breaking his silence. "Where are they?"

"Oh, them – they live in Bloomfield. They call themselves the '3% Chosen' or something dumb like that. I gather supplies for them, so they leave me alone."

"Bloomfield? Is that east of here?"

"You guys aren't going that way, are you?"

"We were considering it," Henry said. "Are these people we need to avoid?"

"They'll take everything you have. For sure those vehicles."

"We can spare one if it gets us by," Timothy said. "Are they not reasonable at all?"

"Their leader, CJ, he spent time in prison. One of the guys told me he stormed a federal building in D.C. a long time ago."

"Great," Robby said. "I knew we'd run into a band of post-apocalyptic assholes sooner or later."

Chapter Thirty-Two

Mariya scrubbed the gnarled feet propped before her with a pumice stone.

Week one of salon indentured servitude was hell.

When visitors walked in on her crying, most showed pity, saying they would return later. A few stuck around for shoddy nail care. Others stomped off to complain.

She dropped the stone in the soaking tub, knocking her out of her sad daydream. She inched forward to administer the mandated calf massage.

The customer cleared her throat.

"*What?*" Mariya said with zero customer service.

"Don't jip me, little girl," the woman said. "You're supposed to apply lotion for the calf massage."

"We ran out of a whole tub. There's a limited supply, you know."

"I know for a *fact* there are miles of storage tunnels, and lotion is in stock," the woman said, looking down her nose past her bulbous neck fat. "I know you have a stash, so do your job, missy!"

"My job? This is slavery."

"Honey, we were the slaves, working in that coal mine while y'all lounged about. This is *fair*."

"Oh, *you* worked in the coal mine?"

"Don't sass me! Just...finish up."

Mariya grabbed a sponge and squeezed. Before she could soak it in dirty feet water and throw it, the salon door opened.

Natalie Brynn entered with her tablet in hand.

Mariya met her at the door. "Look...I can't do this. I don't know the first thing about pedicures. I used to run an urban farm, I'm a certified butcher and veterinarian. I work with animals, not people who act like animals."

"*Excuse me?*"

"You heard me, Karen."

"It's Tammy! Why does everyone keep calling me Karen around here?"

Natalie slid between to play peacemaker. "Sorry, Tammy," she said. "Allow me to have a word with Ms. Ichinose. Perhaps you can return in a week or two?"

"She needs to learn her damn manners!" Tammy said, huffing and puffing out the door.

Mariya's face flushed red. "I'd rather sit in a cell the rest of my sentence than deal with her again."

"She's awful, but I'm not here for that," Natalie said, locking the door behind the latest dissatisfied salon customer. "I overheard something, and I didn't know who to go to."

Mariya's anger gave way to curiosity.

"I check in with Ashley and Grant daily. Today, I went up to the suite and they weren't there. It was open, so I got nosy. I went into the bedroom, saw the trapdoor Timothy Spencer climbed through...and then they walked in. I was about to greet them, but they were in a heated discussion."

"I'm listening."

"They're afraid of what Marcus Trencher might do when he returns. He won't be happy Henry and Robby are gone, but they even think he'll be upset Timothy Spencer was exiled to the surface."

"I'm worried, too. You know he shot two people before he left."

"Since the trial, people have conjured all sorts of conspiracy theories absolving Marcus of any blame. Grant and Ashley think people will do whatever he says, and if he says to toss them out, the people will."

"What are they planning to do about it?"

"Grant convinced Ashley that they were no more than pawns to Marcus, and that it's best Marcus doesn't make it back."

Mariya peered through the salon curtains. She looked across the bunker proper at the tinted windows above the hospital where Marcus Trencher once secluded himself, and where Ashley and Grant now dictated their lives.

"I guess we warn Marcus when he arrives?"

"They're not waiting for him. By the time I snuck down the trapdoor and walked back around, Grant was gathering a bag to leave for Bloomington. He's going to assassinate Marcus before he can return."

"I don't know what any of us can do about it. They have guards watching us. It's too late."

"It's not. You need to get to your friend, Kent."

"The-Computer-Guy Kent?"

"Yes – the cable to Bloomington was hooked up yesterday. Kent is doing tech stuff to get it online.

Nobody knows about it yet. Ashley and Grant want to control communication outside the bunker."

Natalie unlocked the salon door but turned back before opening it.

"I know Marcus is odd, and I'm fully aware he has done deplorable things...but I knew his mother from school. I watched him grow up. Deep down, he's a good person."

* * *

Mariya entered the server room where the IT brains of the bunker were held. It was unlocked and unguarded.

Kent Grieves stood at a tiny table with his laptop open before a wall of black boxes and blinking lights. He looked over, saw Mariya, and sighed.

"Don't tech-guy-sigh at me," Mariya said.

"Sorry, I've been at this for hours. We're being integrated into a network with the other bunkers."

"That's why I'm here. Is your guard on break?"

"Guard? No, nobody watches me. Ashley checks in often though."

"Okay, I'll make this quick. Grant left for Bloomington earlier today to hunt Marcus down. We need to warn him. Can you send messages yet?"

"Sure, but only on this terminal for now. I'm working with a former co-worker from *Trencher Industries*. It's crazy – this guy, Gene, had a sex-change *right* before the news broke about the end of the world and now goes by Genie."

"I hope Genie didn't hate working for Marcus. Ask her if she has seen him."

Kent typed the message on a black screen with plain text and received a quick response.

"She says he left Bloomington a while ago...he was in a bunker in Indianapolis, and last she heard, headed to Louisville, but trying to get back here."

"Ask if she can get him a message. Tell her to tell him, 'Don't trust Grant. He plans to assassinate you. Ashley and Grant sent Henry, Robby, and Timothy to the surface.'"

He looked at her to see how serious she was. "Assassination? Alright, one sec..."

More terminal text appeared. She leaned over Kent to read for herself.

"He shows offline 2 days, will leave him message on...metaverse?"

"They run a metaverse across all the bunkers. That's what's giving me so much trouble compiling and meshing—"

"Save your breath," she said. "Just confirm your friend sends that message to Marcus. I better get out of here before Ashley drops in."

* * *

Grant Maniego hopped out of a pickup truck at the train station in Bloomington. Hitching a ride with the tunnel construction crew was made possible by the unfortunate disappearance of Adam Terry. The crew even gave him the front passenger seat.

He was greeted by Jim Cox, the bunker architect and unofficial welcoming committee chairman.

"What a pleasant surprise," Jim said as Grant climbed the platform. "To heck with quarantine, come on up. What brings you back to the Quarry so soon?"

"I wish I could say it was for something better."

Jim smiled and waved at the returning tunnel workers.

"Did Adam Terry stay back at your place?"

Grant glanced around. They walked down the platform for privacy.

"Remember that badly injured girl we sent your way a few days back?"

"Of course. Jenna Doth-something? She's stable. We'll transfer her to Indy once the train comes our way. Their hospital facilities are tops in the network."

"The reason I bring it up, is that her injuries were inflicted from an assault – and we believe the assault came from Adam Terry."

"I can't imagine why he would do such a thing."

"This is no excuse, but alcohol was served at our tunnel breakthrough celebration. He was seen with Ms. Dothmayer throughout the night."

Jim frowned. "I didn't think Adam even liked women. We'll need a formal investigation. Is he in your custody?"

"Unfortunately, no. Our men pursued Mr. Terry, and he somehow escaped to the surface."

"The *surface*-surface?"

"I don't know how he did it. We all assumed someone like Marcus Trencher could override the lock, but Adam managed to get through. Does that make any sense to you?"

"Actually, it does," Jim said. "Adam was an engineer, and he designed our vault doors. I imagine he knew a way to open them up."

"I think you solved a big piece of the puzzle."

"Between you and me, Adam had an edge about him that made me uneasy."

Grant's framing of Adam Terry was off to a spectacular start.

"Can't say I got a good read on him." He paused to let it sink in how above passing judgement he was. "I was wondering if Marcus Trencher has returned?"

"Not yet. He went to Indianapolis but didn't say how long he planned on staying."

"I'd like to keep off the communications lines. News of this delicate matter is best delivered in person. Do you have any emergency vehicles?"

"We do. If you know how to ride, I recommend the electric motorcycle. Should get you to Indy on a single charge."

Chapter Thirty-Three

Marcus peered from his hollow pallet. The platform was on the opposite side of the tracks from where it was in Speedway. He had made it to the Mega Caverns bunker of Louisville.

"Mr. Trencher?" a girl's voice called from below. "My name's Jayla, and this is my dad. Are you here?"

The platform was empty other than the girl and a big man. He stood.

"It's safe. You can come down."

He climbed to the base of the railcar and hopped to the platform. He had to look up to the man.

"I'll be damned, it is him..." the man said, extending a hand. "Name's Ellis Caldwell. This is my daughter, Jayla."

Marcus's hand was engulfed. Ellis was six-foot-nine, lanky, and sported a shiny bald head.

"If any other man climbed off that train, I would've tied him to the tracks. My daughter was way too trusting to a stranger on the internet."

"Kids these days and their metaverse..." Marcus said, sounding 70-years-old. "I'll vouch for Jayla's friend, Trevion. He's a good kid."

"That's a relief." He ruffled Jayla's hair. "But I still don't think we're ready for no boyfriend drama."

"He's not my boyfriend! He's a boy-that-is-a-friend!"

"Alright, lady. We'll meet your friend when this interbunker league starts up."

"You play basketball?"

"You could say that," Ellis said, amused by the lack of recognition.

"Trevion's father, Taveon, plays, too."

"Taveon, from Indy? Played at Butler? I might know who you are talking about."

"You know everybody," Jayla said.

Workers began to trickle onto the platform to unload the train.

"And everybody acts like they know me," Ellis said, looking over Marcus's head. "Folks might get excited seeing a man such as yourself. They see me all the time and still talk trash because I chose UK over Louisville."

"The United Kingdom?"

"Nah, man – University of Kentucky."

Ellis and Jayla led him through a set of doors off the platform and out to a concrete mezzanine overlooking a cavern alcove.

Calcified streaks dripped down the walls where lights at the base sent shadows climbing upward. A paved road complete with painted lines looped around a limestone pillar. At the top of the bend, trucks waited in loading docks.

"We're at the upper end," Ellis said. "If you look over the train station, up the slope, you'll see the old gift shop from when this was just a tourist attraction. The surface door is somewhere up there. Shows how much was excavated."

Forty feet above, windowpanes sealed off a rectangle of cavern wall. The rubble slope below it was steep but scalable. Stern signs warned against the idea.

Ellis covered Jayla's ears. "Those signs ain't lying – they shoot if you climb up there. You can still see bloodstains from a fool who tried."

"They, as in military?"

Ellis nodded.

"I already knew that happened," Jayla said, pushing her dad's hands away. "I found out in school."

"They teaching you about a guy getting shot?"

"No, all the kids were talking about it."

Ellis stepped to an open edge and grabbed a zipline handlebar rigged overhead. The line was so long it disappeared in the distance.

"If you want to zipline down, be my guest. I don't trust the harness."

"I'll pass," Marcus said. "I didn't survive the end of the world to die in a freak ziplining accident."

"My man, I said the same thing."

They descended grated stairs to the street level and climbed into the first truck in the loading dock. Ellis tapped the top to get the attention of a man on a forklift, who then loaded a pallet in the back.

"Is there a large military presence here?"

"There is. They dug the place out, constructed all the buildings, and administered the move in. I heard a rumor there's a separate tunnel down to Fort Knox. We're not living under Marshall Law. It ain't bad."

Another pallet was placed on the truck. The forklift driver tooted his horn.

"Alright, now the tour truly begins."

They rounded the limestone pillar into a narrow straight, and after two-hundred yards, emerged into a wider cavern, like leaving a fjord for the ocean. They descended to a village straight out of a Christmas movie, minus the snow.

Four-story buildings with colorful 19th century facades lined the road. Bunker planners simply built as if it were the outdoors. There was ample space.

"The interior buildings house public services, restaurants, doctors' offices, stuff like that. Buildings along the cavern walls are residential. They go way back into the rock. We're talking quarter-mile hallways. Population is supposedly around 75,000."

"Impressive."

"Not as impressive as what we started with. When the asteroid hit, an entire cavern collapsed. Thousands of folks were back there. It was a tent city, but they were going to build it up. We had a memorial service a few days back."

Marcus was certain the catastrophe was planned. The puppeteers brought thousands in to die – put them in an ancillary cavern and buried them – leaving the survivors convinced there was an asteroid.

They stopped before a fountain-centered roundabout. Cyclists zoomed by. A flock of women crossed the street wearing flamboyant dresses and elaborate hats.

"This is the Audubon hood," Ellis said, as he gave a two-finger-steering-wheel wave at the women. "Down cavern, there's Poplar Level, Cherokee, and Butchertown, where we're headed."

"They're villages, but dad calls them hoods. Each one looks different. And don't forget Deer Park where people exercise. Oh, and we have a lake."

Buildings surrounded each pillar, leaving alleys filled with cafés and outdoor seating. As impressed as Marcus was with the architecture, engineering, and community planning, he was still distracted by what people wore. A flock of teenagers walked by decked out in Versace and Chanel.

"You'll want a jacket when we start walking around. It's 58-degrees year-round down here."

Jayla handed him a puffy black jacket.

He flattened it out and read the big white letters printed on the back: GUCCI.

"Okay – what is up with the luxury brands? And those old ladies dressed to the nines?"

Ellis and Jayla burst out laughing.

"We were waiting to see how long it took you to say something!" Jayla said.

"Legend goes that a cargo plane full of luxury goods happened to be at the Louisville airport when the asteroid announcement went down. Somehow it all ended up down here, along with everything else in every warehouse in the city. Now we have folks walking around like it's the Kentucky Derby every day."

"Or the *Hunger Games*," Marcus said.

"You know the *Hunger Games*?" Jayla asked, leaning between the front seats. "I met the lead actress! She lives here! Those movies came out forever ago, so she is an old lady now."

"Old lady? You goofball," Ellis said.

They drove by a turf lawn hosting a yoga class. The architecture made a sudden modernist shift on the other side of it.

"We are now entering Butchertown, home to our bunker's primary industry."

"Let me guess, meat?"

"Not just any meat – the lab-grown stuff."

"I wasn't a fan when I tried some a few years ago. It was almost more psychological than the taste."

"I was the same, but they nailed the fish fillets. Jayla won't eat anything not lab-grown."

"It tastes the same and you don't have to kill animals. Y'all are the weird ones for needing to murder something for it to taste good. The chicken nuggets are fire."

Ellis backed the truck up to a beige building.

"Run in and tell Vince we have his bath water."

Jayla jumped out and disappeared through a teal door. A moment later, the dock door opened.

"Did you say *bath water*?"

Ellis tilted his head back and laughed.

"The plastic drums we're dropping off are filled with a nutrient mix they produce up in Indy. They take cultured cells from cows, chickens, pigs, you name it, and 'bathe' it in the nutrient wash, and the meat grows. We started calling the stuff bath water as a joke."

A group of people wearing lab coats stepped out. Marcus sunk in his seat and put a hand over his face.

"Take a mask from the glove box. People wear them all the time down here, pandemic style."

Marcus did so and felt a little more secure in his anonymity. The remaining pallet was removed from the truck and Jayla returned.

"That's it for us," Ellis said. "The other guys can deliver the rest."

"Can I go to the library? I need to tell Trevion that Mr. Trencher made it."

"I wouldn't mind checking in with a few people myself," Marcus said.

* * *

Grant Maniego revved the electric engine one more time as he came to a stop at the Speedway Bunker train platform. The Bloomington tunnel was rough, but the paved lane to Indianapolis was a breeze. He pushed the bike beyond 90-miles-per-hour for much of the journey. He preferred burning fuel, but the electric bike wasn't half bad.

The platform was empty, save for a teenage boy on sweeping duty. Grant climbed the platform stairs on the bike.

"Sick bike. Are you from Louisville?" the boy asked, leaning on his broom.

"The Quarry, in Bloomington," Grant said. "Say, kid, maybe you could help me. My friend Marcus Trencher came through here a few days ago. You know, the billionaire inventor? You wouldn't happen to know where he is, would you?"

"You're a friend of Mr. Trencher?"

"Sure am. And between you and me, he could use a friend right now."

The boy looked around the empty platform.

"There were some suits from Carmel looking for him. We snuck him on a train to Louisville yesterday. I have a friend there and—"

"Louisville, yesterday?"

"Yes, sir. Do you want me to tell him you are coming? I can contact him."

"Nah, I'll talk to him in person. But thank you for your help. What's your name, kid?"

"Trevion."

"Thanks again, Trevion. Got anywhere I can charge this bike?"

* * *

They entered the Mega Caverns Library, a sprawling complex that put the Speedway library to shame.

"I'ma hit up the front desk to get the books I have on hold," Ellis said. "I know where to find y'all."

Jayla led the way to a study room with cameras on the walls that assisted with motion capture, just like the one in the Speedway library. Marcus grabbed the public use headset and wiped it down.

"Tre isn't on yet," Jayla said already wearing her headset. "He had to sweep but he said he'd be done by now."

"We'll give him a minute," Marcus said. "I'll reach out to another friend of mine."

231

He joined Jayla in her digital hangout decorated with pop star video screens, gaming trophies, and windows facing out to an alien world.

He summoned Genie, who soon showed up as her centaur avatar. She activated her bucking and whinnying animation. Jayla burst out laughing.

"Are you a minotaur?" Jayla asked.

"God no, honey. I'm a centaur – horse body, human torso. Who are you?"

"This is Jayla, she helped smuggle me to safety. She's cool."

"I have good news and bad news. We're in the final stages of UAT testing with your bunker. You'll get to visit your friends in the metaverse in a couple days. I didn't realize you had Kent with you!"

"Kent is great. I presume that's the good news?"

"Correct. The bad news is, a man by the name of Grant Maniego departed your bunker yesterday to find and assassinate you."

"Jesus, Genie. When the news is that bad, lead with it! Why would that mercenary want to kill me?"

"He and a woman named Ashley are afraid of what you might do when you get back. I don't know what went down, but your friends Robby and Henry, and our pal Timothy, were all exiled to the surface."

"That can't be. Those are the only people I want..." Marcus trailed off. "...and I need Timothy. Can you put me through to Kent? *Metaverse, contact Kent Grieves.*"

"Sorry, hon, he's not on here yet. We've only exchanged messages through a terminal."

"Did he say anything else?"

232

"Adam Terry was tossed out as well. Now they're trying to keep a diplomatic crisis from breaking out, which is doable considering nobody here cared for the guy. My spies also say the assassin went to Indy, so you might miss him."

A notification that Trevion had joined appeared a second before his avatar materialized.

"Whoa, is that a minotaur?" Trevion asked.

"No! I'm a centaur. Don't you kids know the difference?"

Trevion apologized and turned to Marcus.

"Hey, Mr. Trencher. I just talked to one of your friends. He came in on a sweet motorcycle from Bloomington."

"Did you catch his name?"

"Uh, no. He knew you were in trouble and wanted to help. He wore army pants."

"That wasn't my friend. Is he still in Speedway?"

"He charged his bike up and left for Louisville. He said he was going to help. Sorry, I didn't know."

"Don't sweat it, Tre. It's no big deal."

Ellis, entered the real room.

"Y'all about ready? I need something to eat."

Marcus disconnected the headset. Jayla had the courtesy to say, "Bye."

"Ellis, would you happen to know any other big guys like yourself?"

He gave a cool nod.

"Someone decided to bring down ball players like myself as some kind of morale boosters. I got a whole team of All-Americans, and ain't none of us under six-five. I'll gather the boys."

Chapter Thirty-Four

Timothy woke up shivering cold in his room at the Park Inn and immediately scrambled to put a shirt on. He tried the light, to no avail.

There was a knock at the door.

"Timothy, the power's out," Henry said.

He arrived in the lobby to find the others crowded in the back office around the *Trencher Industries Monolith* unit panel.

"This is like the third place this month," Cameron said. "I don't understand why."

"Let me take a look," Timothy said. "I designed those things."

They moved aside. The temperature had already plummeted to freezing inside. Timothy began maneuvering through the interface.

"Went out at midnight on the dot. What time is it now? 12:40? Interesting."

"You know what's interesting? Places with heat. It's freezing," Robby said.

"If there's no power, how is the panel on?" Adam asked.

"The panels always get power if there is any coursing through the grid, which is a good sign. In this case, the unit just fell off the grid."

"Why would it do that?"

He clicked to another screen. After a look of puzzlement, he laughed. "It was booted off the grid because the method of payment expired."

"Method of... the freaking credit card?"

"Says here the card on file expired four months ago and apparently that's the limit the company set to be overdue before it's kicked off the grid."

"Let's get somewhere warm and figure it out later," Robby said.

"I know a few places that should have power," Cameron said. "They're just a few blocks away."

* * *

They left the least valuable vehicle hidden behind the Park Inn and followed Cameron's snowplow down a residential street to a house that still had power.

The wheels were spinning in Timothy's head.

"What is it, Timothy? Spit it out," Robby said.

"Our *Monolith* units function 'off grid' as long as a solar array or wind turbine or whatever else feeds them. The other option was to subscribe to the grid, where power is shared with other units in the area.

"When the sun was shining or the wind was blowing, power was essentially free, and some even banked credit for producing back into the grid. Obviously, that's no longer the case with the sun blotted out, so the credit cards are starting to get

235

billed. If those cards are expired, the smart contracts are broken, and they are booted off the grid."

"Smart contracts?" Robby said. "Sorry, I never bothered learning how all this shit works."

"It was an automated billing function in the blockchain. If there is no credit banked up from excess production back into the grid, and no up-to-date method of payment, the unit automatically disengages from the grid and reverts to being a standalone unit. The Park Inn apparently wasn't producing its own power. The card declined, it exceeded payment delinquency, so it was booted at midnight."

"Wouldn't this require Visa and Mastercard and all the financial institutions to still be operating?" Adam said.

"Everything was so highly automated it wouldn't surprise if all sorts of systems were still carrying on. I don't know if it's the payment failures or if it's the expirations, but the results are the same."

"Basically, the entire grid is decaying," Henry said. "Cameron, didn't you say other places have lost power recently?"

"Yeah, three that I've broken into at least."

"Starting tomorrow, you need to find homes or businesses with wind turbines and *Monoliths*. Figure out how to install turbines on a bunch of houses in a tight radius. You'll need to setup your own microgrid and get ahead of this."

"That will have to wait," Timothy said. "Cameron, you're coming with us to Bloomfield."

"I am?"

"We'll need your help getting past that gang you work with. If we want to save the grid from collapse, we need to get to Bloomington, and we need to get to Marcus Trencher."

Chapter Thirty-Five

Ellis and crew looked busy while a single headlight approached from down the tunnel. It was no train. The train was already there, pulled beyond the platform to the maintenance bay.

As expected, the approaching visitor was on a bike. Grant Maniego rolled up and dismounted.

"Welcome, stranger. C'mon up," Ellis said. "What brings you to Louisville?"

Grant did a double take upon seeing how tall Ellis and the rest of his crew were.

"I'm tracking down a guy that came this way. He arrived yesterday."

"Wouldn't happen to be Marcus Trencher, would it That rich prick treated us like peasants the moment he stepped on our platform."

Grant was thrilled. His job just got easier.

"It would happen to be Marcus Trencher. Let's just say he's needed back home. If you gentlemen can help me track him down, I could send a thank you gift the next time the train makes a lap."

"We might be able to help you."

"I can send wine, coffee beans, you name it. I'll throw together a gift basket if you can get me to him."

"You got yourself a deal. But first, we need to get your quarantine paperwork sorted. Don't want to get caught in the cavern without it."

Grant sighed.

"Relax, my man. I'll scribble on the paper like a doctor, and you'll be good."

He led Grant to the quarantine area.

The crew followed close behind. Ellis ducked to clear the doorway into a narrow hall.

Grant grew nervous and tried to make small talk.

"What were you guys before? CIA?"

"Nah, man – NBA," one of the men said.

"In here, my man. We'll get this paperwork knocked right out..."

Grant hesitated but entered.

Marcus Trencher sat there, waiting.

The crew rushed Grant. They stripped the duffel bag from his shoulder and wrestled the strap from his hand.

"Alright, alright," Grant said, giving up the fight.

A man pulled out a compact assault rifle.

"Damn, this thing real?"

The others gathered to examine the weapon and empty the rest of the bag. Ellis stayed by Grant, encouraging him to take the seat across from Marcus.

"Lieutenant, whatever were you planning to do with that rifle?" Marcus said.

"Protect myself...and to protect you. I heard someone was looking for you in Indianapolis?"

"Cut the bullshit."

"What? Why would I? You saved my life."

"How are Henry, Robby, and Timothy doing?"

Grant exhaled through his nostrils. "Timothy Spencer was a problem – for both of us. Your friend Henry volunteered to go with him. Robby went on his own. Why do you care about Timothy, anyway? He ruined everything."

"If we want to reclaim the surface within our lifetime, there are two people that can make it happen sooner rather than later. I am one of them, Timothy Spencer is the other. I need him alive."

"*These dudes talking about the surface-surface?*" one of the crewmen whispered to another.

Marcus stood and began to pace.

"I heard an interesting story when I was at the Quarry. Allegedly, authorities here in Louisville sent a 'lice-infested rapist' to Bloomington without explanation. Ellis, did you hear about this?"

"Sure did, it was the talk of the caverns. It was a politician's drug-addicted kid. I heard the Hoosiers up there were pissed."

"I doubt anyone would be surprised if Bloomington sent Lieutenant Maniego here as payback. This man is a murderer. If you don't mind, Ellis, call the authorities to apprehend him. I'll have Bloomington send the details of his crime."

"Hold up! I can help you," Grant said. "I can track your friends on the surface."

Marcus raised a hand to stop Ellis.

"I need Timothy *alive*, along with the rest of my friends."

"I'll find them, I'll guarantee it."

"Why should I trust you?"

Grant looked back at the giant athletes hovering behind him.

"Gentlemen, can you give us a moment?"

The men filed out, taking Grant's belongings with them. Marcus moved his chair closer.

"Ashley and I have struck up a relationship," Grant said.

"Congratulations?"

"She's pregnant."

Marcus sat back. He steeled his expression.

"From my understanding, there's overlap between our *interactions* with her."

"The kid isn't mine. Impossible."

"You and I know it is possible. But I can fix it."

"What do you mean 'fix it'?"

"I'll claim the kid. Unless he or she starts solving calculus in the cradle, nobody will be any wiser."

"We have DNA testing capabilities. There's a geneticist. Is...is Jenna Dothmayer still alive?"

"The woman you shot?"

A fire lit in Marcus's eyes, which darted to the doorway. Before he could call the men, Grant reneged.

"She survived. So did the chef, Brad. There was another incident with the girl, but that's not your concern. She's in Bloomington awaiting transport to the hospital in Indy."

Marcus shook his head. "This is not the most pressing issue. I need Timothy and my friends. You'll be outfitted in Bloomington, then transported to my bunker. From there, you'll go straight to the surface. I want them alive. Ellis, we're done here!"

The crew filed back into the room.

"Let the authorities know this man is wanted for a murder in the bunker west of Bloomington. He is to be extradited on the next train north. I'll be taking his bike."

"What about the gun and this big ass blade?" a crew man asked, holding both.

"I don't care, just don't give it back to him."

Chapter Thirty-Six

Henry, Robby, Timothy, and Adam packed supplies for the journey east to Bloomfield, and then the city of Bloomington beyond there.

"I'll need to swing by the Park Inn and load up a trailer of loot," Cameron said. "We better not show up empty handed. Ricky and CJ wouldn't like that."

"Make it quick," Timothy said. "There's a break in the weather."

It was -40-degrees, but the snow stopped, and the wind died down from brutal to biting. Conditions remained life threatening, but they could at least see a hundred yards ahead.

"Can we get my Cybertruck?" Robby asked. "That snowmobile will be a good bargaining chip."

"There's a chain in the back of the snowplow," Cameron said.

"You and Henry see if you can dislodge it," Timothy said. "Adam and I will go with Cameron to the motel and load everything up."

* * *

They found the Cybertruck beneath the sign with a snowbank accumulated along the passenger side up to the truck bed. The snowmobile and trailer were buried. They detached it and pulled it away first.

The truck was certainly lodged, and the tires sat in grooves of ice, but they made short work of towing it out with the half-track and chain.

"Back in business," Robby said. "I'll let you lead the way."

Back at the Park Inn, Robby announced their arrival by doing donuts in the parking lot.

* * *

They packed a trailer of food, clothes, and various trinkets. The charging stations in the parking lot were on the municipal grid. Once the Cybertruck was charged, they were good to go.

"We just have to load the guns," Cameron said.

Timothy opened room 101. "Sheesh, it's like the Waco compound in here."

Cameron had an arsenal. Three dozen rifles were piled on the bed and no surface was without firearms or ammo, including the floor.

"Waco?" Cameron asked.

"Before your time, kid. Let's get on with it."

"Linton loves firearms. So does CJ and the gang in Bloomfield."

"Do you get anything in return?" Robby asked.

"They gave me a PlayStation 3 and some games last trip, and some food."

They loaded dozens of rifles, handguns, and ammunition, still having to leave several behind.

Cameron rummaged through his stash of goods and found enough two-way radios, so each had one.

They departed the Park Inn in a convoy headed east on State Road 54. The temperature readings remained in the -40-degree range. The sky was hazy grey, absent even a pale dot where the sun hid. The ground was covered in pristine snow after the previous storm, but with a snowplow leading the way, the road was passable.

Bloomfield was a mere twelve miles away, straight and flat. The snow and ice did not push away easily, but at a steady pace, they would make it within the hour. It was far better than the first leg of their journey from Sherman to Linton.

They passed a high school gymnasium with "Wolverines" written on the side. A water tower blended in with the sky, floating black letters that read, "Switz City." It was generous to call such a tiny town a city. They had reached the halfway point between Linton and Bloomfield.

"Cameron, do these people know we're coming?" Timothy asked, breaking the radio silence. "I don't want to drive into an ambush."

"A guy named Brant lives around here," Cameron said. "He guards the fuel depot. By now, he's been on the CB."

"I hope they know we come in peace."

"They'll recognize my snowplow."

They crossed a bridge spanning the White River. After a mile of fields and a cluster of billboards, they entered Bloomfield. Other than the road plowed clear to the cement, there were no signs of life. Cameron took a right to the local high school, his regular drop location.

He got out and began pulling the tarp off his trailer. Timothy, Adam, Henry, and Robby parked behind him and reluctantly got out to help.

"Where is everyone?" Timothy asked.

"They'll be here any minute. Start unloading stuff onto the curb but stop when they get here. Keep your hands where they can see them."

By the time they got their gloves on, a rumble of diesel engines stole their attention. Eight jacked-up trucks flew up the drive and formed a semi-circle around them in the parking lot.

The lead truck flew rebel flags from welded pipes on the back of the cab. Men aimed guns from the windows. A wiry country boy not dressed for the cold hopped down from his Chevy.

"Hey, Ricky," Cameron said. "I brought in a good haul for you guys."

Ricky sized Timothy up and glared at the others.

"Who are these guys?"

"They come from Sherman. They're unarmed."

"We're only hoping to pass through," Timothy said. "With your blessing, of course."

"Where you headed?"

"Bloomington. We want to see if some family and friends survived."

Ricky laughed.

"You hear that, boys? These fellers want to go to Bloomington. Sounds like we got a bunch of fucking liberals on our hands."

"What? No, nothing political, just...survival."

"It's always political. How you think we got in this mess? I ain't see no asteroid. Someone's pulling this shit on us. I bet it was the fucking Democrats."

"You could be on to something."

"Damn right I am," Ricky said. He motioned to the second truck and two men in camouflage got out. Ricky's eyes drifted to the trailer. "What'd you get us this time, Cam?"

"More guns, mostly. Oh! And I found a video game system in an attic. It's called a *Dreamcast*. Had six games with it. It works offline."

"Hell yeah, brother. I found a couple PS3 games up in Worthington. I'll swap you."

Timothy, Adam, Robby, and Henry stood by, cold and confused.

"Newer game systems require being online," Cameron said. "The internet is down, so you can't play anything. The old stuff is gold."

"If we find any in Bloomington, we'll bring it back to you all," Timothy said. "And any guns."

"Not so fast, partner," Ricky said. "I ain't the one that makes them decisions."

"If it helps, we brought a special gift."

Robby went to pull the cover off the snowmobile.

"Stop right there, Gumby," Ricky said. He motioned for his men to do the unveiling.

"The fuck we need a jet ski for?" one of the men said after pulling the tarp.

"You dipshit, that's a snowmobile," the other said. "Always wanted me one of these!"

"You used to make $30K a year at the county garage, dumbass. Why the hell would you buy a snowmobile in Indiana?"

"Fuck off, Joe! One would be pretty handy now, don't you think?"

"Shut up, both of you!" Ricky said. "CJ might like this. But you know what he might like more? That there Cybertruck. Might just be your ticket through our town."

Robby inched forward. Henry pulled him back.

"If it gets us by, we'd be willing to part with it," Timothy said.

"I'm freezing my nuts off. Let's take you boys to the tower to meet CJ."

* * *

They piled into Cameron's snowplow and were escorted by a redneck motorcade. The tower Ricky spoke of was a seven-story structure, formally of Section 8 housing. Men patted them down in the lobby.

"A few folks live around town, but a bunch of us moved in here," Ricky said. "Easier to keep one place warm. Now, hands together."

They zip-tied their wrists.

They ascended a dingy stairwell to the second floor. Residents stood in doorways to catch a glimpse of the strange visitors from the west.

Ricky stepped into an apartment to give the mysterious CJ the rundown. He reemerged and motioned them in.

They squeezed past stacked crates of cigarettes. The stench hit them all at once – a smell from the distant past. The rest of the apartment was cluttered with looted junk food. A large man sat behind a messy desk, sporting a bandana and a full beard.

"Cam, my boy, introduce me to your friends."

Cameron did so, forgetting Adam's name and mixing Henry and Robby's.

"Ricky tells me you all wish to pass through to get to the sinners' snake pit of Bloomington. Is that so?"

"It is, sir," Timothy said. "We're searching for friends and family."

CJ cocked his head, his beard barely moving.

"City folk didn't fare so well. Too trusting of their godless government and fake news networks."

"We understand the odds, but we have to try. We'll come back this way and tell you what we saw, then continue back to Sherman."

"Sherman? That's where y'all come from? Home of the world-famous Marcus Trencher! Shut down all our coal mines because of his little invention..."

CJ broke into a coughing fit before lighting another cigarette.

"God chose us to rule this little corner of the new world and we got to be careful who crosses it. We refused to let the National Guard shove us into a bunker, and God rewarded us. We're his chosen.

"People called us crazy, saying we was conspiracy wackos, made fun of our forums and news sources, but they was the ones telling the truth! We knew all along there wasn't going to be no asteroid. You do know there wasn't one, right?"

"We didn't watch the skies," Timothy said. "But, yes, it became clear we were lied to."

"Damn right we was lied to! I *did* watch the skies – right from the roof of my trailer. There wasn't no space rock! And there ain't no way in hell all them people fit in bunkers. The government went and killed everybody, and we have proof."

"Proof? Where were they taken?"

"Closer to your neck of the woods. The old underground mine on the Knox County line. Been shut down for years. They emptied the entire Greene County population out in a day using the railroad. We sent men that way a week later and the mine was collapsed. They put all them people down there and blowed it up.

CJ took a long drag off his cigarette. "God has a plan for us. As for your plan, there's one issue. We ain't cleared the road east, and that's on purpose. We don't want to make it easy for liberal city folk fleeing to us here in Bloomfield."

"We can take our half-track vehicle and not plow the way," Timothy said. "We'll stop short of the city and do our search on foot. The next snowstorm will cover our tracks."

CJ stroked his beard as he thought it over.

Then, the power went out.

"Daggonit! This shit's got to stop!"

Men scrambled to light candles placed around the room. CJ lit a lantern on his desk. It appeared to be a recurring issue.

Henry tugged on Timothy's sleeve. With only a look, he asked, *should we tell them?* Timothy shook his head.

"Same things happening in Linton," Cameron said. Timothy glared at him. "...but I'm not sure what's causing it."

"We know what's causing it," CJ said, rolling his chair to the window to let in natural light. "It's those damn *Trencher* machines. We have an electrician and he says the credit cards are expiring. I ain't never trusted that Marcus Trencher and I sure as hell ain't never trusted banks!"

He knocked over a stack of ramen noodle bundles while rolling back to his desk.

"Get this shit out of here!" he yelled at his men. They scrambled to pick up the noodle packets.

"We'll put y'all up here tonight and decide tomorrow," CJ said, tapping a new pack of cigarettes on the desk. "Now if you'll excuse me, my men and I need to keep this place from freezing over."

Ricky escorted them to rooms on the top floor.

"If the power don't kick on soon, we'll move you. We'll send food up tonight."

"How often has the power gone out?" Henry asked.

"Third time this month. We're installing turbines on the roof, but ain't got around to it yet. I imagine we're about to do that now."

He clipped the zip ties from their wrists.

"I think the boss likes y'all. Don't do nothing stupid and fuck it up."

Chapter Thirty-Seven

Marcus made the hundred-mile journey from Louisville to the Quarry on the electric motorcycle confiscated from Grant Maniego. He rode with an abundance of caution.

Jim Cox, bunker architect and tour guide, was once again there to greet him.

"Wasn't expecting that to be you. Welcome!"

"Good to see you," Marcus said, dismounting from the bike. "Do you hang out on the platform all day and wait for arrivals?"

Jim laughed. "No, we have cameras in the east tunnel that notify me of arrivals. Say, isn't that the bike we loaned Lieutenant Maniego?"

"It is. About that – I'm going to need your help."

* * *

Jim's office in the engineering department was little more than a broom closet.

"I'll cut to the chase. Lieutenant Maniego was not hunting me down to help me. He was attempting a coup on my bunker."

"Oh my. If I would have known..."

"It's fine, he's been apprehended, but I need help. In two days, he will arrive as a prisoner transfer. Louisville is awaiting details of his crime. I told them he is wanted for murder."

"I know a guy that can send the report."

"Good. When he arrives here, he will need a survival pack and winter gear. Have him transferred under armed guard to my bunker immediately."

"You want me to have winter clothes waiting for him? Why?"

"He exiled friends of mine to the surface. Adam Terry is up there as well, alive or dead, I don't know. Maniego might be able to find them and bring them back."

"Do you trust him to right his wrongs like that?"

"Hardly, but I need to exercise every option. My friends are far more important to me than his punishment."

Jim shook his head. "You know, he told me Adam escaped to the surface after he allegedly assaulted a woman. Her name was Jenna..."

"Dothmayer? Is she okay?"

"Yes, that's her. She is here actually, in stable condition. We'll transfer her to Indy on the next train."

"Could I see her?"

* * *

Audrey Bruni was working a double shift in the burgeoning bunker maternity ward. Despite famine and chaos, there were seven pregnancies and two recent births. The babies were healthy and cherubic. Many saw it as a sign of hope and optimism. She did not.

She wanted her own.

No patient brought about these feelings more than Melonie. She carried the child of the only man she desired in that godforsaken place. The man that rejected her, burdening her only with the guilt, shame, and the cruel hope of a sexual affair.

She grieved the loss of Robby privately, as if she did not have the right.

Melonie's appointments were kept clinical. Her baby was perfectly healthy. She was perfect. Young, beautiful, bubbly. It made her sick.

"Thanks, Audrey!" Melonie said.

Ashley Cameron wobbled in as Melonie exited. She never made appointments, but the staff always made time for her before the other women.

"Alright, let's get this over with," Ashley said.

Audrey, on the brink of tears, fought to remember what Ashley needed checked. She flipped through her chart.

"We are up for an ultrasound. How exciting."

"See if we can make it quick."

Audrey applied the ultrasound gel and revealed the image of a baby on the screen.

"There's a hand, you can see the feet there. Do you want to know the gender?"

"Sure. I've had enough surprises lately."

"You will be having a boy, and if everything continues as is, a perfectly healthy baby boy. Congratulations."

She stared at the screen in silence. It was the closest she had come to showing emotion about bringing a life into the world, at least in front of Audrey.

A tear ran down Audrey's cheek.

"You had a thing for Robby Reed, didn't you?"

Audrey wiped the tear away. "Sorry?"

Ashley laughed. "Trust me, I know how it feels to be overlooked. It's a tragedy he chose that young girl over you. She's beautiful, I'll give her that, but so are you. I'd kill to look like either one of you."

"I'm okay, I'm just tired from—"

"It's particularly rough when the other is so inferior. What is she, a hairdresser? You're a doctor! Men are just scared of strong, intelligent women."

Audrey rolled her eyes in agreement.

"And your friends take her side. I'm always catching the tail end of conversations. Everybody just *loves* Melonie!"

Audrey's shoulders slumped. She knew of no sides being taken.

"Gosh, I'm blathering," Ashley said. "It's just your friends – along with gossiping about you – are up to something, but I don't know what it is..."

She put her hand on Audrey's.

"How about I sign off on getting you a few days of rest? Come by my suite. We'll crack open a bottle of wine and talk about whatever you want, since it seems like you don't—"

"They know Grant is going to kill Marcus," Audrey said. "They sent a message to warn him."

The artificial warmth left Ashley's demeanor.

"How?"

255

"Through a computer, I think? I guess they connected a cable in the tunnel?"

Ashley pulled her shirt over her belly and flashed a flagrantly fake smile.

"You've earned some time off. We'll be talking."

* * *

Marcus was led through a maze of dimly lit hallways in the Quarry hospital. A no-nonsense nurse stopped him at the door. He looked in at Jenna Dothmayer, all hooked up to machines and tubes.

"Ms. Dothmayer sustained very abnormal injuries," the nurse said. "Her fingers have been broken, and her tongue is lacerated. She suffered blunt force trauma and we were surprised to discover a gunshot wound that had received prior treatment."

"She has had a rough go," Marcus said.

"She can't speak, but she is awake. You have five minutes."

He crept to her bedside, hovering into her sight range. She looked up through bloodshot, glassy eyes. They widened in terror. Lines danced on the screen and monitors beeped.

"I wanted to apologize for hurting you. You don't have to forgive me. I wouldn't if I were you. I lost myself, but I'm trying to make things right."

He reached out and brushed the hair from her forehead. She flinched.

"I also came to forgive you. Your dad was in the Bureau, right? Interesting program he signed you up for – children of agents receive a crash course in corporate espionage, get into a company, pass secrets. For what, student loan forgiveness?"

He took her hand, careful not to jostle the peripheral IV in her vein.

"I'll tell you what you were sent to seduce from me. My power grid – the one the government so desperately wanted control over – can in fact be manipulated. It only requires a machine I happen to be carrying...a bit of my blood, a bit of Timothy Spencer's, a few keystrokes, and voila."

Through the swelling and fright, she was still beautiful. He thought about what could have been.

"Did they tell you why they wanted it? There's an army of killer drones up there that require charging as they fly around wiping survivors out. They want it to finish depopulating the earth. I've decided not to let that happen. I am going to reveal whoever is orchestrating this culling of humankind."

He lifted her hand and kissed the bandaging.

"Get well, Jenna. I want you to be there to see it."

257

Chapter Thirty-Eight

Power returned to the tower before temperatures dipped far enough to force a move. Ricky brought them bowls of ramen with an egg for dinner.

As brutal as Cameron made CJ and the gang out to be, Timothy did not see it. They were rough around the edges and prone to conspiracy, but there *was* a conspiracy. They were more right than wrong.

"I don't think we're in a bad spot," Timothy said. "We give them the truck, snowmobile, all the loot Cameron gathered...we can replace that. I think they are going to let us through."

"Should we tell them we're really going to Bloomington to fix the grid?" Henry asked. "That'll help them more than anything."

"Let's keep that in our back pocket. CJ already indicated he is no fan of Marcus."

"The less they know the better," Adam said.

Adam and Cameron split off to the other apartment, leaving Henry, Robby, and Timothy in the other. They were in bed before the lights-out curfew.

At some point, all of their racing thoughts fell away and they slipped into sleep.

It felt as though no time passed before they were awakened by shouting and flashlight beams. Dark figures pulled Timothy out of bed.

"Everybody up! CJ wants to see you!"

"What's going?" Timothy asked.

"Shut up and walk!"

They carried him into a cramped elevator.

"Where are you taking me?"

"I done told you. CJ wants to see you."

Timothy was shoved down the hall and into CJ's cluttered apartment.

"Welcome back Timothy...Spencer, is it?" CJ said. "How's come you didn't tell us who you really was? That's one thing I don't like – dishonesty."

CJ tossed a copy of *Tech World* magazine on the desk, turned to an article on *Trencher Industries*. There was a full-page picture of him and Marcus posing with their first prototype.

"One of the boys recognized you. Ran across town to the library and dug this old magazine up."

"Yes, that's me."

CJ's lackeys herded Adam, Cameron, Henry, and a combative Robby into the room.

"I have a few buddies over in Sherman. It was an open secret he was digging a hole out in those stripper pits. It was a bunker, wadn't it?"

"Yes, he built a bunker. We were in it, but men took over and we were exiled."

"Your pal Trencher threw you out?"

"He had left the bunker, through a tunnel to Bloomington."

"The big tunnel projects! Them billionaires have been digging for the past decade. Sumbitches knew all along. Now quit bullshittin', why are really wanting to go to Bloomington?"

"We developed a key to the grid. Let's us take it over, which is supposed to be impossible."

"So, these blackouts we've been experiencing, y'all can remedy that?"

"If we get to Bloomington and get to Marcus Trencher, yes. We can drain entire towns and route power here, and we will, if you let us through."

CJ smiled, flashing a silver tooth amongst the missing and yellowed.

"Maybe I'm just redneck from Greene County, but is this, like, an old skeleton key?"

"It's a piece of computer hardware. It requires both Marcus and I to use it."

"Can't say I get it, but it sounds like you're pretty important, and sounds like you boys need to get to Bloomington."

Timothy gave a sigh of relief.

"But not you, Mr. Spencer. You'll stick around. The rest of y'all can bring Marcus Trencher back. I'd like to meet him. Maybe I'll watch y'all do this key thing."

Ricky and Joe grabbed Timothy by the arms and dragged him from the room.

"Now that bigshot is out of the room, let's get you boys ready for your big trip."

* * *

Henry, Robby, Adam, and Cameron piled into the snowplow and turned east on State Road 54. They followed their captors to a garage on the edge of town.

"Alright, listen up," Ricky said in front of a jacked-up truck rigged with a snowplow blade. "Me and Joe will get you to the quarry. From there, you're on your own."

"Where'd you guys take Timothy?" Henry asked.

"You'll see your pal when you come back with Trencher. Now let's get. We're losing daylight."

The first truck cleared the top layers of snow. The second truck, and Cameron's, took care of the rest. State Road 54 provided only minor challenges. I-69 was slow going, but uneventful. They were put back on edge when they exited down to the local roads south of Bloomington.

The first road off the highway was ordinary, but they turned off onto a country lane. There were no signs advertising the Rooftop Quarry, but they came to a stop before a rusty gate.

"This is it," Adam said.

"Y'all thought we was lost, didn't ya?" Ricky said over the radio. "Back up, I want to ram this thing."

They gave him room, and he got his thrill in. They circled the vehicles in a lot surrounded by snow-covered peaks of excavated limestone.

Ricky ran out to their vehicle. "Here's the maps. I reckon you keep on down this lane."

Ricky peeled out and they left the way they came.

Cameron drove down the lane to an old lumber mill. The surrounding lot was filled with military transport vehicles. Adam was the first to get out.

"We have to go inside and disable the turrets," Adam said.

"In this janky building? Wait, the *what*?" Henry said.

261

"Gun turrets, at the vault doors. We can't just walk up and knock."

Adam cleared snow from a number pad at a side entrance on the mill. He punched in a code, pressed his thumb to a sensor, and opened the door.

The inside was nothing like the rusted corrugate outside. The building was retrofitted to serve as the bunker's above-ground construction headquarters. Lights clicked on, and air began to blow from vents. They followed Adam to his former office. He pulled keys from a desk drawer and tossed them to Robby.

"Open that gun safe. We don't know what kind of reception we'll get when those vault doors open."

Robby grabbed military-grade assault rifles and passed them out. Adam grabbed a hiking backpack from the floor behind his desk. He grabbed a couple rappelling carabiners from the drawer and tossed them in the bag. They backtracked out of the office to a control room.

"Step one, we disable the turrets," Adam said, as he booted up a computer. "This will set off alarm bells down below, so we'll have to move fast."

"Then what?" Robby asked.

"We head down to the Quarry."

Chapter Thirty-Nine

Marcus called a meeting in Jim Cox's office that brought the humble Midwesterner together with Genie, the colorful computer programmer. They needed to hash out details of the prisoner transfer.

Genie, pleasure to meet you," Jim said, shaking her hand. "The criminal report has been sent to Louisville. We have a task force ready to welcome Maniego at the platform, and transportation on standby to take him to your bunker."

"Wow, Jim, you are on it," Marcus said. "Genie, I need you to reach out to Kent and get a pulse on whether it's safe for me to return. If so, I'll see Maniego to the surface myself."

"We might have an issue there," Genie said. "Kent got pulled off the project, and now I'm dealing with some kid who doesn't have a clue. He says Ashley intervened. Know her?"

"I do. She is a traitor along with Maniego."

A bell chimed from Jim's computer. He tapped the spacebar. "Looks like we have an unexpected visitor." He put his glasses on. "That's odd. Do you think Louisville is sending Maniego early?"

Jim turned the laptop to show the tunnel camera snapshot of a black SUV barreling down the service lane.

"They're not from Louisville. Those are the suits from Carmel that chased me out of Speedway."

"What do they want from you?" Genie asked.

"Blood, if I were to guess. Jim – can you distract them at the platform? I'll take the bike and get back to my bunker. I can handle my people there."

Before he could answer, Jim's computer made a louder, more-alarming noise.

"More visitors?" Genie asked.

Jim squinted at the screen in disbelief. "I don't...this can't be right. The defensive apparatus at the vault doors has been disabled."

"Who has access to do that?"

"Down here? A half-dozen military men. But on the surface – where this command was inputted – I only know of one."

Marcus bolted upright, knocking his chair back.

"Adam Terry! My friends could be with him. Alright, new plan..."

* * *

Cameron rolled to a stop somewhere between the mill and the Rooftop Quarry. A massive slab of limestone blocked the road.

"We do the rest on foot," Adam said.

They climbed out of the truck into deep snow. They walked the road for fifty yards before Adam spotted a tree with a red ribbon tied around it.

"The road continues down to the quarry bottom. We need to go to the ridge above the doors. Trust me, there's a trail here."

They followed him into the mixture of woods, overgrowth, and heaps of limestone. The deep snow was littered with fallen limbs and rocks. Wind cut through the skeletal trees.

A loud *crack!* froze them in place, echoing like a gunshot.

"Holy sh—" Henry said, ducking. "Is someone shooting at us?"

Robby and Henry lied flat. Adam crouched. Cameron remained standing.

"Cameron, get down!" Henry said.

"Guys, that wasn't a gunshot."

"He's right," Adam said, pointing at a maple tree. It had a three-foot gash near the root where it had burst open. "The sap is freezing and expanding. I think the wind set one off."

"Glad I can't feel my face. It won't hurt when tree shrapnel blasts it," Robby said.

They trekked warily through the trees until there were none. They entered another lot of excavated limestone. After rounding a stack of slabs, the ridge overlooking the Rooftop Quarry came into view. They peered into the pit.

"Where are the doors?"

"Right below us, a little to the right," Adam said.

"Then why are we up here?"

Adam motioned them over to a standalone block of limestone. He cleared away the snow sticking to its side and found a notch. He turned a knob, and after a few shoulder checks, opened a compartment. The rock was fake.

"Bolt cutters, please."

Adam clipped a cheap chain and opened an encasement over a Frankenstein electrical switch.

"The clock really starts to tick after I throw this. It sends power to the engines that open the vault. We'll have a matter of minutes to get down there before someone inside cuts the power feed."

"Double back to the road? That'll take another half hour," Henry said.

"No time for that. We'll rappel into the quarry. You guys climb?"

Adam tossed his backpack to the ground and pulled out reams of rope, clips, and harnesses.

"This is crazy."

"I've never done anything like this," Cameron said. "I don't like heights."

"You two go first and we'll pull the harnesses back up," Adam said. "I'll flip the switch and take Cameron down with me."

Adam secured the climbing rope around the false rock. They helped each other don the harnesses over their heavy winter suits, and after a thorough safety check, stepped to the quarry ledge.

"I can't do this," Henry said. "It's been years..."

"Lean back and hop down the wall or scrape down the side," Adam said. "Doesn't matter to me."

"Okay, okay. Just ease me down."

Robby and Henry lined up on the edge and began to inch backward. Despite every instinct to buckle his knees and fold, Henry kept them locked. Robby did just fine. Once parallel, they did their first hop-and-descent, successfully.

Robby hit bottom first. Henry lost his footing on the final hop but made a soft landing. They tugged the ropes to signal they were clear.

Adam rigged Cameron's harness to his and did all the work. Cameron screamed the entire way down.

"See, that wasn't so bad," Adam said.

The vault doors were set in the face of the wall they rappelled, twenty yards south. The imposing steel barrier was camouflaged. Dormant gun turrets sat perched at the corners.

Adam opened a hidden panel to the side.

* * *

Alarms sounded across the Quarry. A woman announced that all bunker citizens must shelter in their rooms in the Stacks immediately.

"Our visitors are opening the vault doors," Jim said. "It's Adam. It must be."

"What's the protocol here?" Marcus asked.

"People will think it's a drill. We haven't had one in a couple months."

The bunker began to shake.

"Oh, wow. Maybe it isn't a drill," Jim said.

"It's fake," Marcus said. "C'mon, we need to get up there."

"It doesn't feel fake," Genie said.

"I mean it's manufactured. None of this is real."

"Huh?" Jim said, dumfounded.

"Now's not the time to explain. We need to go."

Red lights blinked and the lockdown message played on repeat. People walked with varying levels of urgency. Guards waved people along.

When clear, they ran to a stairwell door. Jim badged them in.

Soldiers jogged by, ignoring them. They filed in and began the ascent. Jim lasted two floors before he was out of breath.

"Go on. I'll catch up."

Genie kept pace. Why she even chose to come along, Marcus did not know.

The stairs seemed endless. Marcus lost track after ten flights, and he was sure they doubled that. Finally, they emerged at the vault bay behind a group of equally exhausted soldiers.

The horizontal vault doors yawned like a giant beast. Its steel teeth were the size of grown men. Blinding light poured in as the lower jaw sank into the ground. A blast of cold air swept in.

Soldiers organized in a firing line. Figures of authority emerged from a cargo elevator.

The doors screeched to a stop. Eyes adjusted to the light. Four silhouettes stepped across the threshold.

"Stop right there!" a soldier yelled. "Drop your weapons!"

The visitors did so.

"My name is Adam Terry. I'm a resident here!"

One of the authority figures motioned for the men to lower their guns.

Marcus rubbed his eyes. *If that was Adam, the others must be...*

"Henry! Robby!" Marcus yelled. He ran forward.

Soldiers intercepted.

"Those are my friends. Let them in!"

The starstruck soldiers looked at their superiors and let go. Marcus ran to Henry and hugged him, then Robby.

"Where's Timothy? Is he not with you?" Marcus asked, panicked.

"He's in Bloomfield," Henry said. "Are my parents here?"

"They are. We'll get this settled and see them."

The cargo elevator doors opened once again.

The suits from Carmel stepped out.

Chapter Forty

"Apprehend that man!" a woman said.

Dr. Roger Cooley, chairman of the Quarry bunker committee, intervened. "Whoa, let's all take a step back. Under whose authority? This is not your jurisdiction."

The suits drew handguns. Soldiers pointed their weapons at the suits.

"It is classified. Marcus Trencher comes with us."

Adam Terry approached the standoff, hands raised.

"How about a sidebar conversation? I think we can resolve this peacefully."

The suits lowered their weapons. Adam, the agents, and Dr. Cooley convened.

"Marcus, who are those people?" Henry asked.

"I don't know, but I have a feeling they are after the blood key."

"They know about that?"

"I doubt it, but I don't think the people who were trying to take our grid have given up."

They watched the negotiations from a distance. Adam, usually stoic, was animated and all smiles.

Was he betraying them? Finally, he made his way back to them.

"Alright, shut the fuck up and listen," he said, maintaining a smile. "We have sixty seconds until they approach to arrest you, Marcus, so I need you to answer one question. Is the blood key in that bag on your shoulder?"

"Yes."

Adam tilted his head back, pretending to laugh.

"Alright – we're making a run for it. When I say go, pick up the guns. Bonus points to whoever fires off a round first. I'll activate closure of the vault doors. It can't be interrupted, but it won't be quick. Stay close to the quarry wall. Don't stop until you reach the inlet road."

The suits began their approach.

"Okay, guys. Step back...calmly....and....*Go!*"

Robby and Cameron got to the guns first. Henry grabbed his, but didn't know how to work it, so took the lead in running away with Marcus. Cameron fired his automatic rifle nowhere near anyone, but it had the desired effect. People scattered.

Adam pressed his thumb to the panel. He punched in a code and leaned in for an eye scan. Robby covered him, firing his first shots in the general direction of the suits. They returned fire.

A bullet ricocheted close by.

"All good, let's go!"

The vault doors slowly began to close. The suits pursued and slid out to the quarry floor, two of the men flailing onto the ice. Robby popped off a few more shots before joining the sprint.

Several rounds were fired in their direction. They were no exploding trees. The sweat on Marcus's brow, produced during the sprint up the stairwell, froze. The shocking cold amplified the out of body experience of running for his life.

"Keep going!"

They kept to the quarry wall, as instructed. It ever-so-slightly bent to their favor. The gunfire grew distant and less menacing. No one could aim in that cold, at that range. The inlet road came within sight.

They turned the corner and collapsed on the incline. In the distance, they heard a gun blaze of a whole other caliber.

"What the hell was that?" Henry said.

"I activated...the turrets. Everybody...catch your breath," Adam said. "Cameron, give Marcus your hat. Henry, gloves."

Marcus was dazed by the extreme cold. Robby snatched the hat from Cameron and put it on Marcus's head. Henry shoved Marcus's fists in the gloves. Adam ran back down the hill, clutching his side, to see if they were being pursued.

"We're clear, but let's not wait around. Light jog to the truck. Let's go."

They piled into Cameron's snowplow. He floored it in reverse, pivoting at the mill. He flew past the crashed gate onto a county road.

Henry shed layers and passed them to Marcus, who was in an early stage of hypothermia. Cameron turned onto the I-69 ramp.

"Whoo!" Robby yelled. "We fucking made it!"

They hugged and slapped each other on the backs. Robby grabbed Adam by the shoulders and shook him. He grimaced in pain.

"You deserve a steak dinner, my friend I've said it once and I'll say it again. I'm glad I peeled you off that vent...Hey, are you okay?"

Adam slumped forward, revealing a dark splotch on his jacket beneath his right shoulder blade.

"It's nothing."

"Shit, they got him. Cam, is there a first-aid kit in here?"

"Yeah, um, under the seat."

Robby rummaged through energy drink cans and pulled out a plastic case. He removed Adam's jacket and lifted his shirt. Bright blood bubbled from the wound.

Henry picked out the bandages, Robby fumbled them.

Adam lurched forward and grabbed Marcus's arm.

"My parents were...involved with..." Adam said, struggling for air. "These people...are trying to kill...Don't let them do it. Don't let them do it!"

"Take it easy," Robby said. "We're going to get you help."

"I need to hear you say it!" Adam said, gasping.

"I...I won't," Marcus said.

"Say it!" Adam hacked up blood onto Cameron's headrest. His grip on Marcus's arm released. He slumped back, paler than before, unconscious.

"I won't let them do it."

Chapter Forty-One

Somewhere between Bloomfield and Bloomington, Adam Terry stopped breathing.

"Stay with us, buddy," Robby said, tapping him on his pale cheek. "Guys, he's not doing so hot."

Robby cursed under his breath, pinched Adam's nose, and breathed into his mouth.

Henry grabbed Adam's wrist. "No pulse. Cam, pull over."

They dragged Adam's lifeless body to the shoulder of State Road 54. Robby began what he knew of CPR, to no avail.

Adam Terry was dead.

"Let's get him back in. Cam, how much longer until Bloomfield? Maybe they can shock him or some shit. Want me to drive?"

"He's gone," Henry said. "You did all you could."

Robby walked away. The crunch beneath his feet was the only sound. For the first time since they were on the surface, the wind was still.

Cameron and Henry placed the body in the truck bed. Marcus never left the front passenger seat. He stared out the window in the opposite direction.

* * *

Cameron announced their approach on the radio. They were greeted at the garage east of town by CJ's henchmen, Ricky and Joe.

"Y'all made good time," Ricky said.

Henry and Robby laid Adam's frozen-stiff body on the concrete.

"What the hell went down at that quarry?"

"They weren't keen on letting us leave," Henry said. "This man got us in and out. He sacrificed himself. Anywhere we can bury him?"

"Can't dig an inch through the permafrost," Ricky said. "We have a crematorium in town. We'll do right by the dead. Now, we better take you all to CJ. Keep your jackets on. Power's out again."

Joe stood slack-jawed, staring not at the body, but at Marcus.

You're—"

"Yes."

* * *

They followed Ricky and Joe's jacked up trucks through town. Marcus had hardly spoken a word. He left death and destruction when he fled the bunker and brought more the moment they reunited.

"My name is Cameron, but the way. It's an honor to meet you."

"Nice to meet you," Marcus said. He glanced at Henry and Robby in the back seat. "I'm glad you guys are alive."

"Are you?" Robby said. "Because we almost weren't, a couple times."

Marcus tilted his head back against the headrest and took a deep breath.

"I'm sorry, for everything. I'm going to make things right." He turned to look Robby in the eye. "I'm happy for you and Melonie. I hate myself for what I said."

The wound was deep, but it wasn't worth letting it fester. Robby relented.

"Water under the bridge."

Henry, ever the peacemaker, was more relieved than the both of them. But there were more pressing issues at hand.

"I hate to break up the kumbaya moment, but this CJ guy can be a loose cannon," Henry said. "I don't think he is a fan, Marcus."

"Did I hear right? Their power was out?"

"The grid is dying. Blackouts are starting to roll through."

"Then it's simple. They can give us Timothy, or they can freeze to death."

* * *

Henry begged Marcus to consider a softer approach. Marcus assured him everything would be fine. Ricky ushered them into the apartment with unnecessary roughness.

Timothy sat tied to a chair. A drip of blood ran down his forehead into his right eyebrow.

"Hello, Marcus," Timothy said.

"Timothy, you look...well."

276

He hugged his duffel bag to his chest, showing a clear outline of the blood key.

CJ sat behind his desk in a winter coat and lumberjack hat, cigarette lit.

"What an honor to finally meet *the* Marcus Trencher. Heard you boys had a hell of a time getting out of Bloomington."

"Pleasure to be here, CJ. Can I call you that? And before we begin, could you put out that cigarette? I am sensitive to smoke."

CJ looked at his men and laughed.

"The balls on this one! I'm gonna smoke until we loot every pack of cigarettes from here to Kokomo."

"I'll manage," Marcus said. "But *man* is it cold."

"We installed a whole rig of wind turbines on the roof, and the damn wind dies down!"

"I imagine Timothy explained how we can help alleviate that."

"We had a chat while y'all was gone. Sounds like this is what you're looking for."

He smeared the blood on Timothy's forehead and showed his red thumb.

"It's not that simple. We will need samples drawn. If you have the medical personnel and equipment, we'd be grateful. We will also need free passage back to Sherman to access the grid controls."

"Is that it? The key?" CJ said, looking at the bag Marcus was hugging. "What's to stop me from drawing y'alls blood and figuring it out on my own?"

"You won't, with all due respect."

CJ sat back down and put his cigarette out.

"I got old Lucille over on Sand Hollar Road freezing her tits off. Refuses to move, so we deliver firewood every day. My people are scrambling around the county for houses with heat. They look to me."

"We'll route power to Bloomfield as soon as tonight. Problem solved."

CJ stared into Marcus's eyes. Marcus never broke his gaze in return.

"We'll fetch Kathy to come take your blood," CJ said. "Then, you and Mr. Spencer will head off to Sherman and turn on our heat."

"Excellent decision. You won't regret it."

"Cameron and these two fellows stay. Do what you promise, and they're free to go. If we get no power, then...well, it's best that don't happen."

Henry and Robby gave the okay.

"You have yourself a deal, CJ."

Chapter Forty-Two

Bloomfield's grid was on its last leg. There were not enough homes with heat to support the population of approximately 300, and their stock of firewood was depleting fast.

Despite waning daylight, and a long day in which Timothy was beaten and Marcus made a harrowing escape from Bloomington, they prepared to depart for Sherman – blood vials and blood key in hand.

They just hoped their decade old machine still worked. There was no guarantee.

"Y'all can take that Cybertruck," Ricky said. "We're diesel 'til we die, or there's not a drop left."

Marcus handed the keys to Timothy. "I'm still not much for driving."

"Meter says -24 Fahrenheit, practically a record high these days," Ricky said. "Ain't no wind either."

"Then we better get to it," Marcus said. "I expect my friends to be released tomorrow morning."

"We get power, they're free to go. CJ's word."

They departed west on State Road 54 toward a strange, alien sky. Somewhere beyond the dense atmosphere, the sun was setting. The bruised palette of color was beautiful and frightening.

Timothy Spencer and Marcus Trencher, back together. There was more than a road ahead to navigate.

"The first thing I wanted to do when I saw you again was to punch you in the face," Timothy said.

"I can let you if you want. I deserve it."

"You're not off the hook. Once we get the grid configured, we go straight to the bunker to get my daughters. They better be okay."

They crossed the high frozen waters of the White River and approached Switz City. An old man stood at the side of the road, as if checking his mailbox.

The man waved. They waved back.

They drove straight through Linton, where the roads were paved clear of snow and ice. It was dark, quiet, and eerie.

Marcus had more guilt weighing on him. It was difficult to bring up, as the pain it caused Timothy was excruciating.

"I'm sorry about Shelley," Marcus said. "I feel responsible."

Timothy was quiet, measuring his thoughts and words.

"Shelley was too good for this world. I wish our daughters were enough, I wish I was enough, but we weren't. You didn't cause anything. This was all just too much for her to take."

Marcus watched the snow-covered farmland pass by. As cold as the world was, the people could be colder. He didn't want to be that way.

"Back in the day when we were building the company, I don't think either of us would've eaten more than a meal a day if it wasn't for Shelley."

Timothy laughed.

"That, and bathing," Timothy said. "She used to drag me to the shower."

"Remember the time she marched in and handed me a stick of deodorant and said, '*Wear it*'?"

Timothy laughed. "Fun times..."

They left it at that, each occasionally exhaling a small laugh as they replayed the memories.

"I don't know how I'm going to face the people."

"Don't worry about that. They've concocted all sorts of conspiracy theories in your favor. They blamed the outsiders, and the jealous co-founder of *Trencher Industries*."

They both laughed. Outside, they crossed the Greene-Sherman County line.

"Last question, then I'll let it rest. Did you just want me in the bunker because you knew this day would come, and you'd need my blood?"

"C'mon..."

Seriously, let it all out. Come clean."

"It wasn't the key. I thought if you were at least close, maybe we'd get over our issues someday."

"I'm touched, but the blood key...You knew this day, right now, was going to come, didn't you?"

"I would've taken the blood key down anyway, just as a keepsake. Once I wrapped my head around there being no asteroid, I thought about the grid. When Senator Granger started spouting off about some greater power pulling the strings on this apocalypse, and killer drones, I started to develop some ideas."

"Want to run some of those by me?"

* * *

The grid in Sherman was still powered. With nearly every home with a unit, and Marcus having rigged *Trencher Industries* to foot the bill as a gift to the town, it was far better off than Bloomfield.

They turned off Trencher Street at flashing traffic lights and pulled up before the old headquarters on the courthouse square. Marcus was a little disappointed in the broken windows.

They went to Timothy's old office. It was left untouched since his unceremonious firing.

"You left everything here, how sweet."

Timothy sat at the computer and tried his old username and password. It worked.

"You never deleted my access? I could've brought the whole company down."

"We had you banned outside the home network." Marcus paused. "I think."

They said a silent prayer, then inserted their tubes of blood.

"Here goes nothing," Marcus said.

Mechanisms pulled the tubes inside. They winced at every grinding noise as the blood moved to the extraction needles. They called play-by-play what they hoped was happening inside.

"The samples should be moving into the flow cells," Timothy said. "I hope they're still good."

"We should've waited until the room warmed."

"Shut up, it's going to work."

After another spurt of excruciating hardware noises, a USB drive was ejected from a slot at the bottom of the machine. They both lunged for it, but Timothy was too fast.

He plugged it in. A prompt requested two passwords.

"I remember mine," Timothy said, as he typed it in. "If you don't remember yours, I am going to murder you."

Marcus typed his password in. Success.

"We're in," Timothy said. "Looks like our company satellites are still in orbit."

He opened a program monitoring the grid in real time. A map of the Midwest filled the screen, with Indiana dead center.

"This is ugly," Marcus said.

"You're not lying," Timothy said. "Blue dots are live, red means dead. This is a bloodbath."

"Wave all the late fees. That'll leave only the units that are damaged or malfunctioning in the red."

He flew through screens, typing like a hacker in the movies. He compiled his code and flipped back to the map.

"Boom! Blue everywhere!"

"Eh, except up there," Marcus said. "Where is that? Crawfordsville? Must've been a tornado."

He switched to a screen showing where power was flowing. It looked like a cardiovascular system with a blockade in Crawfordsville.

"Downed lines for sure," Timothy said. "Whoa, checkout north of there. What's cranking out that kind of power?"

"Wind farms, and look, there's more west of Lafayette."

"No way those windmills are functioning without maintenance."

"Forget the Region for now, let's fix up Bloomfield. Test if we can drain units from nearby."

"You choose."

"Uh, select that town, Loogootee."

"Apologies to anyone in Loogootee. All your power belongs to Bloomfield."

In a matter of keystrokes, power began to move from the already decayed grid of Loogootee to that of Bloomfield.

"It's working. This is God mode."

"Set Bloomfield to priority routing. Once their local grid hits capacity, revert back. I don't want to freeze some poor soul in Loogootee."

They stared at the screen, watching the grid coursing power like blood to the reactivated units across the state. They zoomed out to view the entire Midwest grid. They could blackout Ohio and drain its power to Indiana if they wanted.

They controlled it all.

Chapter Forty-Three

Robby and Henry were held captive in an old house a block from the tower. With nothing to do but wait, they dozed off on couches before the fireplace, hoping to wake up to power the next morning.

When the power suddenly kicked on that evening, sleep was not an option.

Residents ran door-to-door, checking every home with a *Trencher* unit. Battery percentages were rising. The town lit up. The grid roared back to life. The jubilation seemed to warm the night air.

Marcus and Timothy did it.

CJ called his men back to the tower to celebration. Henry and Robby were dragged along.

It was a rowdy redneck affair. Hard rock, country, and the obligatory Mellencamp blared long into the night. They had a few drinks, but it was too wild, even for Robby. There were people smoking methamphetamine.

Partygoers passed out on the lobby furniture. To their amusement, Cameron left the tower with a girl around his age. CJ, Ricky, and Joe led a contingency to a downtown bar. Henry and Robby took the opportunity to exit the scene. They went upstairs to the rooms they were previously sequestered to and called it a night.

* * *

The next morning, searing light poured through the tower windows.

"Sheesh, is that the sun?" Robby groaned. "What time is it?"

"I don't know, but dang that is bright," Henry said. "Let's head down and see if we are free to leave."

They took the elevator to the lobby. It looked like a bomb had gone off.

Bodies were slouched on the mishmash of couches. A few people fell asleep with their heads resting on the tables, which were otherwise covered in empty beer cans, bottles of hard liquor, and drug paraphernalia.

An elderly lady snuck up and placed a hand on Robby's arm, startling him.

"Do you boys know if they are serving breakfast this morning?" the old lady asked.

They didn't notice her amongst all the bodies. She was of nursing home age and bundled up. She must have walked to the tower that morning.

"Sorry ma'am, looks like everyone had a long night."

"Drats. I have eggs back home. I can still do my own cooking, you know. That nice boy CJ got me an electric stove!"

Henry contemplated searching the kitchen to cook for the poor lady, but she shuffled toward the bright entrance vestibule.

"At least it's a lovely day," she said before stepping out.

"I could use some of her optimism," Robby said.

"She is easily the oldest person I've seen since...you know," Henry said.

They thought it best to speak to someone before they left town, but nobody of authority was there, and everyone else was unconscious.

Robby grabbed a pack of cigarettes and a lighter from a table.

"I'm going to step out and smoke a cigarette in this beautiful day that old Lucille speaks so highly of."

"You don't smoke."

"If there was ever a time to start, it's when there isn't enough supply to get hooked."

"I'll look for food. I'm not ready for the cold yet."

Robby zipped up his jacket and put on a hat and gloves. He squinted at the brightness. He lit the cigarette, braced for the cold, and pushed through the vestibule door.

His first inhale was through a cigarette. At least it was warm.

He took in the scenery. The snowmobile was pulled up in front of the tower and surrounded by empty beer cans.

A sense of confusion froze him. The extreme cold always did that, but it didn't feel the same. Was it the nicotine?

He stood still and listened. Water dripped off the eaves. He breathed in and out but did not see his breath. He rubbed his forehead. It felt warm. Was he that hungover? He flicked the cigarette into the snow and ran back inside.

"Henry, get out here!"

Henry came around the corner with a spatula. "What? I don't feel like putting my jacket on."

"You don't need one. C'mon."

He rolled his eyes but joined Robby outside. He was struck by the same confusion.

"Am I losing my mind, or is it...warm?"

"It's like 60 degrees! I'm sweating!"

"What the... What is going on?"

"They must've stopped pumping that shit into the atmosphere, or moved that solar shade, or something. It's what, late July, or August?"

"It's like I can't believe my senses. Look, the sky is clearing up."

They shielded their eyes. When tears welled up, they wiped them away and kept looking. The sky was the palest shade of blue. The sun was a white dot, breaking through the thinning clouds.

"Hey, do you see that thing up there?" Robby asked.

"The sun?"

"No, over there," Robby said, pointing and taking two steps forward. "Is that a fucking UFO?"

Something hovered high in the sky. Henry's stomach dropped. "I think it's a drone."

The glimmering dot sparked. Before they could make sense of it, a missile blazed above their heads and slammed into the tower.

The blast threw them thirty feet into the yard. Henry came to face down in the wet snow. Robby ran to him and lifted him upright. He yelled inches from Henry's face, but Henry heard nothing.

He pulled him to the snowmobile and made him wrap his arms around him.

Robby fired up the snowmobile and ramped a concrete ledge down to the city street. They slid off the melting snow in the gutter and onto the road. The tracks still took on the wet concrete.

Another bomb dropped somewhere behind them, deeper in town. They sped past the inlet road to the high school and down a hill to the White River floodplain.

Robby veered off-road into a snowy field. There were brown dots in the distance. When he got closer, he realized it was a herd of deer. He'd seen twenty in a field before, but never one-hundred-and-twenty.

Above, a dense swarm of blackbirds swooped in the skies. Animals had migrated with the warmth.

Robby headed for the herd. If the drones had any issue with differentiating between humans and animals, he thought their signature could be hidden.

The deer took off toward the river. Near the tree-lined bank, they darted south in unison.

He kept straight toward a gap in the tree line – a boat ramp to the White River. The snowmobile slid on the river ice as he turned south. He picked up speed and spotted a clearing on the opposite bank, short of the State Road 54 bridge.

The blackbirds above parted. A streak of smoke and fire rained down.

A plume of water and thick ice shot into the sky. The river exploded before them. The snowmobile splashed into freezing waters.

Henry was catapulted over the hole in the ice. He landed on his head and slid thirty feet, leaving a streak of blood.

He turned back to the carnage.

There was no snowmobile. There was no Robby.

"*Robby!*"

He slid to the edge of the hole. The blast left a near perfect circle in the ice. Large opaque blocks clinked against each other in the swirling waters. He scanned frantically for Robby.

He spotted his hand between two of the blocks, pinned more than clinging. One of the blocks gave and tumbled in the current. Robby's hand began to sink.

Henry dove.

He grasped Robby's forearm before shock stole his breath. He pulled up, which took him under. He resurfaced and brought Robby's head above water. He clutched his back to his chest and dug through the ice before reaching the edge of the hole.

His first attempt to heave Robby up to the solid ice was pathetic. Robby's head rolled to his shoulder.

"Robby! Wake up! We ne-, we need to climb!" Henry cried. "I can't...I can't lift you!"

His attempts only grew weaker from there. Cold seeped in while hope left. He approached the point where, if he let go, he may have enough strength to save himself.

He couldn't. He held onto his friend. This is how it ends, he thought.

"Robby...we..." He trailed off in sobs.

A doe stood on the east bank, watching them die. He looked into her eyes. He stopped shivering, overcome with calm. She perked up and looked past them, startled.

He closed his eyes – for a second, maybe two. It reminded him of when he was a kid waking up for school, and he would turn off his alarm and slip back into sleep. His mother would come in and pull his covers.

He opened his eyes, back from black.

The doe darted off.

Before he could return to the peaceful void, perhaps for good, something splashed before them.

"*Grab it, boy!*" a strange voice said.

A rope floated in front of him. Still, it didn't register to make use of it.

A hand grabbed Henry by the breast. Another pried Robby from his embrace.

"*Let go, son! You hang on now.*"

Two blurry arms moved above his head. They fashioned the rope beneath Robby's arms, then disappeared. Henry looked on, curious and dumb.

Suddenly, Robby's lifeless body was pulled from the waters and slid away.

The hands and arms returned to pull him out as well.

He lied on the ice, staring at the sideways world. A man beat on Robby's chest and breathed into his mouth. He wanted to keep watching, to see what happened, but he slipped into a comfortable sleep.

Chapter Forty-Four

Marcus and Timothy stood on the porch of Henry's parents' house where they stayed overnight. The bright, warm day they awoke to was unexpected.

"This should be a good thing," Timothy said, reaching out to water dripping off the porch. "But I have a feeling this is not a good thing."

"I don't think this is a coincidence," Marcus said. "We've drawn attention."

Timothy stepped down from the porch and looked up. "The sky is clearing. It's almost blue."

Marcus joined him.

"We need to get to the bunker."

* * *

The roads were slush but passable. It was the brightest it had been since they resurfaced. The reflection off the snow was blinding. A mile from the bunker site, they spotted movement above.

A massive flock of birds danced in a mesmerizing murmuration.

They pulled through the gate and parked next to Robby's old Jeep. They trekked across the slick snow to the concrete dome housing the elevator.

"They changed the code," Timothy said.

"Change it all they want, mine will still work."

Timothy stepped away to watch the birds ripple and sway in the sky. All at once, the flock darted east. Something else caught his eye.

"Hey, uh, Marcus. I think we have company..."

"Ugh, I always mess up at least once," he said, fumbling at the numerical pad. "What were you—"

The glimmer in the sky was a drone. The second glimmer was a missile. Robby's Jeep and the Cybertruck were obliterated by a pounding strike. The blast knocked Timothy down.

He scrambled to his feet and flattened himself against the door. "Hurry!"

Marcus punched the code, and they rushed inside.

* * *

When the elevator came to a halt, they were greeted by Ashley Cameron and two men.

"Marcus? You're...you're alive," Ashley said.

"Surprised?" Marcus said. He looked to the men, who had sheathed their nightsticks. "Deputy Miller, Deputy Lowell."

"Welcome back, Mr. Trencher," Deputy Miller said. "What's it like up there?"

"About seventy, and sunny," Marcus said. "Could you guys do me a favor and round up my friends, and Timothy's daughters?"

"Sure thing, Mr. Trencher."

The deputies left the decontamination room. Ashley fidgeted, pushing her hair behind her ear over and over.

"Thank God you are alive. I was so—"

"I know you and that mercenary planned to kill me. Maniego should be here any moment."

Ashley's expression flashed panic before transforming into whatever look she thought would help her get her way.

"I didn't want to go along. I couldn't stop him!"

"Oh, Ashley..." Marcus said, shaking his head. "You were a useful idiot – until you weren't."

"I can still help! And..and I'm carrying—"

"Carrying what? My child?"

Marcus removed the blood key machine from his duffel bag. He ejected a blood sample and tossed it at Ashley.

"Run a DNA test. The kid is not mine."

"How can you be so sure? The timing..."

"Vasectomy. I decided early on that I did not want to bring a child into the world. Not this one."

Her sniffles turned to sobs. "What are you going to do with me?"

"I'll see that you find a new home. You might like Carmel. You know what they do in that bunker?"

She shook her head.

"They drive golf carts around roundabouts all day."

Neither Ashley nor Timothy got the joke.

Deputy Miller re-entered the room.

"Your friends are starting to file in."

"Impeccable response time, deputy. If you don't mind, please walk her out."

The deputy took Ashley for a walk of shame. Marcus reverted the surface door passcode for Henry and Robby from a panel on the wall. He dragged it out, stalling.

"I might need your help in there. They have every right to hate me."

Timothy put his hand on his shoulder. "Just be honest with them. I've got your back."

* * *

Marcus entered the room, knocking it silent. Brad Farris – the man he shot before fleeing down the tunnel – happened to be standing closest to the door, along with his wife, Becky.

"Brad...Sorry I, uh, shot you..."

"No worries," Brad said. "It's cool."

Becky looked at Brad in utter disbelief.

"*That's it?*" Becky said. "No worries? He shot you – with a *gun* – and you're 'cool'?"

Brad shrugged. "It's like every man's secret fantasy to survive a gunshot wound with no permanent damage, other than a sweet scar."

Becky slapped him beneath the wound.

"*Fucking men...*"

Marcus stood where, a lifetime ago, they watched the presidential public announcement about the asteroid, when only he knew it was all fake. He propagated the lie then, but now was time to be truthful.

"I want to apologize for what I put you all through. I understand if you want to leave. I can help arrange that. Bloomington and Louisville are nice."

"Where is Henry?" Mariya said.

"And Robby!" Melonie said.

The others voiced their concurrence.

"They are on the way, from a few towns over."

He realized they didn't care about him. They cared about the people they loved.

The door out to the greater bunker opened. Deputy Miller peered in.

"Sorry to interrupt. Had to get a few ladies out of school. And, uh, the computer guy."

Timothy's daughters, Liza and Madeleine, sprinted into the room. "Daddy!" they said in unison. He fell to his knees to embrace them.

Deputy Lowell approached Marcus.

"We have visitors at the train platform. Said they're here for a prisoner transfer."

"Bring him next door."

He watched the reunion carry on. Everyone took turns welcoming Timothy. He went to Steve.

"I might need your muscle. Our friend Grant is waiting next door."

Marcus tapped Timothy on the shoulder and informed him as well.

"Girls, I'll be right back," Timothy said. "When I return, we'll get ice cream. How's that sound?"

The girls cheered.

"Brad, please tell me you have ice cream somewhere," Timothy said.

"I might be aware of a stash that I have *not* been pilfering from the past several months," Brad said.

* * *

Marcus, Steve, and Timothy entered the decontamination room. The deputies stood by Grant, who was restrained with zip-ties.

"Did he come with a pack?" Marcus asked.

"Yes, bag full of clothes."

"Free his hands and legs. We'll handle him from here."

The deputies did so and departed. Marcus opened the elevator doors.

"Not wasting any time, are we?" Grant said.

"Timothy, what was the temperature this morning? -40 degrees?"

"It was frigid, that's for sure," Timothy said.

They rode the platform up to the concrete dome. Marcus tossed the bag of clothes to a far corner.

"Take your shirt off," Marcus said. "Pants, too."

"You've got to be kidding! It's -40 out there!"

"Should we let him keep his boots? Yeah, we'll let him keep his boots."

Maniego sat down on the grated platform and removed his pants. He stood, wearing only boxer briefs and boots.

Timothy and Steve each took an arm. Marcus counted to three. They tossed Maniego out and slammed the door behind him.

"Good riddance," Timothy said.

Steve was not as satisfied.

"Got no love for that guy, but I don't feel good about all that," Steve said. "Makes us no better than he was."

"Relax, Steve. It's almost 70 degrees out there," Timothy said.

* * *

As the ice cream party went on, Marcus grew more and more concerned. He pulled Timothy and Steve aside.

"If Henry and Robby are not here within the hour, we send out a search party, drones or no drones. I'm starting to get worried."

Chapter Forty-Five

Henry awoke on a couch in the living room of an old country home. He was layered in blankets and sweating. A grandfather clock ticked away.

He sat up, setting off a killer migraine. His side ached. He lifted his blanket and saw he was down to his underwear. His wet clothes sat folded on the floor beside the couch. He heard movement in the kitchen.

"Ah, you're awake!" A man said. "You took a nasty spill in the river! Pretty good knock to the head, too. Patched you up while you slept. Had to get your wet clothes off you to warm you up. Name's Brant. I have coffee brewing. Would you like a cup?"

"Where is my friend?"

"The tall feller is in the bedroom. He was a little worse off. Don't think either of you would've made it if it weren't for this heat wave! Pulled y'all out and dragged you up to the house on my ATV. Lucky the power kicked back on. Didn't want to start no fire. I bet them birds shooting up Bloomfield attract to things like chimney smoke. I was seeing them in the sky all morning, but nobody was answering the radio. I sure hope folks are okay. Anyhow, I think the water in your pal's lungs got him more than the cold. Last I checked in, he was still sleeping it off."

"Thank you, you saved our lives. We owe you."

He changed into dry clothes and went to check on Robby. He was tucked in up to his neck, pale and bruised. He took a hit to the head as well. He opened his eyes and sighed a long, drawn-out F-word.

"Thought I lost you there," Henry said.

"What happened?"

"We escaped Bloomfield on the snowmobile after a drone blew up the tower. You drove onto to the river and a missile hit right in front of us. You don't remember any of that?"

"I don't but sounds pretty badass."

"I'll have nightmares the rest of my life, but yeah, it was pretty badass."

It was evening time, as they had slept most of the day. Brant warmed up cans of soup and ran their wet clothes through the dryer.

"They are going to wonder where we are," Henry said. "We were expected at the bunker by now."

"How are we going to get there?"

"You boys might be in luck."

Brant brought in a change of clothes for Robby and coffee.

"There's a mean storm on the horizon. We had these roll through right before the weather went cold. Real nasty things. Green sky, lightning, tornadoes. No drones going to fly around in that. Won't be easy travel, but you'll have cover. My question is, y'all feel up for it? You're welcome to stay until you get right."

"Could you help us with transportation?"

"Sure thing. Let's head out to the barn."

They stepped outside and saw the ominous westward sky. They scanned, fearful of drones, but the sky was already clouded above them.

Brant flicked the lights on in a cavernous barn. The first thing they saw was a combine tractor. The next, a pristine black 1970 Chevelle SS with two wide white stripes.

"Oh, hell yeah," Robby said.

"Now, I ain't that nice!" Brant said. "What I had in mind for y'all is over here."

It was a small electric Chevy pickup truck with an ATV in the back. It would more than suffice.

"How could we ever repay you?" Henry said.

"I'd like to get some winter wheat in the ground come September, but this old gal is broken down. Keep your eye out for a good John Deere and send word along."

"Will do," Henry said, not knowing the first thing about tractors. "Hopefully those drones move along, and we can come back this way."

"I'm always watching the road. Good luck, and God bless."

* * *

They departed west into the storm. The sky pulsated with distant lightning and rain began to fall.

Robby drove as fast as he reasonably could through the slush on State Road 54. By the time they reached Linton, it was raining too hard to speed.

Then, as suddenly as the storm came, it cleared. There was even some twilight left on the other side.

"It's a little too clear," Robby said.

"Those drones can't cover everywhere, so I bet they are programmed to prioritize populated places, or main routes."

"So take the back roads?"

"We both know them, and it's way shorter."

They crossed the Sherman County line and turned off on a paved back road through old coal mining lands. The sky continued to clear. They navigated the debris filled route before coming across the far end of the bunker site fence line. They still had another mile or more to get to the gate.

"I know a shortcut," Robby said.

"Really? There's another entrance?"

"There is now."

Robby bounced through a ditch and rammed the fence. The truck took a section out before getting caught in mangled chain link and barbed wire.

"Gah, you could've warned me!"

"Time to get the four-wheeler out."

They pulled the hatch down and laid the tracks. Robby backed the ATV out and got it within the bunker site boundary. Henry climbed on.

The rode around the rim of the half-empty manmade lake. The concrete dome over the elevator was a dot in the distance. They approached the gravel parking lot, where there were remnants of two obliterated vehicles.

They examined the carnage. No sign of bodies.

"Damnit! That was my Jeep and my Cybertruck!"

They ran to the concrete dome. Footprints darkened by the rain led away from the vehicles – a good sign. Another set of tracks, even fresher and made by boots, led west toward the house they first went to when they were thrown out.

* * *

The elevator doors opened. Marcus was there, alone, waiting for them.

"I thought I told you not to put a scratch on my Cybertruck," Robby said.

Marcus laughed and wiped a tear away.

"Come on, people who want to see you."

They stepped into the media room to cheers.

Mariya ran to Henry and walloped him on the arm. "Don't you ever leave me again!" She jumped into his arms.

Robby hugged and kissed Melonie, then fell to his knees to kiss her belly.

"Promise me you'll stay," she said, tearful.

"I promise. I can't wait to raise this baby with you. If it's a boy, when he's about five, we'll let him grow the nastiest little mullet..."

The others crowded in to get their hugs. Henry, Robby, and Timothy shared heroic stories of the surface. Marcus stood to the side.

Audrey looked on, distant and jealous, perhaps stricken with guilt for her collusion with Ashley. While Henry and Marcus spoke with Melonie, Robby went to her.

"I wanted to let you know I'm leaving," Audrey said. "Going to try the travelling nurse gig. I'll find Jenna, see if they need help where she is."

"I hope you find happiness. I really do."

Timothy found the group and gave them pats on the back. His daughters played with Steve and Mercedes, happy and healthy.

"Well, what's next?"

They looked to Marcus.

"It's time I address the entire bunker."

* * *

An announcement was broadcast across the bunker. Hundreds gathered in the chamber on the other side, as they did during the trial weeks prior. Nobody wanted to miss hearing Marcus Trencher speak.

It was a confusing time to be alive, for all. There were rumors that they were both saved and enslaved by Marcus Trencher. There were rumors that there was never an asteroid, yet the surface was freezing in the middle of summer. Nobody knew what to believe, but they were inclined to trust the genius born in their small Indiana town for whom they had so much admiration and pride.

When he emerged from the tunnel, the crowd hushed. He ascended the ramp before the drab green door and took the microphone that waited.

"Ten years ago, I was called upon to join a top-secret program to help design massive doomsday bunkers, with the understanding that they would soon be necessary. I was promised one of my own to oversee, which I would fill with people of my choosing. When the time came, I chose all of you.

"A year before move in, the powers that be reneged and left me only fifteen bids. I schemed a way to separate myself and the few I was allowed to choose from the other half of the bunker, which was to be filled by whomever the government sent. It was spiteful, but I was angry after all I put into the program, and into this place.

"Six months before move in, I was informed of a plot to kill me and take the bunker entirely. The plot was foiled, and long story short, all of you are here. I alone made the decision to stick with the division between the two halves. I kept my friends ignorant of your existence. It was selfish, but I also didn't know who was coming down that tunnel when it broke through. It's no excuse. It was wrong, and you all suffered for it. For that I am deeply sorry, and I beg your forgiveness.

"I also want to inform you of the reality we face. There was never an asteroid. What there is, up there, is a deliberate, systematic effort to depopulate the planet. I'm afraid whoever is orchestrating this effort has been terribly successful. I want to change that – but I'll need your help.

"The skies began to clear this morning. Unfortunately, drones are sweeping the area, hunting signs of human life. These machines require access to the grid we built, the grid my dear friend Timothy and I now have control over. We will find a way to starve these machines, here and across the Midwest. That is where we need you.

"There is infrastructure to secure. We will learn their weaknesses and expose the evil cowards behind these crimes. We will not be bystanders to the worst atrocity in human history. We must unite with the other bunkers and the pockets of survivors on the surface. We will reclaim the surface."

He paused to scan their awestruck faces.

"We fight back – starting today!"

The crowd erupted. A woman rushed forward to touch him. Another handed him a baby. Men expressed devotion to their new cause. They were given a mission, a purpose.

Marcus Trencher was given forgiveness – and a small army.

About the Author

Shane Noble is originally from Sullivan, Indiana, and now resides in Louisville, Kentucky. He graduated from Bellarmine University and taught middle school for six years before moving on to the private sector. He aspires to someday earn enough money to own things.

Thank you for reading!

Stay tuned for the final book of the trilogy, coming soon!

Best way to follow for future releases, for now, is the **Trencher's Bunker** *Facebook page or the* Shane Noble *Amazon author page.*

www.ingramcontent.com/pod-product-compliance
Lightning Source LLC
Chambersburg PA
CBHW020539020726
47494CB00006B/1827